THE STOLEN CHASE

Also by Cap Daniels

The Chase Fulton Novels Series
Book One: *The Opening Chase*
Book Two: *The Broken Chase*
Book Three: *The Stronger Chase*
Book Four: *The Unending Chase*
Book Five: *The Distant Chase*
Book Six: *The Entangled Chase*
Book Seven: *The Devil's Chase*
Book Eight: *The Angel's Chase*
Book Nine: *The Forgotten Chase*
Book Ten: *The Emerald Chase*
Book Eleven: *The Polar Chase*
Book Twelve: *The Burning Chase*
Book Thirteen: *The Poison Chase*
Book Fourteen: *The Bitter Chase*
Book Fifteen: *The Blind Chase*
Book Sixteen: *The Smuggler's Chase*
Book Seventeen: *The Hollow Chase*
Book Eighteen: *The Sunken Chase*
Book Nineteen: *The Darker Chase*
Book Twenty: *The Abandoned Chase*
Book Twenty-One: *The Gambler's Chase*
Book Twenty-Two: *The Arctic Chase*
Book Twenty-Three: *The Diamond Chase*
Book Twenty-Four: *The Phantom Chase*
Book Twenty-Five: *The Crimson Chase*
Book Twenty-Six: *The Silent Chase*
Book Twenty-Seven: *The Shepherd's Chase*
Book Twenty-Eight: *The Scorpion's Chase*
Book Twenty-Nine: *The Creole Chase*
Book Thirty: *The Calling Chase*
Book Thirty-One: *The Capitol Chase*
Book Thirty-Two: *The Stolen Chase*
Book Thirty-Three: *The Widow's Chase*

The Avenging Angel – Seven Deadly Sins Series
Book One: *The Russian's Pride*
Book Two: *The Russian's Greed*
Book Three: *The Russian's Gluttony*
Book Four: *The Russian's Lust*
Book Five: *The Russian's Sloth*
Book Six: *The Russian's Envy*
Book Seven: *The Russian's Wrath*

Stand-Alone Novels
We Were Brave
Singer – Memoir of a Christian Sniper

Novellas
The Chase is On
I Am Gypsy

THE STOLEN CHASE

CHASE FULTON NOVEL #32

CAP DANIELS

ANCHOR WATCH
PUBLISHING
** USA **

The Stolen Chase
Chase Fulton Novel #32
Cap Daniels

This is a work of fiction. Names, characters, places, historical events, and incidents are the product of the author's imagination or have been used fictitiously. Although many locations such as marinas, airports, hotels, restaurants, etc. used in this work actually exist, they are used fictitiously and may have been relocated, exaggerated, or otherwise modified by creative license for the purpose of this work. Although many characters are based on personalities, physical attributes, skills, or intellect of actual individuals, all the characters in this work are products of the author's imagination.

Published by:
ANCHOR WATCH
PUBLISHING
** USA **

All rights reserved. No part of this book may be reproduced or transmitted in any form or by any means, electronic or mechanical, including information storage and retrieval systems as well as artificial intelligence without written permission from the publisher, except by a reviewer who may quote brief passages in a review.

13 Digit ISBN: 978-1-951021-73-3
Library of Congress Control Number: 2025945691
Copyright © 2025 Cap Daniels – All Rights Reserved

Cover Design: German Creative

Printed in the United States of America

The Stolen Chase

CAP DANIELS

Chapter 1
Freshwater Mermaids

Late Spring 2016 – York River, north of Camp Peary, VA

I handpicked the operators for the highly classified mission, and there's no one on Earth I would've rather had by my side in that unforgiving and often deadly environment. Our target was a pair of boys who believed themselves to be men, but my team was about to disavow them of that belief in a world where we felt superbly confident, but they did not.

They were well trained, strong, and capable of handling themselves both individually and while working as a team. The intelligence we had on our prey was extensive and strong, but even without knowing everything that could be known about the pair, I had faith that my team could—and would—take them on a terrifying ride they would never forget.

The playing field was level in one respect: both predator and prey required the same tools to sustain life in the unforgiving and otherworldly realm where the conflict would occur. The home court advantage, however, was undeniably in our hands. Our victims didn't know we were lying in wait for them, but the men around me weren't the most unbelievable part of the coming scenario. When it's time to break things and kill bad guys, I had precisely the band of marauders to make it happen, but when I needed to lead young men astray, the tools in my kit were far superior to those of most covert operator teams. My favorite secret weapons were something our targets could never anticipate or prepare to encounter, and those weapons of psychological warfare were two of the most capable women who've ever lived.

Anastasia "Anya" Burinkova was a former SVR assassin of the Russian Federation and one of the most physically beautiful people to ever grace the planet. Her partner on that day, Elizabeth "Skipper" Woodley, could've been right at home on a fashion runway in Paris or Milan, but the stunning young woman who I'd always see as my little sister chose a path with far fewer spotlights and photographers. Skipper was one of the finest intelligence analysts in the game, but her tradecraft in the field was impeccable and expanding by the day. Beautiful women are distractions everywhere they go, but in the world that we inhabited on that day, they were the last thing on the minds of our unwitting victims.

The voice-activated communication system built into our full facemasks gave my team the ability to talk with each other where most divers could not, but that wasn't the limit of our technological superiority in the murky depths of the York River. Each of us, excluding Skipper and Anya, wore Draeger Mark V fully enclosed rebreathers to avoid dispensing the telltale exhalation bubbles of conventional scuba gear. The word *conventional* would never describe my team. We could move and communicate in near silence, but when we hit our target, silence would quickly become utter chaos of the highest order.

Anya and Skipper would make first contact, but they would not participate in the inevitable fight that would follow their performance.

Shawn, a former Navy SEAL, hovered motionless just to my left and had more hours spent underwater than the rest of my team combined. No one in the water that day believed themselves to be superior to Shawn in the murk of the York River, twenty miles upstream of Chesapeake Bay.

Gator, the youngest and most physically fit member of my team, lingered behind me with one hand resting on my left ankle so I would always know exactly where he was. A former all-American free safety from K-State, Gator refocused the physicality and mental acuity of the gridiron into a battlefield mindset unlike anyone I've ever known. He was fast, strong, and fearless, just like I had been in my twenties. Now, almost two decades his senior, I saw Gator as a stalwart force for what is right and good. He was still unjaded by experience, and I envied that in him. I'm not sure I had the same strength of character when I was his age, but having a teammate with such zeal and intensity was a treasure that I would never stop nurturing.

On my right, a freight train of a man hovered only inches above the muddy bottom of the river. Mongo, a former Green Beret at 6'8" and almost 300 pounds, looked more like Goliath than David, the boy king, but he was one of the gentlest people who ever lived . . . right up until the point when the need for gentleness dissolved away and the demand for violence took center stage. I never saw the big man lose a fight, and on the battlefield, he had no equal when toe to toe with an enemy. Completely independent of his physical strength and size, inside his skull rested the mind of a philosopher, professor, and mechanical engineer. Every team should be so fortunate to have such a combination in its ranks.

Somewhere above and upstream of us waited the three remaining members of my elite tactical team. Singer, our sniper and moral compass, sat on the starboard tube of our rigid hull inflatable boat, most likely with his eyes closed and his lips and heart talking to God. Kodiak, a retired Green Beret and arctic warfare specialist of the highest order, was probably lounging in the bow of the RHIB, waiting for his turn to dance with the devils the rest of us would pull from the deep. Undoubtedly, at the boat's helm stood Disco, the oldest of our knuckle-draggers and a retired Air Force colonel with more combat hours in the A-10 Warthog than anybody else. Although he cut his teeth in the cockpit, we turned the hardened fighter pilot into a commanding presence on the ground when he joined our team. He could fly anything with wings or rotors, drive any vehicle with a steering wheel like Mario Andretti, and pilot anything on the surface or beneath the waves.

One more small advantage in our column was the ability to hear our prey talking to each other via their underwater comms. That capability was delivered by our resident mad scientist, Dr. Celeste Mankiller, a former technical services officer with the U.S. Department of Justice. She held a filing cabinet full of patents and kept my team well stocked with gadgetry and weapons that made us one of the deadliest small-unit forces in existence.

I glanced at the dive computer strapped to my wrist. "Is everybody ready? It's almost showtime."

Everyone reported ready, with Anya and Skipper checking in last.

I said, "I'm bringing their comms online now. Remember, they don't know we're here, so let's have a little fun with them before we make those boys sully their wetsuits."

The voice of the first man was weak due to the distance separating us, but the amplifiers built into Dr. Mankiller's eavesdropping system performed perfectly. "What's your count?"

The second man said, "Nine hundred meters. We should reach the objective in another sixty seconds."

I said, "Get on your toes, ladies. Here they come."

Anya answered, "Mermaids do not have toes."

Her lingering Russian accent amused me, even though she had the ability to speak flawless English devoid of any accent when the situation demanded it.

Target number one said, "Nine hundred fifty meters. Keep your eyes open."

"I think I've got it," number two said. "Holy . . . ! What was that?"

Ah. The first sound of panic, confusion, and distraction filled my ears, and my plan was already working perfectly.

Number one said, "I don't have any idea, but whatever it was, it was fast."

Skipper said, "Here I come!"

A few seconds later, number one yelled into his comms. "Whatever it was, there it comes again."

"Is that a . . . wait! No way. Did you get a good look at it that time?"

Number one said, "You're going to think I've lost my mind, but it looked like a mermaid."

Anya would soon make her turn and accelerate back toward the approaching divers. She would propel herself between the two men with the powerful ducted-fan thrust device built into the body of her single fin.

One of the men groaned. "It hit me!"

"Are you hurt?"

"What is that thing, and are there two of them?"

I said, "That's enough, ladies. Nice work. We're moving in."

"I've got point," Shawn said, and Gator and I fell in line behind him. Mongo brought up the rear because no one could see around him if he was in front.

We didn't have the benefit of propellers built into dry suits like our mermaids, but each of us was clipped to a diver propulsion vehicle that looked like a torpedo with a steering wheel. The DPVs were capable of jetting most of us through the water at eight to ten knots, but not Mongo. Squeezing six knots out of the machine while pulling the behemoth through the water was the best we could hope for.

Shawn single-handed his DPV and drew a small hairdryer-shaped device from his kit, focusing it dead ahead. The technology was another of Dr. Mankiller's creations—a self-contained sonar detecting and ranging system. She called it SODAR, but the rest of the team called it "Shawn's favorite toy." Getting the tool away from our SEAL would've been only slightly less dangerous than pulling polar bear teeth.

The piece of aquatic magic did its silent work by bouncing sound waves off objects ahead and returning them to the receiver built into the front of the gadget. Anything bigger than a softball showed up in grainy relief on the gray screen.

"Got 'em," Shawn said. "Twelve o'clock and twenty meters."

I made the first safety call of the operation. "Are my mermaids clear of the strike zone?"

Skipper answered, "Affirmative. We're back on the surface and well clear of the playing field. Hit 'em hard, Chase."

"That's the only way I know how to hit 'em."

My team of subaquatic warriors would protect the underwater transmission line carrying telephone, electricity, and internet from the west bank of the river to the east, but foiling the attackers' mission was only item number one on our mission checklist. The fun part of our assignment was to discourage the two saboteurs from ever trying again.

Every mission has rules of engagement, and our watery work that day was no exception. Everything short of killing the aggressors was on the table. Somebody rang the dinner bell, and we served up every dish we knew how to cook.

We killed and sank our DPVs, and it was no surprise to anyone when Shawn struck the first blow. He hit the lead diver from above and forced the man's face into the mud, but that was far from the limit of Shawn's attack. Adding insult to muddy injury, he drew his knife and pierced the diver's buoyancy compensation device.

Just as we'd planned before we splashed into the river, the second diver belonged to Gator, as long as he didn't screw it up. He did not, and I was pleased to see his speed, efficiency, and conservation of energy. He rolled his target diver faceup and sent a crushing knee strike between the man's legs.

Every boy who ever played organized sports knows exactly how that particular strike feels, and everyone does exactly the same thing when it happens. He doubles over forward, grabs the injured region of his body, and takes a long, deep breath in what is usually a wasted effort to quell the pain. Gator understood the sequential reaction scheme, and he took full advantage of it. The instant the diver reached to grab his body, my all-American sent a palm strike to his target's chin, sending his facemask off and clear of his head. The move eliminated the diver's source of air and left him disoriented with his mouth, nose, and eyes full of filthy river water.

To my surprise, the diver reacted to being demasked in textbook fashion. He kicked away from Gator, pulled his alternate air source from his BCD, and stuck it in his mouth. Without a mask, his vision was blurry at best, but he was once again breathing air from his tank.

His next move concerned me and would likely send the coming underwater skirmish down a path no one wanted. Instead of working to recover his full facemask, he drew a compact dive mask from a pocket, slid it over his head, and cleared it with practiced precision.

I watched closely as the diver assessed his situation. He clearly wasn't panicked, but he was outnumbered. Something in his posture told me to join the fight before it turned deadly, but I had no way to know how quickly that was going to happen.

I finned with every ounce of strength my lungs and legs could create, but the diver drew a knife from somewhere inside his kit before I was within striking distance. Gator seemed to identify the weapon at the same instant as I did, but his reaction time was a fraction of a second too slow. The shimmering blade sliced through the water with unmatched speed and precision. Its razor's edge caught Gator's dry suit inches below his left shoulder.

As his suit filled with water, Gator's mobility diminished in a breath. Suddenly, he was dragging around the weight of his gear, his own body, and a six-foot-long rubber bag of river water that only seconds before had been his dry suit. I wasn't concerned about depth. We were within inches of the bottom and only two dozen feet beneath the surface of the docile river. My concerns lay with the aggression of the diver who'd turned himself from victim to avenger in an instant.

The diver kicked hard, propelling himself toward Gator, and I considered that to be my cue to end the fight before one of the good guys took a blade deeper than the skin of his suit. When I believed I was close enough to reach my mark, I grabbed the yellow, low-pressure hose feeding the diver's alternate air source between his lips. I hit my mark and yanked the man's lifeline from his mouth. Doing so gave me a leash with which to steer the man away from Gator and get him under control before the whole operation went off the rails.

He changed hands and gripped his knife firmly in his right. With well-aimed swipes, he threw his fist in a large arc above and behind himself... exactly where I thought was the safest place to be. I dodged the knife, but the fight was far from over. The primary advantage I had was my team, and coming in a very close second was the fact that I had air to breathe and my adversary did not.

His lungs had to be on fire, but the fight inside of him remained. He swung the blade ever closer with every revolution until he caught the elastic straps holding my facemask in place. The blow was powerful, leaving me reeling as my mask fell away and stars circled my head.

How badly am I cut?

Where's Gator?

Don't let the guy get away!

My brain talked to my body, but an obvious disconnect stood like a barricade between the two. I was definitely hurt, and the entire operation was in serious jeopardy. Afraid the diver was still more than an arm's length away, I kicked hard, begging my fins to put a little more distance between me and that knife. Once I believed I was far enough away to survive for a few more seconds, I shoved my mask back onto my face, cleared it of water, and yelled into the built-in, waterproof mic. "Abort! Abort! Abort!"

Chapter 2
Lost and Found

With the universal signal to "knock it off," I brought both hands in front of my face and waved off the man who'd sliced Gator's dry suit. It was the same signal I'd learned when I endured training at The Ranch at Camp Peary. The training scenario my team participated in had turned into a train wreck in a swamp, and I had to stop it before anyone else was seriously injured.

Using the same hand signal I'd made, Shawn ended his wrestling match with the first diver, and his adversary backed off, no doubt relieved that the bullfight with a far superior matador was over.

I turned to find Mongo, which should've been a simple task. His bulk made him hard to miss in almost every environment, but in spite of his size, the big man was nowhere to be seen.

"Sierra Two, Sierra One. Say position."

A few seconds later, Mongo said, "I'm thirty meters downstream in pursuit of diver number two."

I spun in the water, completing a full turn in seconds, and discovered that Mongo wasn't the only missing man. The diver with the knife had vanished as well.

"Do you have him in sight?" I asked.

"Negative," came Mongo's winded reply. "He fled to the south after knocking your mask off, and that's the last I saw of him."

"Let him go. He'll surface when he realizes what's going on."

Mongo said, "Roger, boss. I'll see you on the surface."

Shawn escorted his man twenty feet to the surface of the York River while I cut Gator out of his flooded dry suit. By the time he and I made the surface, Mongo was back in our midst, and our RHIB was hovering nearby.

The first diver shucked off his mask and shook his head. "What was that all about?"

"It was all part of the exercise," I said. "It was our job to stop you from rigging the explosives on the trunk line."

He huffed. "I'd say you guys won. Who are you, anyway?"

Mongo answered before I could. "We're just a bunch of misfit toys a long way from their island."

The diver shot a thumb downstream. "Were those two, uh . . . whatever they were, part of the exercise?"

I motioned toward our boat, where Anya and Skipper sat in the bow, waving like Miss Americas.

He laughed. "I guess I'm glad to know I wasn't losing my mind."

"Where's your partner?" I asked.

"I don't know. I guess we bombed this exercise, huh?"

"You weren't expected to do well," I said. "The purpose of the exercise was to make you aware of how vulnerable you are in an underwater scenario. We've been doing this a long time, kid, so you weren't going to win no matter what happened down there."

He scanned the surface of the river. "I'm concerned about my partner."

Shawn asked, "What was your contingency plan in the event of separation?"

The diver wiped water from his face. "Had this been a *real* operation, the plan would've been to continue the mission, but since it was a training exercise, our plan was to search for the missing man for one minute on the bottom and then meet on the surface."

I motioned toward his mask. "See if you still have comms with him."

He pressed the mask to his face. "Bravo One, Bravo Two, over." He waited several seconds, tried again, then looked up at me. "Nothing."

I yelled to Disco at the helm of the RHIB. "Get search and rescue out here. We've got a missing diver. He should've been on the surface by now according to the pre-dive safety plan, but he didn't come up."

Disco lifted the mic from the boat's radio and made the call. Five minutes later, there were a dozen divers and three more RHIBs in the water.

"How much air do you have left?" I asked Bravo Two.

He lifted his gauge cluster. "Four hundred pounds."

"How does your buddy's breathing rate compare to yours?"

"He's a little better, but not much. He usually hits the surface with a couple hundred more than me."

Even if he had six hundred pounds, that would only give him minutes of air if his heart rate was elevated and he was on the run.

"He wouldn't have gone upstream, would he?" Shawn asked.

Bravo Two said, "I wouldn't think so, but I didn't expect him to cut and run, either. It's not like him."

We scoured the river bottom for almost an hour before I threw my arms across the portside tube of the command-and-control boat. "No luck."

The commander was a man I hadn't met prior to the exercise, but everything about him said competent, thorough, and experienced.

He scratched his beard and checked his watch. "There's no way he's got any air left. If he's still in the water, he washed out of Chesapeake Bay by now, and our search zone is the whole North Atlantic."

"You're in charge," I said. "What's the call?"

"You're sure he wasn't injured, right?"

"I didn't hurt him, and he shucked Gator off with a knife."

"A knife he wasn't supposed to have," the commander said.

I drifted beside his boat until he offered a hand and pulled me aboard. He said, "Call off your team, and I'll get some more help out here."

I shook like a dog, shedding water from my hair and beard. "My guys aren't going to like being called out of the water before we find your boy."

He said, "Leave 'em if you want, but I've got two teams of SEALs from Special Boat Team Twenty on their way from Little Creek. If he's still in the water, they'll find him, and if he's ashore, he'll find us."

I pulled my mask to my face. "All Sierra elements, this is Sierra One. Recover to the RHIB."

My team climbed aboard our boat and motored alongside the command vessel.

"Is everybody all right?" I asked.

"We're good," Mongo said. "Did somebody find him?"

I shook my head, and he asked, "Then, why are we calling off the search?"

"We're not," I said. "We're handing it off to the SEALs. They're on their way from Little Creek."

Shawn perked up. "Special Boat Crew guys?"

I nodded, and he said, "If you don't mind, I'd like to stay in the water with them."

"Everybody who wants to be in the water is welcome to stay. I'm heading back to the office with these guys to read the file on the lost diver."

No one was surprised when my entire team, including my mermaids, slid overboard and back into the water.

The commander extended a hand. "Of course I know who you are, Dr. Fulton, but we've not been formally introduced. I'm William King. They gave me Gunny's office when he retired."

I shook his hand. "It's nice to officially meet you, Mr. King. Please call me Chase."

"All right. Chase it is. And you can call me Will."

I said, "I like that you didn't claim to take Gunny's place. You said they gave you his office."

He chuckled. "Replacing Gunny isn't possible. Nobody can fill those boots, but I'm doing the best I can."

I nestled onto one of the unpadded seats on the RHIB. "Tell me about the missing man."

Will pressed the throttles forward. "Let's have that conversation in my office."

* * *

When I walked through the door, I pointed toward the blade-shaped hole in Gunny's metal filing cabinet. "Would you like me to autograph that?"

Will furrowed his brow. "What do you mean?"

"Gunny made that entrance wound with a Ka-Bar during a fight with me a long time ago."

Will chuckled. "I've always wondered how that happened. Have a seat. Can I get you anything?"

"A bottle of water would be great. Thanks."

He tossed the bottle and slid the missing diver's file across his desk. "Take a look and tell me what you see."

I downed the bottle and opened the file. On my first pass through the paperwork, I skimmed and flipped pages quickly, but on my second pass, I was far more thorough and came to a stop on page three. "Pre-law and political science from Rutgers. Interesting."

Will nodded. "Yes, it is, and his GPA was three point eight. He also rowed crew and played rugby."

"Crew and rugby? Are those real sports?"

"Depends on who you ask, I suppose. Keep digging. It gets better."

I continued through the file until I came to a page that's often called the "dream sheet." I said, "He applied to NSA and CIA."

Will continued nodding. "That's right. And he was never officially turned down by either organization. Keep reading."

I turned the page. "The Navy?"

Will tossed a second bottle of water. "Yep, and they said no thanks."

"Why?"

"I'm not sure. Apparently, he wanted a guaranteed slot on the Teams and a safety net as an intelligence officer. The Navy doesn't do that."

"Doesn't do what?" I asked.

"Make guarantees like that. I'm sure they'd love to have him, but there's no shortage of smart college grads standing in line for a naval career. It's supply-side economics at its finest. They can be as picky as they want when they have that many well-qualified applicants."

I turned to the background page and read his family history twice. "His father was a shipwright at Norfolk."

Will said, "Yes, he was, and his mother was a schoolteacher."

"So, he's first-generation."

He took a long breath. "For intelligence work? Is that what you mean?"

"Yes. What made him want to be in the intel business so badly?"

"Beats me, but he's a good kid, and he'll make a decent operator. He's done well here at The Ranch, but he hasn't excelled at any one thing. He's solid across the board, though."

I closed the file. "How did he come to us?"

"We went to him, actually. After he applied to NSA and CIA, our antennae went up. We get some good recruits who don't make the cut at the agencies."

"So, you recruited him?"

"Not me, personally, but the Board liked him and sent somebody to talk with him."

"Did he jump at the opportunity?" I asked.

"No, it took some selling to hook him. It's all detailed in the recruitment section in the back."

I flipped to the final pages of the file and read the transcript of his interview. "He's well-spoken and articulate. I'll give him that, but he was awfully quick to swing a knife at my man in the river."

Will raised a finger. "That's one of the things that bothers me about this situation. Both divers were supposed to be completely unarmed. We didn't want to risk one of them getting in a lucky shot on one of your guys."

"I appreciate that, but there's no question he had a knife."

"Is your man okay, by the way?"

"He's fine. He made a nice move to avoid getting cut, but his dry suit didn't fare so well."

Will said, "We'll replace the dry suit."

I waved him off. "Save your budget. We've got plenty of spares."

He tapped his fingers on the desk. "Go ahead and ask the question."

I gave him a half smile. "Why would he run?"

Will made a sound like a ringing bell. "We have a winner. Tell him what he's won, Johnny."

I said, "I've never met the kid before today, and I don't even know his name."

Will leaned back in his chair. "Did you hurt him?"

"No. Gator got a little rough with him, but he didn't do any real damage."

"No blood?"

I said, "No. Gator didn't even pull his knife."

"What about you?"

"I jerked him around by a hose, but your team did a lot worse in the pool, I'm sure."

"Yeah, we're not exactly gentle. He's never shied away from anything until today. The boy's been fearless throughout the program. He's practically finished with training."

"Where were you going to send him?" I asked.

"We don't know yet. I planned to talk with you about picking him up. That's part of the reason I asked you to come play OPFOR. I want you to see him in action."

"We don't need anybody. I have the best team any leader could ask for."

"I see. Care for a drink?"

I waved a hand. "No, thank you. I'd like to get back in the water with my team."

"Mind if I have one?"

"Of course not. You're the boss."

"Zookeeper is more like it." He poured three fingers of scotch, and after a sip, he dialed a number and slid his phone onto the desk.

"Hello, Chief."

Will said, "You're on speaker. How's it going out there?"

The man said, "The SEALs are here, but we've not found any sign of our guy. To be honest, I'm starting to get a little concerned."

"Sonar?" Will asked.

"Yes, sir. We're running active sonar on every surface vessel, and Chase's team has a handheld sonar, but no one's getting any hits."

"How's the tide?"

"It's outgoing at just over two knots."

Will let out a low whistle. "That's not good."

"No, sir, it's not. From where they were, anything that's not pinned to the bottom is out in the Atlantic by now."

Will laid his head back and closed his eyes. "What do the SEALs have to say?"

"Nothing."

"Who's in command?"

The man said, "A lieutenant named Dobson. I've never met him before, but he seems squared away."

Will bore the weighty burden of command and said, "Turn it off and go to ground."

"Yes, sir."

He pocketed the phone. "What do you think?"

I said, "I think you made the right call. If he's in the water, it's salt water by now, and chances are he's on the bank somewhere."

"Yeah, that's my rationale as well, but if he's dry, I don't know why he hasn't made contact with somebody."

"Tell me about his dive buddy," I said.

He pulled a second file from the wounded cabinet. "Solid as a rock. Excellent shooter, no fear, and he can run a hundred miles without breaking a sweat."

"Do you mind if I interview him?"

"Be my guest, but you remember how we do things around here. Trainees aren't allowed to tell each other anything about themselves — not even their names."

I said, "I remember, but if these guys have been training together for a year, they know a lot more about each other than they realize."

Will leaned forward. "Are you going to hypnotize him?"

"Absolutely. You're welcome to sit in if you'd like, but you'd probably make him as nervous as Gunny made me all those years ago."

"In that case," Will said, "I think I'll just listen in."

Chapter 3
We Don't Dream

As Will led me down a long subterranean corridor, we met head-on with an old friend, and I threw open my arms. "Dr. Fred, how are you?"

Other than the lines of time, Fred Kennedy, The Ranch's psychiatrist, looked the same as he had when we first met in nineteen ninety-seven.

He stepped into my embrace. "Chase. What a nice surprise. What brings you to our little secret in the woods?"

Out of courtesy, I turned to Will. "May I tell him?"

Will nodded. "Of course. Fred knows everything, even when no one tells him anything."

"It's nice to hear you still have your ear to the ground," I said.

"You know how it is. Playing around inside people's heads makes us clairvoyant."

"You're a little more than clairvoyant, but that's a discussion for another day. My team and I came up at the behest of Mr. King here. He asked us to take a look at a couple of hard-charging head knockers."

Fred frowned. "So, this is a recruiting trip."

"Not exactly," I said. "I thought we were just going to harass some trainees in the water, but it turned into a missing man mission."

Fred snapped his attention to Will. "Which one?"

Will huffed. "Bravo One."

Fred cocked his head. "Missing, as in disappeared or dead?"

"We hope for the first, but we fear both may be true. He broke away during an underwater exercise in the river."

Fred stared at the ceiling for a moment. "Have you seen his file, Chase?"

"Yes, I read it twice."

"Theories?" he asked.

"None yet, but I'm about to have a little one-on-one with Bravo Two."

"Fighting or talking?"

I tried not to laugh. "Come on, Doc. You know I'm a lover, not a fighter."

"Yeah, that's you, ol' lover boy Chase. Speaking of love, when was the last time you saw Anya?"

I dug in. "Penny, my wife, is doing great. She spends a lot of time in California writing screenplays."

Fred smirked. "Nice deflection, but you forget — I'm the neuro-ninja, and I can see your thoughts. You've spent more time with Anya than with Penny lately."

"That's true, but—"

"There is no *but* after the truth, my boy. Truth simply is. Tell the terrifying Russian I said hello next time you see her."

"Will do, Doc. Say, do you want to sit in with me when I talk to Bravo Two?"

Fred checked the spot on his arm where a watch would be if he owned one. "Don't waste your time trying to hypnotize him. He won't go down."

"In that case," I said, "I'll have to beat the truth out of him."

Fred laughed. "Sure. Give that a try. He's fifteen years younger and in the best shape of his life."

"Then maybe we'll just talk."

Fred motioned down the hall. "Meet me in Psych Two. I'll be there in five minutes."

The Ranch had two areas devoted to psychological well-being.

Psych One was a cold, sterile room that echoed every word spoken above a whisper. When Dr. Fred wanted to scare the stuffing out of a trainee, Psych One was his preferred playground.

Psych Two, on the other hand, was quite different, and it had been upgraded since my time in the hallowed halls of The Ranch. Three Herman Miller chairs with footstools rested on a gorgeous, antique Persian rug. A curved, plush sofa sat adjacent to the chairs, and the lighting was perfect.

I took in the surroundings. "When did you do all of this?"

Fred said, "It's only a few months old. Check out the paint."

I tried to focus on the color, but the more intensely I peered at the wall, the less certain I was of the actual color. "Is there blue in that?"

"Good eye. There is the faintest touch of blue inside the gray. Our eyes can't really see it, but our brains feel it. It's calming and peaceful. That's what we practice in this room . . . xin."

Will laughed. "I see you two have some catching up to do, so I'll go get our boy."

I said, "Don't stress him out. I don't want him thinking something negative will come from this little get-together."

Will flattened a palm against his chest. "Me? I'm offended that you think I'd put somebody under stress."

"I'm sure you're quite the calming force in the lives of the young men under your direction."

Fred and I settled into two Herman Millers, and he said, "Aren't these nice?"

I rubbed my palms over the arms. "I have two of these in my office, and I love them."

"Best chairs on Earth."

A tap came at the door, and I stood. Fred did not. The young man I'd last seen in the York River came through the door first, with Will on his heels.

I stuck out a hand. "We've not officially met yet. I'm Chase, and I'm sure you already know Dr. Kennedy."

Bravo Two nodded toward Fred and shook my hand. "I'm not sure what all of this is about, but you were there. You know I didn't do anything to get Bravo One hurt."

I motioned toward the sofa. "Relax, and have a seat. You didn't do anything wrong."

He settled onto the sofa. "Yeah, unless you count losing my dive buddy and failing to complete the primary mission."

"You weren't expected to complete the mission," I said. "My team and I were there to make sure of that."

"That's why they disarmed us, wasn't it?"

I nodded. "Yes, your training officers didn't want you to have any weapons you might be able to hurt or kill us with. You obviously followed that directive, but your buddy did not."

Two furrowed his brow. "Are you saying he had a weapon?"

"Yes, he pulled a knife on one of my men and sliced open his dry suit."

Two shook his head. "Not possible. I double-checked his dive gear before we went into the water, and he wasn't wearing a knife."

I leaned back and crossed my prosthetic ankle across my left knee. "Nobody's blaming you. What happened wasn't your fault."

He groaned. "My dive buddy is my responsibility, and . . ."

I softened my tone. "Yes, of course he is, but this case is unique. You were ambushed by a superior force. Your concern for your dive buddy is admirable and noble, but please understand that you are not responsible for whatever happened to him. What's his name, by the way?"

Two stared between Fred and me. "Are you kidding me with this? I don't know his name any more than he knows mine."

"What's yours?" I asked, still in my relaxed posture.

"Not a chance," he said.

I lifted the yellow legal pad from a side table. "They tell me you've got the endurance of a gazelle. Have you always been a runner?"

"Not really. I played other sports, but not track."

I ignored him. "They also tell me you can really shoot. Do you enjoy it?"

"I used to, but to be honest, this place kinda took the fun out of it."

"I get that. You won't be here forever, so you'll have plenty of time to learn to enjoy the sport of shooting again when you're not expected to put ten thousand rounds through the same hole."

His shoulders fell almost imperceptibly, and Fred noticed, too.

"Tell me about Bravo One," I said.

He stiffened again, and Fred said, "Relax. You've done nothing wrong, and you're not going to be held responsible for anything that happened to Bravo One."

He licked his lips and finally let his eyes settle on me. "So, who are you?"

Fred leaned forward. "Who Chase is isn't important. What you need to understand—"

I laid a hand on Fred's arm. "It's okay. There's no reason to play games in here. We're dealing with a missing man, and finding him is our number one priority."

Fred leaned back. "Okay, let's put all of our cards on the table. Go ahead, Chase."

I kept my tone soft. "I'm Dr. Chase Fulton. I'm a psychologist by education and license, but that's not my full-time gig. I lead a tactical team under the direction of the same board of directors that oversees the training you're undergoing here at The Ranch."

Two narrowed his gaze. "So, you're what *I'm* trying to become, is that it?"

"Not exactly. You're working to join a team of operators like ours, but you won't start out running that team. You're essentially finished here. Now, it's time for your real training to begin."

Fred took in every pause, every sigh, and every change of focus. "Your turn, Ben."

The young man looked as if he'd seen a ghost, and Fred almost laughed. "Strange, isn't it? Not hearing your own name for eighteen months makes us uber-sensitive to the sound. It's okay, Ben. Chase has both clearance and the need to know. You can be completely honest with him."

Ben let out a breath. "No offense, Dr. Kennedy, but I'm not breaking the code until one of the training officers makes it clear that I'm allowed to."

Fred pushed himself from his seat and slapped me on the shoulder. "See? I told you he was a good one. I'll be right back."

Fred was gone for no more than thirty seconds before returning with William King in tow.

Will looked down at me and said, "I hear you need some authorization from me."

I pointed toward Ben. "Not me. Him. He's being a little stubborn about his real name."

Will stepped toward Ben and extended his hand. The kid hesitantly stood and took it.

Will said, "Congratulations, Bravo Two, Benjamin Thomas Gaines. You've now completed your training at The Ranch, a facility you will never mention again."

Ben's eyes fluttered around the room. "Are you serious? Is it really over? Is Bravo One okay?"

Will said, "Now we're on an even playing field. Everybody in the room has successfully completed this training. As the senior training director and your current direct supervisor, I'm authorizing you to answer Chase's questions honestly."

Ben said, "Yes, sir."

Will gave the young man a gentle push back toward the sofa. "Chill out, man. We're all on the same team."

Will stepped from the room, and I studied Ben's expression. "So, let's have it."

He said, "Well, you've already got my name, but I suspect you knew it already."

I said, "Believe it or not, I didn't know your name, and I still don't know Bravo One's name."

Ben said, "I don't know it, either. He and I both took the rules of this place pretty seriously. I learned on day one that following the rules made all of this a lot easier."

I said, "I remember that lesson well. Mine came in the form of a wrecked truck in a cesspool."

Ben clapped his hands. "They're still doing that one. I thought I was dead when they pulled it on me."

"The classics never go out of style. Tell me about the sports you played."

"I played lacrosse and rowed crew."

"That explains the stamina," I said. "You and Bravo One had rowing in common then."

Ben's blank expression was either ultimate sincerity, or he was ready for an acting career in one of Penny's movies.

"You never talked about rowing with Bravo One?"

"I told you, we didn't break the rules."

"Bravo One did. He had a knife when he was supposed to be unarmed."

Ben held up his hands. "Maybe some of that's on me for not checking more closely when we did our pre-dive checks, but I'm telling you, he didn't have a knife on any of his gear."

"It's not your responsibility," I said. "You've got nothing to worry about other than helping us find our missing man."

He squirmed in his seat. "I swear to you I don't know what happened to him. One of your guys put my face in the mud, turned off my air, and tried to drown me."

"Nobody tried to drown you," I said. "You can rest assured that if our mission had been to kill you, nobody would've ever heard from you again."

He tilted his head. "Kinda like what's happening to Bravo One?"

"We didn't kill him, either. He bought himself a little time when he cut Gator's dry suit. We had to deal with that issue before we could continue harassing your buddy. That's when he disappeared."

Ben said, "I'm sorry. I don't know anything that can help."

"You're probably wrong about that. You likely know a lot more about Bravo One than you realize. You've lived, trained, and worked together for months. I want to take a look inside your head and pull out the information you don't realize you have."

He straightened up. "What are we talking about here? You're not talking about opening up my skull like a lobotomy, are you?"

I chuckled. "I'm not that kind of doctor, and we don't have any current technology that allows us to pull that kind of information out of your brain with surgery. The technique I'm talking about is having you relax and just answer my questions."

"Except for the relaxing part, that's what we're doing, isn't it?"

"Yes, but the relaxation part is what's important right now. I'd like for you to make yourself comfortable. Take off your shoes. Loosen your belt. Lie down, and close your eyes."

Ben pointed at Fred. "He's already tried this with me, and it doesn't work."

"Don't think about him right now. Just do as I say. Rest assured that I won't do anything destructive, and you will have one hundred percent control of the situation throughout."

He moved with hesitation, but Ben finally did as I asked and nestled onto his back. "I'm telling you. It isn't going to work."

I spoke gently and quietly until Ben's eyelids batted and his breathing became slow and rhythmic. Fred shook his head, and I gave him a wink.

"Okay, Ben. You're doing great," I said. "Let's talk about training. What did you do better than Bravo One?"

He took in a long breath. "Running. I'm faster and have better endurance."

"What else are you good at?"

He sighed. "I like hand-to-hand and CQB."

"Me too, Ben. Let's think about Bravo One now. What was he good at?"

"He's good with knives."

"Yes, he is. What else?"

"He's good at looking scary."

I fought back the laughter that wanted to explode from my chest. "What do you mean?"

Ben said, "I don't know. Sometimes, when I'd look over at him, he'd have this face like, I don't know . . . a serial killer or something."

"We call that the face of war, Ben. You have it too, but you'll never see your own. Tell me more about him. Did he do anything strange? Anything that didn't make sense?"

Ben chewed his bottom lip for a moment. "He talked in his sleep sometimes."

Fred and I locked eyes, and I said, "Oh, really? What did he talk about?"

"I don't know."

I leaned toward Ben. "How do you not know? You slept in the same hooch with him most nights."

"Yeah, but I don't speak that language."

I tried to hide the surprise on my face. "What language, Ben?"

"It must've been Russian, or maybe Ukrainian. I don't speak either of those, but that's what it sounded like."

I leaned back and turned to Fred, who wore the same expression as I did. "We don't dream in foreign languages. We dream in the first language we learned as a child."

Chapter 4
Not Exactly True

The interview was over, but the process was not. I helped Ben achieve a level of relaxation that wasn't natural, so I owed it to him to help him find his way out of the tunnel.

I sat forward on the edge of my chair. "You're doing great, Ben. I don't have any more questions for you about your dive buddy, but if there's anything else you'd like to tell us, please feel free to do so now."

He opened his eyes, but he didn't appear to focus on anything. "It's just his look. It's not normal, but nothing here is normal."

"Okay," I said. "That's all we need to know. Here's what I'd like for you to do. Just stay where you are and enjoy the rest. You've been running at full steam for eighteen months. You've earned the sleep. You may close your eyes and sleep as long as you'd like. When you wake, you'll feel fully refreshed and ready for what comes next. For now, just breathe and enjoy the silence."

Fred and I stepped from Psych Two and into his office.

Before either of us sat, he said, "I think we should get Will in here."

"I agree. This thing just got sticky, and if we don't play it right, Will's going to get it all over himself."

Fred dialed a number. "Will, it's Fred. Drop whatever you're doing and join us in my office. Something came up that you need to know."

While waiting for Will, Fred said, "It's not entirely true, you know."

"What's that?"

"Sometimes, we do dream in foreign languages if we're bilingual."

I said, "You're right, but not in this environment. When was the last time a trainee here at The Ranch wasn't physically and mentally exhausted when they hit the bunk at night?"

He sighed. "You've got a point, but it's still not unheard of."

I reached across his desk and lifted the missing man's file, but Will came through the door without knocking before I could dig into it.

"What's going on?" he asked as he slid onto the chair beside me.

Fred motioned to me. "Go ahead. You tell him."

"Your missing man dreams in Russian."

Will screwed up his face. "How do you know?"

"I talked Ben into taking a little nap and answering a few questions. He volunteered a piece of information that surprised us."

Will crossed his legs. "What did he say?"

"He told us Bravo One talks in his sleep sometimes, and that it sounds like Russian."

Will pointed toward my lap. "Is that his file?"

I handed it to him, and he thumbed to page five. "He's got elementary Mandarin, conversational German and Spanish, but nothing close to Russian."

I said, "I didn't pull it out of Ben. He volunteered it, so it isn't contrived. He believes the language is Slavic."

Will adjusted in the chair. "A minute ago, you said Russian, and now it's Slavic."

"Ben doesn't speak or understand Russian, so he couldn't specifically identify the language. He said it sounded like Russian or maybe Ukrainian."

Will planted both boots on the floor. "Let's get our story straight. You're accusing one of my trainees of being a Russian plant based on a second-hand account of him speaking a language that another trainee doesn't know. Is that what's happening here?"

I held up a hand. "Let's slow down. I'm not accusing you—or anyone—of anything. I'm sharing a piece of data we collected. That's all. It's way too early to assume anything, but it is something we have to consider."

Will ground his palms into his temples. "No way. There's no way he got this far without being detected. There are too many checks and balances—too many eyes and ears for something like this to slip through the cracks. There aren't any cracks."

Fred took the reins. "Nobody's throwing any punches in this room. We're still reeling from the uppercut we took in Psych Two."

Will tossed the file back onto Fred's desk. "How does that kid in there know what Russian sounds like if he doesn't speak it?"

Fred bounced a racquetball off the wall of his office and caught it several times. "Because Russian sounds like Klingon, and everyone knows that sound. The somniloquy isn't the only thing Ben mentioned."

I grimaced at the can of worms Fred was about to open, but he kept talking before I could intervene. "He also told us that Bravo One looks like a serial killer."

Will huffed. "Are you kidding me with this? If you can make it through this course *without* looking like a serial killer, there's something seriously wrong with you."

I jumped in to minimize the damage. "The look isn't important, and the language may be a big misunderstanding, but it's not something we have the luxury of ignoring. We've got a missing trainee who had a contraband knife that he used to attack an active operator. That's what we're investigating."

Will said, "No, Chase. *We* aren't investigating anything. You were here as part of the opposing force for a training exercise and to evaluate a couple of trainees for placement in the field. That's the limit of your involvement in this."

I took a gentler tack. "We work for the same people, Will, and ultimately, it's up to those people how we handle this. Sweeping it under the rug isn't possible. If we think he's dead, we have a responsibility to notify his family. If we think he ran, we have a responsibility to find him. Either way, we have to notify the Board."

Will pinched his eyes closed and groaned. "I didn't need this today."

"None of us did," I said, "but we're in it, and we'll get out of it together."

He maintained the distressed posture. "Dear God, I hope this kid is dead."

Silence consumed the room for a moment until Fred laughed. Odd reactions from Dr. Fred were nothing new, but laughter was the last thing I expected.

He composed himself and said, "Think about how bad it is when all three of us would prefer a dead trainee over the alternative. You're not in this alone, Will. If this dude is a plant, and I missed it, I'm finished. My career is over. You inherited Bravo One. I'm the one who conducted his psych evals. I have to wear this one, not you."

Will shook his head. "I'm not looking for somebody to blame. I just can't believe we let a mole get this deep into our operation."

I said, "Let's set up a call with the Board and tell them what we know. Ultimately, they're the decision-makers in this thing."

Fred made the call and arranged a video conference for ninety minutes later. That gave us just enough time to talk with the SEAL commander and our teams.

We found Lieutenant Dobson sitting on the bank of the York River, wearing the look of a man with the weight of the world on his shoulders.

I took a seat beside him. "How's it going, Lieutenant?"

"I've had better days. It's good to see you're finally getting some work out of Shawn. He dragged his feet the whole time he was in the Navy. How'd you do it?"

I appreciated his attempt at humor. "I just pay him what he's worth."

"Why didn't I think of that?" Dobson said.

We sat in silence for a moment until he finally said, "What's the story with this kid we're looking for?"

I broke it down for him. "He brought a knife to a fight when he was told to go unarmed."

"Smart kid," he said. "I'd do the same thing."

"You wouldn't have done it at BUD/S."

He plucked a piece of grass from the ground and stuck it in his mouth. "No, I guess you're right. They would've washed me out for disobeying orders, but this ain't BUD/S."

I tapped a stone with my boot and watched it roll into the water. "No, it's not, but we're just as serious about the rules."

He shot a thumb across his shoulder. "Do you work for the schoolhouse?"

"No, I'm a contractor like most of your guys will be when they leave the Navy."

"How's the pay?"

"Not bad," I said. "Do you have any theories on what happened to the lost diver?"

He stared into the sky. "Was this guy confident in the water?"

"He wasn't bad. He chose to stay and fight instead of running immediately."

The lieutenant pulled the blade of grass from his mouth and studied it thoroughly. "Is there any way this guy thought you were real-world aggressors trying to end him?"

"What makes you ask that?"

He shrugged. "It just doesn't feel right. If he knew it was all part of the training scenario, he would've never pulled the knife. Surely, he's smart enough to know that would get him thrown out of the program. If I've got the story right, this kid did exactly what I would do if I believed I was in mortal danger. I'd fight back with every tool in my arsenal—including contraband knives—and I'd haul ass out of there at the first opportunity."

Special operations commanders look at every situation through a very different lens than the rest of the world, and I should've seen precisely the same thing Lt. Dobson perceived.

I laid a hand on his back. "Don't leave, L.T. I may need you in a briefing in twenty minutes."

"Nope. Not interested. We're here on a search and recovery mission. The agency isn't going to hang this one around my neck. I'm a SEAL, not a scapegoat. You guys are on your own when you start handing out the blame cards."

"You've got the wrong impression," I said. "If you're right about our missing boy, this thing just got a lot bigger than any of us."

"Precisely my point," Dobson said. "When you find a ship that needs sinking or a dock that needs to be blown to high heaven, I'm your man, but you can have your briefing without involving my team and me."

"I get it, and I won't drag you into the mud with us, but I really appreciate your willingness to help out here in the water."

"It's what we do," he said. "Good luck with all of this, but for what it's worth, I don't believe this guy got washed out to sea. I think he believes he got busted running a deep-cover op and ran for his life."

* * *

The conference room at The Ranch wasn't as modern and plush as ours back at Bonaventure Plantation, but it was efficient. The Board appeared on a monitor mounted on one wall of the room, and Fred opened the meeting.

"We've had an incident here at The Ranch," he began. "During an underwater training exercise, one of our trainees drew an unauthorized knife and attacked one of the OPFOR players. There were no injuries, but the trainee is now missing."

"For how long?" a man on the monitor asked.

Will checked his watch. "Almost three hours."

The same man asked, "Who is the trainee?"

Fred said, "Timothy Martin Taylor, call sign Bravo One."

"That explains what Chase is doing there. We had him loosely earmarked for Team Twenty-one," the man said.

I shook my head. "We don't need anyone new, but thanks for thinking of us."

The man ignored me and asked, "Theories?"

Fred said, "There are only three possibilities. One, he's dead and rolling in the deep blue North Atlantic. Two, he's on the riverbank and hasn't made contact with anyone yet. Or three . . ."

The man from the Board interrupted. "Stop right there, Dr. Kennedy. I want to hear from Mr. King."

Will looked up at the camera. "All indications point to him being dead, but that's tough for me to swallow. He wasn't injured in the skirmish. He likely had a few hundred pounds of air left, so he could've made the surface and swam ashore, but apparently, he didn't do that. The only remaining possibility is exactly what Dr. Kennedy was about to say."

The man from the Board held up a finger. "Give us two minutes."

The screen turned gray and silent, and I unplugged our microphone. "What are they talking about, Fred?"

"I don't know, but you can bet your boots they'll have an assignment for somebody when that camera comes back on."

Almost exactly two minutes later, the Board returned to the screen. The same man who'd done all of the talking on their behalf said, "Mr. King, you're now in charge of the perimeter-contained manhunt. Figure out how far it's possible for Taylor to have traveled since he was last seen. That's your search area. If he's inside that circle, recover him and return him for questioning by Dr. Kennedy."

Will sighed. "It's busywork, isn't it. You don't think he's inside that perimeter, do you?"

"We have to cover all of our bases, Mr. King. Assemble your team and get to work. You have unlimited resources, but keep it out of the news."

Will rose. "Understood, sir."

He left, and Fred and I remained well within the Board's sights.

"Dr. Kennedy, we'd like you to review every detail of Mr. Taylor's recruitment, background, and psychological profile. If you need additional personnel, we'll be glad to authorize the expenditure."

Fred said, "I'd rather keep it in-house for now. My staff and I can manage without more help."

"Good," the man said. "Now, it comes down to Dr. Fulton."

I looked up in anticipation of being told to butt out and go home, but I couldn't have been more wrong.

He said, "Dr. Fulton, your assignment is to brief your handler within the next ten minutes and go find Timothy Martin Taylor for us. We've got a few questions we'd like him to answer."

Chapter 5
Looking Smart

Clark Johnson, retired Green Beret and my handler, is the only person in my life who never fails to answer the phone when I call. No matter the hour or day of the week, when I dial his number, Clark says, "Hello, College Boy." His answering streak remained intact that day.

"Good afternoon, boss."

"I don't like the sound of that," he said. "You only call me boss when you need a favor or you're about to stab me with a piece of bad news and break it off somewhere under my skin."

"I'm not calling to ask for anything."

He moaned. "Oh, boy. Let me guess. You've let your dollar mouth overload your nickel butt again."

"That might be an accurate description for what's going on, but it's going to get a lot worse before it gets better."

"Don't make me wait any longer. Let's have it."

I said, "You know we're at The Ranch, right?"

"Yeah, I know about that. How'd the kindergarteners do? Are you bringing one of them home with you?"

"Not exactly. One of them did a little too well. He lashed out and tried to gut Gator in the river."

"Wait a minute," he said. "They weren't supposed to be armed. Please don't tell me a trainee took a knife away from Gator."

"No, he had one of his own tucked away nice and neat. Gator's okay, but I can't say the same for his dry suit."

"I hope you made the swordsman pay for his indiscretion."

"We plan to."

Clark raised his volume. "You plan to? You mean you let him get away with it in the water?"

"We didn't actually let him do anything. I intervened to protect Gator, and the kid escaped."

"Escaped? What does that mean?"

I said, "I'm sorry. I didn't mean to use a big word you don't understand. He got away, as in, he's missing, and not even the SEALs can find him."

"What SEALs?"

"William King, the new commander at The Ranch, called in the Special Boat Team out of Little Creek. They spent three hours in the water, along with my guys and a bunch of cadre from the schoolhouse. The boy is just gone, but that's not the worst part."

Clark said, "Hang on a minute. I get the feeling I'm going to need another drink for this fairy tale."

"Better make it a double. It's possible the trainee is a Russian plant."

The line went silent until the sound of ice cubes falling into a sink reverberated through the phone. "This calls for bourbon straight up. Break it down for me."

I told him everything we knew about Timothy Martin Taylor and covered every conversation we had that day.

When I finished, Clark said, "Is Skipper on it already?"

"Not yet, but she will be soon. I'm planning to get her back in the op center at Bonaventure while I spend some quality time with Taylor's parents in Norfolk."

"Are you going alone?"

"No, I'll take the team in case things get sticky."

"Is your girlfriend with you?"

I said, "If you're talking about Anya, she's not my girlfriend, but yes, she's with us."

"Good. Make sure she's inside during the interview with Taylor's folks. She's better at sniffing out communists than anybody I know."

"I'm way ahead of you. She and Mongo are poring over every piece of paper they've got on Taylor here at The Ranch."

He clicked his tongue against his teeth several times. "What's your gut telling you?"

"You don't want to know."

"I wouldn't have asked if I didn't want to know, so give it up."

I sighed. "I think he got caught up in the current and swept toward the Atlantic."

"Toward the ocean, or actually into the ocean?"

I said, "It's impossible to know, but he's strong enough in the water to make land and get back to The Ranch if that's what he wants to do."

"That also means he's strong enough to make land and disappear if that's what he wants to do."

"You're right, but we're just guessing at this point. I'll keep you posted, and I'm sure Skipper will be in your ear as soon as she gets back to Bonaventure."

"You do that," he said. "I'm going to talk with the Board and the new commander up there. What did you say his name is?"

"It's William King, but he told me to call him Will. He took over for Gunny when he retired."

"Got it. Now, go stick your nose to the grindstone while the iron is hot, and figure out what's going on with this Taylor kid."

"I'm starting to believe you do that on purpose," I said.

"Do what on purpose?"

I chuckled. "Never mind. We'll talk again soon. Enjoy your cocktail."

"Better make that plural, College Boy. See ya."

The team was huddled around me for the call, but they gave me a little space when I hung up.

Skipper was first to speak. "I need a ride."

Disco raised a finger. "No problem. I'll have you back in St. Marys before you know it. Mind if I take Gator for the right seat?"

"He's all yours," I said, "but don't drag your feet getting back up here. We have to start at the epicenter of this thing and work out."

Gator, Disco, and Skipper hit their feet, and I took Skipper's hand. "Give me two minutes."

She planted herself back into the chair she'd just abandoned. "What is it?"

I scratched my head. "This is going to sound crazy, but that name —Timothy Martin Taylor—rings a bell in my head, but I can't figure out where I've heard it before. Does it set off any alarms for you?"

She closed one eye and cocked her head. "I'll give it some thought, but it didn't sound familiar when I first heard it. Of course, I'll do a deep dive as soon as I'm in front of my computer back at the op center. If there's any connection between him and anything we've ever worked on, it'll come up."

"Sounds good," I said. "Get some rest on the plane, if you can. If I'm right, this thing will be more of a data game than a shoot-em-up, and everybody knows you're the queen of data."

She squeezed my hand. "Be careful, Chase. I don't like the way this whole thing feels."

"I'm always careful."

She rolled her eyes. "You're never careful. I'll call you as soon as we land."

The analyst and two pilots headed for the Camp Peary landing strip while I slid my seat in front of our giant and asked, "Did you learn anything new?"

Both Mongo and Anya grimaced, and she said, "Is very strange situation. Timothy Martin Taylor's parents still live near Norfolk, but his grandparents are dead."

"All four of them?" I asked.

"Yes. Gloria Martin, Timothy's mother, was raised in Wisconsin, but her parents died when she was in high school. File says they were killed by drunk driver in Thunder Bay, Ontario."

"That's not hard to believe," I said.

Anya shook her head. "No, if it was scenario by itself, it would be sad story, but wait until you hear about paternal grandparents. They disappeared while hiking in Alaska five years after drunk driving crash in Canada."

I pondered the discovery. "Surely, the Board did their due diligence, right?"

Anya shrugged. "I do not know, but I am certain they will say they did."

"We're not that kind of organization," I said. "We aren't going to claim to have done things we didn't do."

Anya asked, "Are you speaking for organization below you or above you?"

"Both."

"Is nice of you to have such loyalty, but you cannot know what happens above your level. You are team commander, but you do not make decisions for all of Board."

I said, "I think I can safely speak at least one level above my head. I have complete faith in Clark, and I felt the same about Dominic before he retired."

She patted my hand. "You have too many bullet holes and too many missing parts of body to be so naïve. It would be wise to double-check everything above Clark."

"You're right. Perhaps my confidence in the Board is a little too high, but they've always kept their word with me, and I never remember walking into a trap they intentionally hid from me."

She leaned close and whispered in Russian, "Faith is good, but blind faith is deadly."

I placed a foot on one of the legs of her chair and rolled her away. "All right, everybody, listen up. Here's how we're going to play this. I'm going to put on a jacket and tie and spend a few minutes talking with Paul and Gloria Taylor. Anya's going with me, but she won't speak."

Anya said, "This does not make sense. Why would I not speak?"

"Because you're there to spot Soviet or Russian culture. We have to approach this intellectually, as if Timothy is a threat, but we can't let his parents know we're considering that possibility."

Anya gave me a look I couldn't identify and stuck out her hand. I didn't take the bait, but she proceeded as if I had. In flawless American English, she said, "Hello, my name is Ana Fulton, and I'm from Georgia."

I smiled back at her. "Okay, if you speak, you have to sound exactly like that. We can't give the Taylors any reason to suspect we're looking for Eastern European ties."

Mongo said, "You're going to be wired for sound, right?"

"Of course," I said. "We'll use our open-channel satellite comms."

The big man asked, "Are you going in before Skipper gets the op center up and running?"

"No. I think it makes more sense to have her record everything we say and hear in there."

Anya said, "I can wear glasses Celeste made for me. They make me look smart, and they have wonderful camera inside."

I scanned the room. "Does anyone have anything else we need to discuss?"

Shawn studied his fingernails a little longer than I liked, so I said, "What's on your mind, Frogman?"

He took a long, deep breath and said, "There's an element here we haven't touched on, and that's the physical risk. I think we'd all feel better if you took a security contingent with you."

I tried to imagine what he was thinking. "You don't think the Taylors are a physical threat, do you?"

"I assume everybody's a physical threat until I know otherwise. That's part of the reason I'm still alive."

"Point taken," I said. "What are you concerned about specifically?"

Shawn said, "There are two possibilities that worry me. The first is that the whole family is working for the Russians and they just found out they got busted."

"What do you mean by busted?"

"Just stay with me for a minute, and I'll take you through it. What if the parents are illegals planted here by the Kremlin, with the sole purpose of raising an American son to go to work for the American intelligence machine? If that's what's going on, and Timothy notified them about the incident in the river, they may be ready to fight back when you confront them."

I let his idea play out in my head for a moment. "Okay, I'm with you. We can't rule that out, but it has to be highly unlikely, right?"

Every shoulder in the room lifted, and Shawn said, "The second scary possibility is that little Timmy ran home to Momma, and he's a coiled cobra ready to strike when you and one of the mermaids show up."

"All right. You sold it. Let's go in force, but I want everyone except Anya and me to stage on the perimeter and be ready to move in if Shawn's theory turns into reality."

That declaration seemed to relieve the bulk of the pressure the team had apparently been feeling, but I asked once more, just to cover all my bases. "Anybody else?"

Heads shook, and I checked the time. "Skipper will be on the ground in half an hour, and she'll have the op center smoking ten minutes after that, so let's get some calories down our throats and see if we can find a sports coat that comes close to fitting me."

Chapter 6
Eleven Roses

"I didn't take your advice."

Those weren't the first words I expected to hear from Skipper's mouth, even though they were true.

"Let me guess," I said. "You didn't rest on the plane."

"You're pretty good at this game. I couldn't rest. My brain is churning at full speed, and you know how I get."

"Yes, we all know exactly how you get when you don your Super-Analyst cape, so let's hear it."

She said, "Let's start with Mamaw and Papaw Taylor. They would be his paternal grandparents. The Board and The Ranch seem to believe they disappeared while hiking in the wilds of Alaska, but I'm not so sure that's the whole story."

"So, they probably *weren't* eaten by bears?"

She didn't laugh. "Maybe they were eaten by bears, but probably not in Alaska. I've never been good at believing the six o'clock news. There's always more to the story. Based on what I've been able to dig up so far, they were hiking—and allegedly—hunting in Alaska when they disappeared. The seaplane pilot who dropped them off said they didn't have enough gear for the fifteen-day trip they claimed was their plan. You'll have to talk to Kodiak about how much gear a couple would need to survive in the Alaskan wilderness for two weeks."

"I think I've got a pretty good idea how much gear that would be, and it probably wouldn't fit in most of the bush planes that serve as aerial Ubers up there."

She continued. "Anyway, he picked them up in Fairbanks and dropped them off near the Yukon–Charley Rivers National Preserve. The Taylors apparently told their pilot they had a mobile radio they could use to call any aircraft they heard or saw overhead, and that pilot could relay the message to the pilot who dropped them off."

"That sounds like a convoluted mess. Did that kind of tunable hand-held radio exist in sixty-nine?"

"Who knows? But remember, Kim was an electrical engineer. Maybe he built one. I don't know. It's not important, though."

I said, "How could it not be important if they disappeared? If they really had this magic radio, why wouldn't they have used it?"

Skipper groaned. "You're making assumptions and getting ahead of me. Stop doing that. Here's the rest of the story. They did get in touch with a Canadian company and arranged to be picked up and taken to Whitehorse in the Yukon Territory of Canada."

"Why?"

"I have no idea, but that's where this whole thing starts to fall apart." She paused, leaving me hanging on every word, before saying, "Let's back up a year or so. Kim was a contractor at Eielson Air Force Base near Fairbanks in the late sixties."

"Slow down. Who's Kim?"

She said, "Sorry. I sometimes forget that you don't know everything I know. Kim and Mary Taylor were Paul Taylor's parents, and Paul was, of course, Timothy's father. Are you caught up now?"

"Kim is a guy?"

She finally giggled. "Yes, silly. Kim can be a man's name, too. Don't be name-ophobic."

"That's not a real word, and I have no phobias of any names."

"Whatever you say. Now, hush and listen. Kim Taylor was an electrical engineer specializing in airborne radar systems. He worked on the Rivet Amber project. Are you familiar?"

"You told me to hush," I said, "so, I'm hushed. But no, I've never heard of Rivet Amber."

"That's what I thought, but don't feel bad. I didn't know about it either until half an hour ago. It was an experimental RC-One-Thirty-Five-Echo with a massive—and I do mean massive—onboard radar system that added over eighteen tons to the airplane's gross weight. That's not all it added, though. Apparently, that thing used so much energy and produced so much heat that an additional APU was installed to provide the necessary power, and a complex radiator system was built specifically to cool the radar. Are you still with me?"

"I'm good. Keep talking."

She cleared her throat. "Now, we've got an overheated, overweighted aircraft that was never designed to manage either of those conditions."

I said, "I feel a crash in our future."

"Bite your tongue," she said. "We don't use the word *crash*."

"Who's word-ophobic now?"

"I'd prefer if you'd hush again. On June fifth, nineteen sixty-nine, the Rivet Amber vanished over the Bering Sea with nineteen crew aboard. The final transmissions with air traffic control were a report of vibrations with an unknown origin. When the controller asked if the crew was declaring an emergency, they received only a radio click and mumbled voices. The next transmission said, 'Crew, go to oxygen.'"

"And that was it?" I asked.

"Yep. The Rivet Amber was never heard from again. And despite a massive search by the Air Force and various other agencies, no wreckage was ever found."

"That's a great story, but what does it have to do with our boy Kim?"

"Keep your shirt on. I'm getting there. The hunting and hiking trip Kim and Mary Taylor went on happened the last week of June, nineteen sixty-nine."

"Oh."

She said, "Oh, exactly. Now, we've come full circle, back to the Canadian company they contacted to take them to Whitehorse. The company sent a pilot in a de Havilland Beaver. That was the only plane they had that was capable of making the nearly four-hundred-mile flight with three adults, two weeks' worth of gear, and a dead moose, all the way to Whitehorse."

I sighed. "Don't tell me. The Beaver never made it to Whitehorse."

"Well done, Doctor Fulton. I'm impressed. But that's not all. Just like the Rivet Amber, no wreckage was ever found."

"If you discovered all of this on your laptop from forty thousand feet, why didn't the Board find it when they ran Timothy's background?"

"I don't know, but I did find out that Kim Taylor was apparently adored by everyone he worked with. They even had a memorial service for him and Mary at Eielson after their disappearance. Apparently, nobody thought they could be spies right in the heart of the Cold War."

I said, "I don't like it, but it's starting to make sense."

Skipper said, "You're not going in there with guns blazing, are you?"

"We don't have enough intel to do any blazing just yet, but I'm not ruling it out before this is over."

She said, "I've got a feeling this thing is a long way from being over."

"Me, too. Do you have anything else before we go talk to Paul and Gloria Taylor?"

"I'm sorry, but that's all I've got for now. If you want, I can put together a full brief on the extended family."

"I do want that, but I don't have time to wait for it. If this thing is already exploding, Timothy could've warned his parents. If that happens, or has already happened, they're likely to run."

She said, "I'll get on it right away. Let me know when you get to the Taylors' house, and I'll grab the audio."

"Anya said something about some glasses Celeste built for her that have video capability. Do you know about that?"

"Oh, yeah. I know all about it, and I definitely think someone should wear them for the interview."

"Who do you recommend?"

She let out an exasperated sigh. "I hate to admit it, but they look pretty natural on Anya. She can probably pull it off better than anyone else."

I tried not to chuckle. "She says they make her look smart."

"If by smart she means slutty librarian, I guess I'll buy it."

"I'll be sure to tell her you think so."

"Maybe that's not the best plan. Just be careful, and try not to miss anything."

"I've got you," I said. "So, if I miss anything, you'll catch it on the audio and video feeds."

"You've got too much faith in me," she said.

"Oh, no, I don't. I have exactly the right amount of faith in you. Now, get back to work. I'll call you when we get to Norfolk."

* * *

I briefed the team on Skipper's discoveries as we drove from Camp Peary to Kings Grant—a community about halfway between Norfolk and Virginia Beach. The hour-long drive gave us plenty of time to spitball theories, and every avenue we explored led to the same place—the Kremlin.

We picked up Disco and Gator at Norfolk International and brought them up to speed. They listened and came to the same conclusion as the rest of us.

"There's the house," Mongo said. "It's nice, but nothing special."

I said, "That's exactly how they'd want it. If they're trying to blend in, they don't want to draw too much attention."

"Blend in?" Singer said. "They've been in this country thirty years or more. They're already blended."

We drove the neighborhood, familiarizing ourselves with every route to a main road. The makeup of the community made it impossible for us to surround the house without neighbors catching us.

From one street behind the Taylors' house, Singer said, "Let me and Gator out here. We can cover the back without being detected while you're inside and the rest of the team waits out front."

Disco flipped a pair of switches beneath the steering wheel, disabling the interior lights as well as the brake lights, before bringing us to a stop. Singer and his protégé slipped from the Suburban and disappeared into the waiting darkness.

I took Disco's seat behind the wheel while he and the rest of the team ducked below the windows of the SUV. I parked on the street in front of the house instead of pulling into the driveway. If a hasty retreat became a requirement, I'd much rather jump into a vehicle at the curb than in front of the garage door.

Anya asked, "How are we playing this?"

I held up my Secret Service credential pack. "Like the bureaucrats we are."

She pulled her cred pack. "I have one, too, but is from Department of Justice."

"Hide that accent," I said. "Don't get us busted in there."

She gave me a mock salute, and we stepped from the Suburban.

I froze in place and turned back. "Somebody call Skipper and let her know we're going in."

A thumbs-up came from behind the middle row of seats, but I couldn't tell who belonged to the hand.

Anya and I strolled up the sidewalk, looking for surveillance cameras or motion sensors. If there were any of either, they were exceptionally well concealed.

"Ready?"

Anya nodded, and I rang the bell.

A television played from inside, and it sounded like the Yankees game.

"That TV's a little loud, don't you think?"

"It's very loud," she said with no discernible accent, as if she were from somewhere in the middle of the country.

Thirty seconds passed, but no one came to the door. I thumbed the bell again and heard the chime over the blaring television inside.

There wouldn't be a third attempt with the doorbell, but I didn't have to tell my partner. She was off the porch and crouched behind the boxwoods before I'd realized she'd moved. Anya peered into each window she passed for only an instant before moving on.

As she continued to the right, I moved left and worked meticulously to get an eye inside every piece of glass in the house.

Anya and I met at the back of the house, and she took a knee. "Anything?"

I shook my head. "Nothing. You?"

She returned the gesture. "We should go inside."

I pulled my pick kit from my pocket, and Anya plucked it from my hand. "I am much better than you at picking."

I didn't offer an argument, and she had the back door open in seconds. There was no telltale beep of an alarm system, and that surprised me. If the Taylors were spies, they had terrible home security habits.

We moved silently from room to room, and nothing looked out of place. Every bed was made. There were no dishes in the sink. And, except for the Yankees fans and announcers, the house was silent. We searched every drawer, closet, and cabinet, and found only what any middle-class home in America might have. There was even a junk drawer in the kitchen, and I considered that to be an extremely American thing.

We checked every window and door for any intrusion indicators. Basic tradecraft called for every intelligence operative to rig an elementary trap to let the agent know if somebody had been messing around in their nest. My favorite was to slip a hair into a hinge. If anybody opened the door, the hair would fall. No one except me would know where the hair had been, and I would know without a doubt that somebody had been snooping. But we found nothing . . . no hairs, no tape, no tiny trails of dust. Nothing.

I tapped my watch and motioned toward the back door. Anya led the way, and I took one more solid look at every detail of the house as we departed.

The second we stepped back into the Suburban, Anya said, "Did you see it?"

"What?" I said. "I didn't see anything that would lead me to believe it's anything other than the typical American working-class house."

She said, "There were eleven roses in vase on kitchen table. Do you remember first time you bought for me roses, Chasechka?"

Chapter 7
Name That Target

"Oh, I remember," I said. "I bought you a beautiful arrangement of a dozen long-stem reds, and your reaction was exactly the opposite of what I hoped for."

"Is good that you remember this lesson, so next time, you can bring for me only eleven, just like Paul brought for Gloria. Even numbers of flowers is for moments of sadness like funeral. Odd number is for love."

"Who made up those rules?" Disco asked.

Anya turned to face him as we pulled away from the house. "Is Russian tradition, and no one knows how it began."

"It's just the way we've always done it," Disco said. "I just love that answer."

I checked the rearview mirror as my team unfolded from their hiding positions, and we rolled to a stop just as Singer and Gator stepped from a line of trees.

With the whole team back together, we continued the discussion as we drove.

Singer spoke up as the eleven roses theory bounced around the interior of the SUV. "Maybe one of the roses died, or she used it to make a corsage or something."

"This is possible," Anya said, "but is also possible that maybe Paul did something bad and roses were apology."

I said, "Sometimes, guys buy flowers for the women they love just because they love them and not because they've done something wrong."

Anya giggled. "This is naivety again. We have to add this one more clue that the Taylors have ties to Russia. Is not enough to declare them to be FSB or SVR yet, but it is one more indication."

Skipper's voice played inside my—and everyone else's—head, thanks to the bone conduction devices implanted on each of our jawbones. She said, "I'm with Anya. The small details are stacking up, and they're hard to ignore."

I asked, "Did you catch the odd number of roses in the vase?"

Skipper huffed. "I'm ashamed to say I missed it, too, but the video came out beautifully. I just wish we had thought about planting a camera before you left so we would know when or if the Taylors come home."

"I thought already of this," Anya said. "And I put motion-activated transmitter on garage door. It is not a camera, but it will tell us if garage door is opened."

"What if they sweep for bugs?" Gator asked.

"This is best part of device I left behind. It is motion-activated, so it does not broadcast unless it is moving. When still, it is silent and impossible to detect. Celeste made it for me."

"She didn't make it just for you," Skipper said. "We all have them, but nice job remembering to bring yours."

Gator said, "Forgive me for being *that guy* by asking, but what do we do now?"

Skipper said, "We wait for Anya's transmitter to come to life while I search the electronic world for Paul and Gloria Taylor."

"I'm not good at waiting," I said. "Do you have anything that might give us a hint where they went?"

The line was silent for a moment, but Skipper finally said, "I'm writing a piece of code to track their passports, credit cards, and a few other goodies. I don't have anything yet, but I'll know as soon as they use any form of ID electronically."

Before I could protest further, my phone chirped. "Hello, this is Chase."

"Chase, it's Will King from The Ranch. We've got a problem. How far away are you?"

"We're down in Norfolk, but we've got the jet. We can be back on the ground at The Ranch in less than half an hour."

He said, "You have one of our Suburbans, right?"

"That's right."

"Good. Leave it at the FBO, and we'll send someone for it. I'll meet you at the airstrip in thirty minutes."

I said, "Before you go, can you give me a hint about what's going on?"

"Not on the phone. It's better if you see it in person."

"We're on our way."

* * *

We touched down at The Ranch ten minutes after taking off from Norfolk, and true to his word, Will was waiting for us when we taxied up.

"Thanks for getting back so quickly. Did you have any luck in Norfolk?"

I said, "We didn't learn much, but we didn't exactly strike out. Nobody was home, but that didn't stop us from doing a little poking around. Nothing jumped out at us except eleven roses in a vase."

He froze in his tracks. "Are you serious?"

I nodded, and he said, "Did you check the trash for the twelfth?"

"We checked everywhere and found nothing. What is it you want us to see so badly?"

He motioned us into the van, and we pulled up in front of the same tiny shelter that was my home for eighteen long months. We dismounted the vehicle and followed him inside. When we stepped into the space, he pulled the string to bring the single, bare bulb to life. It swung freely and spread its weak glow across the room.

On the left side was an empty cot, but on the right stood a second identical cot—with one exception. Lying on his side, Bravo Two, Benjamin Thomas Gaines, rested with white foam encircling his mouth, and his chest, that should've been rising and falling with every breath, was still and silent.

"Was it Taylor?" I asked.

Will shrugged. "We got a perimeter fence alarm that we were certain wasn't an animal, so per our SOP, we searched the compound and buildings. The hootches are last on the checklist, and this is what we found."

I pointed toward the empty cot. "Was that one Taylor's?"

He nodded. "Yes, and before you ask, we already searched it, and nothing was taken. If it was him, he hit Gaines and got out."

"Why would he kill his training partner?" Mongo asked.

"I've got a theory," came a voice from just outside the doorway.

We all turned to see Dr. Fred leaning against the jamb.

"Let's hear it," I said.

Fred picked his fingernails. "He killed him for the same reason you hypnotized him. Taylor knows that nobody on Earth has as much information about him as that dead kid right there. He killed him because he didn't want Gaines working with us to find him."

Mongo contorted his mouth. "Could be, but do we know for sure it was Taylor? Could this be a reaction to something he ate or drank? We need a toxicology report to rule out an environmental condition."

Fred shot a thumb over his shoulder. "The medics are just pulling up. It is two in the morning, after all. We'll have the tox screen and autopsy done in twelve hours."

We moved from the tiny room where I'd slept so long ago, and the medics carried Gaines to the waiting ambulance, but there would be no lights and sirens. The time for those was long gone.

Will said, "The accommodations aren't exactly five-star, but you guys are welcome to crash with us for the night."

"Thanks," I said. "I think we'll take you up on that. I'd like to be here when the toxicology report comes back."

Fred said, "It won't come back from anywhere. We'll do it in-house."

"Even better," I said.

Will took us to a barracks with air conditioning and a water heater that worked.

I said, "I never felt a drop of hot water or cold air conditioning the whole time I was held captive here. You're not going soft, are you?"

Will said, "This place is for VIPs. Back then, you didn't qualify."

I glanced at my watch. "Folks, we've been on our feet and going strong for over twenty hours. Get some rest, and we'll kick some more hornets' nests in a few hours."

No one protested, and we crashed.

The next sound I heard four hours later was Anya coming out of the shower. To my relief, she was wearing shorts and a T-shirt instead of her birthday suit.

I sat up on the edge of my bunk. "That's my shirt."

She pulled at the University of Georgia logo on the front. "Was it?"

"It still is."

She grabbed the bottom of the shirt as if she were going to shuck it over her head. "If you would like, I will take it off, but it probably smells like me, so you cannot take it home to Penny."

One by one, the team emerged from hibernation, and Gator asked, "What time is it?"

"Six thirty," I said. "Let's get moving."

The chow hall hadn't changed, and the eggs were still runny, but no one complained.

Fred walked in and tapped lightly on the end of the table. "We just ran the tox screen. It was a form of cyanide, likely inhaled or ingested."

"So, he was murdered," I said.

Fred slowly nodded.

I called Bonaventure, and Dr. Mankiller answered. "Op center, Celeste."

"It's Chase. Where's Skipper?"

"Oh, hey, Chase. She went down for a nap. I'm covering for her until eight."

"Are you up to speed on the situation?"

"I believe so. Unless something's changed in the past six hours."

"It has. Benjamin Thomas Gaines is dead. He was murdered by cyanide poisoning."

She gasped. "Was it Taylor?"

"That's the prevailing theory at the moment, but we don't have any evidence that isn't purely circumstantial."

"I should probably wake Skipper up."

"No, let her sleep. She needs the rest, and waking her up won't bring Gaines back to life. Has there been any movement by either of the Taylors?"

"Not yet, but it's only been a few hours. They have to buy gas and food sooner or later. We'll catch them."

"Not if they use cash."

Celeste said, "That won't protect them. I set up a facial recognition protocol using the Taylors' driver's license photos as the basis. If their faces show up on a security camera somewhere, we'll get a ping. There will likely be a bunch of false alarms, but it gives us some place to start."

"Great idea," I said. "Keep me posted, and have Skipper call when she relieves you."

"Sure thing. What else?"

"I can't think of anything at the moment, but I'll let you know if something comes up."

She said, "Okay, if that's it, we'll talk soon."

I pocketed the phone and turned back to Fred. "Where was the perimeter alarm?"

He said, "That's not my area, but Will should be here any minute."

Fred was right, and Will made his appearance only minutes later. I asked the same question, and he pointed to the twelve-foot-tall fence with razor wire coiled along the top. "About three hundred yards that way."

I turned on a heel. "Let's have a look."

When we reached the suspected point of entry, Singer—our sniper and master tracker—pointed toward the razor wire. "Right there. See the separation?"

I studied the menacing wire and finally saw what he picked up immediately. "Oh, yeah. That definitely looks like it's been manipulated lately."

I asked Will, "Do you mind if I climb the fence?"

"Knock yourself out," he said. "Just try to stay out of the razor wire."

I climbed the fence and closely inspected the coils. "It's been cut and pressed back together."

Will said, "I guess there's no question now that Taylor came over the fence, took out his former training partner, and vanished back into the night."

I hopped down. "Where'd he get the cyanide?"

He held up a finger. "I'll tell you what I know, but Fred is the subject matter expert. It's apparently a synthetic strain that was manufactured in Europe."

"How do you know?" I asked.

"I don't know. That's chemistry, and I'm a shooter."

"Fair enough," I said. "Where's Fred?"

It took fifteen minutes to get an answer to that question, and I settled onto Fred's sofa in his office. "So, this synthetic strain of cyanide, how specific is the fingerprint?"

He leaned forward. "Do you know anything about the process of synthesizing cyanide?"

"I do not, and I don't want to. I just want to know if you can tell exactly where this one was made."

"We can get close," he said. "Commercially produced cyanide for mining and manufacturing is impossible to trace. It's too basic and simple, but the labs that create cyanide specifically for the purpose of assassination are few and far between. We have samples from most of the labs, and the molecular structure of the compound is practically a signature. It'll take a few hours for the computer to isolate the location of the lab that created this batch, but we should have that information within a couple of days."

"You said definitely Europe, though, right?"

Fred waggled a hand. "Probably Europe, but there's a slight chance it could be Chinese."

I laid my head back. "I think this just became a full-blown, Board-sanctioned mission. Does Gaines's family know yet?"

Fred shook his head. "Not yet, but I'll have to notify them today."

"Are you gonna tell them he was murdered?"

He played with a paperclip beneath his fingertip. "I haven't decided yet."

I said, "I don't know how much they pay you, but I wouldn't do your job for a million dollars a year."

He laughed. "That would be a significant pay cut for you, wouldn't it?"

I stood and turned for the door, and Fred said, "Tell me something, Chase. Can you catch this guy?"

I let his question bounce around inside my skull for a long moment. "Yeah, we can catch him, but I can't guarantee we can do it before he hits whatever his target is."

"Any thoughts on that target?"

I said, "With any luck, I'm the target, and he'll come to us instead of us hunting him down all over the world."

Chapter 8
You're Getting Warmer

The phone that never leaves my side is an absolutely essential part of my world, and the message it delivered on that particular day became the exact turning point the early stages of our investigation needed. I slid the ubiquitous device from my pocket. "Hello, this is Chase."

I didn't check the screen before answering, but the software Skipper and Dr. Mankiller wrote ensured no calls came through from salesmen concerned about my car's extended warranty.

Skipper said, "We've got action at the house in Kings Grant."

"How long ago?"

"Thirty seconds ago."

"What took you so long?"

She didn't find humor in my sarcasm. "Are you going or not?"

"Of course we're going," I said. "But you don't happen to have satellite coverage, do you?"

"I do, but it's worthless. There's a massive thunderstorm pummeling the area, so I can't see anything other than cloud tops and continuous lightning."

I covered the mouthpiece and eyed Disco. "Check the weather at Norfolk. We need to be there now."

Skipper said, "I couldn't understand what you were saying."

"It wasn't for you. I was talking to Disco. We're on our way back to Kings Grant. If we can get in, we'll take the Gulfstream, but if it's as bad as you say, we may be on wheels."

She said, "I just pulled up the weather at Norfolk International. They're reporting four hundred overcast in heavy rain and thunderstorms, south and southeast."

Disco must've gotten the same report because he said, "We can get in. Let's go."

Will dropped us back at the airstrip, and we had the *Grey Ghost*'s twin Rolls-Royce engines whistling their favorite tune in minutes. Although Gator was technically type rated as second-in-command on the Gulfstream, the nasty weather put me in the copilot's seat, and Disco right where he belonged—in the captain's throne on the left.

The air traffic controller said, "*Grey Ghost Four* is cleared direct RUSSL waypoint to join the TERKS TWO arrival. Cross RUSSL at one six thousand and descend via the arrival. Norfolk altimeter is two-niner-two-four."

I was the monitoring pilot, so the radio work was mine while Disco flew the airplane. "Copy the meter, and *Grey Ghost Four* is turning direct RUSSL. We'll cross at one six thousand to join the TERKS TWO and descend as published on the arrival."

She said, "Roger, *Grey Ghost Four*. Norfolk is reporting two hundred overcast in heavy rain."

"*Grey Ghost Four* has Information Charlie at Norfolk, and we request the ILS two-three."

She said, "*Grey Ghost Four*, expect ILS two-three. In the event of a missed approach, fly heading three-two-zero and climb and maintain three thousand."

"If we miss, we'll climb and maintain three thousand on three-two-zero and back to you."

We left flight level two-one-oh for sixteen thousand and buried ourselves in the solid cloud cover. The rain began a few minutes later, and along with it came the turbulence.

"I don't love that," Disco said.

"You're the one who said we could get in."

He kept his attention on the instrumentation—especially the

weather radar. "Yeah, well, just because we can get in doesn't mean we're going to enjoy the ride."

"Speaking of liking," I said, "I'd like for Gator to see this from the front seat. What do you think?"

He said, "Bring him up, but put him in the jump seat. I want this thing in your hands if I curl into the fetal position and cry for my mommy."

"That's comforting."

After squeezing from the cockpit, I got Gator's attention with the curl of my finger, and he made his way forward.

I said, "We want you in the jump seat to watch the approach to minimums."

I returned to my seat, and he perched on his. Jump seats in Seven-Forty-Sevens aren't comfortable or luxurious, and the one in the *Ghost* was only slightly more comfortable than an electric chair.

After beating and banging our way through the turbulence on the arrival, the controller said, "*Grey Ghost Four* is six miles from LUFSY. Turn right heading two-zero-zero, maintain one thousand six hundred until established on the localizer, cleared ILS two-three Norfolk International."

I read it back. "*Grey Ghost Four* is coming right to two-zero-zero, and we'll maintain one thousand six hundred until established. Cleared ILS two-three."

"*Grey Ghost Four*, contact Norfolk Tower on one-two-zero point eight. Godspeed."

I said, "Thanks, approach. We're off to tower on one twenty point eight."

Disco brought the power back and called, "Approach, flaps."

"Approach, flaps set."

Our speed fell, and he said, "Gear down."

I lowered the landing gear handle. "Gear in transit."

I glanced up to see Gator scanning the panel, likely imagining himself at the controls. "Looks like fun, huh?"

He shook his head. "Not one little bit. Why is Disco hand-flying the approach?"

I started to answer, but the captain cut me off. "In this wind and turbulence, the autopilot would work itself to death. Besides, hand-flying approaches to minimums is a good way to keep your skills sharp."

At that instant, we hit what felt like a brick wall in the sky. The *Ghost* shuddered and bucked like a rodeo bronco, but Disco kept cool.

I watched the three lights beneath the gear lever turn green. "Gear down."

Disco nodded as he wrestled the controls keeping the Gulfstream centered on the localizer and glideslope.

I said, "Norfolk Tower, good morning. *Grey Ghost Four* is outside the marker on the ILS two-three."

"Grey Ghost Four, Norfolk Tower. Wind two-five-zero at one eight, gusts three-five, check wheels down, runway two-three clear to land."

"Copy the wind. Gear is down, and *Grey Ghost Four* is clear to land two-three."

I turned to Gator and mouthed, "It's a lot harder than he makes it look."

Gator huffed. "Don't I know it."

The pleasant, feminine, computerized voice of the *Ghost* said, "Five hundred."

The turbulence continued, and so did Disco's wrestling match.

"Four hundred."

I focused through the windshield in search of anything that looked remotely like an airport, but all I saw was the inside of a monstrous gray cloud engulfing us.

"Three hundred. Approaching minimum."

At two hundred feet, we were required to execute the missed approach procedure if we didn't have the runway environment in sight from the cockpit.

The voice said, "Minimums . . . minimums."

I stared through the eerily dark cloud. "Approach, lights in sight."

Disco kept flying and said, "Roger. Continuing."

"Runway in sight," I said as the big, beautiful stretch of concrete lay out in front of us.

Disco glanced at the gear lights and the enunciators. "Three green. No red. Clear to land."

The calming voice of the *Ghost* returned. "Fifty . . . forty . . . thirty . . . twenty . . . ten . . . retard, retard."

The main landing gear touched down as gracefully as a Bolshoi ballerina, and Disco pulled the throttle back and across the detent to deploy the thrust reversers. Our speed bled off, and we made the high-speed turn off.

I called the controller. "Norfolk Ground, *Grey Ghost Four* is off at Golf, request taxi to Signature Aviation."

The controller said, "*Grey Ghost Four*, Norfolk Ground. Taxi to Signature via Golf—Alpha cross runway three-two. And when did you break out?"

I pressed the button on the yoke. "We'll take Golf and Alpha to Signature and cross three-two on Alpha. We broke out right at minimums, with moderate turbulence all the way."

We parked, shut down, and disembarked into the driving rain. The Suburban belonging to The Ranch was still parked exactly where we left it the night before, and we hustled inside as if our lives depended on getting out of the torrential downpour.

"Well, that was exciting," Disco said as he slid behind the wheel.

I shook the rainwater from my hair. "Nice work up there."

He didn't acknowledge the compliment, but he had us headed for Kings Grant in seconds.

A few minutes from the house, I called Bonaventure on speaker, and Skipper said, "How was the flight?"

"Not great," I said, "but we're in the Suburban and headed back to the Taylors' house. Has there been any additional movement from the device?"

She said, "No. It showed movement for about ten seconds, and then, nothing."

I spun in my seat until I could see Anya. "You placed the motion-sensing device on the garage door, right?"

"Yes, this is correct. I put it on bottom corner behind roller so it would be difficult to see."

Skipper said, "If it was on the garage door, then somebody opened the door, but it hasn't moved again, so that could mean they're planning to run in and back out, or they forgot to put the door back down."

The windshield wipers tried, but they were no match for the heavens' seemingly endless waterfall.

I said, "I can't imagine anybody forgetting to close a garage door in this weather."

Skipper said, "Maybe their power's out due to the storm and they had to put the door up by hand."

"We'll know soon. We're pulling into the neighborhood now."

As we headed onto the target street, the world ahead of us turned into a flashing collection of red lights and orange flames.

Shawn leaned between the front two seats. "Oh, boy. This ain't good."

"What is it?" Skipper asked.

I studied the scene as we drew closer and asked, "Are you monitoring EMS, fire, and police in Kings Grant?"

Skipper said, "No, why?"

"Because the Taylors' house is fully involved with flames shooting thirty feet in the air."

"Is the fire department on the scene?" she asked.

"They're here, but they're standing around and watching it burn. Nobody except God is pouring any water on the fire."

A pair of fire trucks passed us with their lights and sirens announcing their presence, and Shawn said, "Oh, good. They brought more firemen to watch it burn."

The first of the two additional trucks turned onto the front lawn of the house, and mud flew from its tires like fountains. When it finally came to a stop, a massive stream of foam poured from a cannon mounted on top of the truck.

The second truck drove past the house and into the neighboring yard. The same fountains of flying mud opened up from the tires of the truck, and the driver showed no regard for the neighbor's landscaping. He left the driveway and forced the truck as close to the inferno as possible. The cannon from the second truck opened up and poured the same stream of white foam into the air.

I motioned toward an SUV with the word "Chief" emblazoned across the door. "Pull in behind the chief."

Disco brought us to a stop behind the truck, and I stepped from the Suburban while pulling my credentials from my pocket. Without asking, I slid onto the front passenger's seat and held up my Secret Service badge and ID. A man in his fifties, with a terrible combover, sat behind the wheel with a phone pressed to his ear. He turned with rage in his eyes, but the rage turned to disappointment in an instant.

I said, "What's going on, Chief?"

"Oh, just a little house fire with people trapped inside, and it's too hot for anybody to go in after them."

"How many people are in there?"

"We don't know, but we believe three people live in the house."

"The Taylors," I said.

"That's right, but why does the Secret Service care about a house fire?"

"I'm not at liberty to discuss that with you, but why is the fire so hot?"

He turned and watched the flames dancing into the liquid sky. "Have you ever seen a house fire with flames that high, Agent?"

"No, but I'm not an expert. Do you have a theory?"

"Accelerant," he said. "There's no question this is either arson or somebody was storing something inside that house that's really good at burning. Most house fires never get above nineteen hundred degrees. We didn't stick a thermometer up this one's butt, but it has to be close to twenty-five hundred or more. I can't send my guys into that monster."

I pondered the possibilities. "If there are people inside, there's no way they could've survived, right?"

"Let's put it this way—if a person got into the bathtub and filled it with water, it would take about two minutes for *that* fire to boil the water out of the tub and cremate anybody inside."

A horrendous noise roared, and the roof of the single-story house collapsed. The dancing flames twisted and coiled around the debris as it fell, and sparking ashes dispersed in every direction.

The chief shook his head. "Now, it's just a matter of protecting the neighboring structures and waiting for that pile of hell to cool enough for the arson investigator to analyze it."

"Have you ever seen this before?"

He frowned. "Arson?"

"No, I meant a house fire this hot."

"No, I've never seen any residential structure burn like a chemical plant, if that's what you're asking."

"Thanks, Chief. Sorry for the interruption."

He grunted and lifted the phone back to his ear.

I braved the still-pouring rain and returned to the Suburban, where the rest of my team was glued to the horrific scene.

"The chief said it's definitely arson, and it's burning at least six hundred degrees hotter than the typical house fire. Apparently, the census records say three people live in the house, and I got him to admit their last name is Taylor."

Anya said, "There is something you need to know about fire." Her tone was that of a frightened child, and she immediately had my attention.

"Okay. Enlighten us."

She said, "This is textbook technique following discovery of a deep-cover operative. We will never know identity of people inside."

"There may not be anybody inside," I said. "The chief believes there *may* be someone in there, but there's no way to know."

Anya sighed. "Believe me. There will be remains of three adult bodies found after fire. Two will be male, and one will be female. They will be burned beyond recognition."

"But they can still identify them by dental records, right?" Gator asked.

Anya said, "KGB did much research on fire and human bodies. They found that exposure to temperatures of one thousand degrees for more than twenty minutes can cause dentin inside teeth to crack from inside and destroy enamel structure of teeth."

Shawn furrowed his brow. "A thousand degrees isn't all that hot. When I did fire training in the Navy, they put us in temperatures up to thirteen hundred degrees, and none of our teeth exploded."

Anya smiled. "This is because inside United States, temperature is measured in Fahrenheit. In Russia, we use Celsius."

I watched the fire continue to rage in spite of the rain and massive volumes of foam the water cannon trucks were still pouring into what remained of the house. "Are you saying the Taylors incinerated themselves to avoid being found out?"

Anya said, "No, they would not do this to themselves. A team of *dvorniki* would do this."

I racked my brain searching for the English equivalent of *dvorniki*, but it wasn't coming. "Translate that for us, please."

Anya shrugged. "Is in English, maybe person who cleans up mess."

I closed my eyes. "And the three bodies we'll find . . . Who are they?"

She said, "We will never know, but I was trained to find homeless people, or especially people using drugs like heroin. It is very easy to convince someone living on street and using drugs to come inside house where it is nice and warm."

I gritted my teeth. "They just didn't know how warm it was going to get."

Chapter 9
Not Coming for Us

I pulled a stack of fast-food napkins from the center console of the Suburban and wiped my face. With my clothes still dripping wet, I locked eyes with Anya. "How certain are you that there will be three bodies in that house?"

Anya frowned. "Is wrong question, Chasechka. There will not *be* three bodies inside. There are *already* three bodies inside, and they died from smoke inhalation."

"If you're right, what are the Taylors doing right now?"

"I cannot say for certain. I can only tell you what my training from KGB and SVR would have *me* do."

Singer said, "Please tell me the protocol is to run home to Mother Russia."

"No, I cannot tell to you this because it would be lie. Paul and Gloria might go home to Russia, but Timothy will not."

"What makes you say that?" I asked.

"Because they are old."

Disco protested. "Hey, they're my age."

Anya said, "Yes, I know this," but she offered no apology. "I do not believe they are on their way back to Russia soon. I have theory about Timothy."

"Quit stalling and spit it out," Kodiak said.

Anya pulled off Kodiak's hat and stuck it on her head. "I am not stalling. I am thinking. Is only new theory, so I do not have all of details worked out yet. This is okay, yes?"

I waved my hand in a circular motion, begging her to spill her theory.

She said, "When FSB or SVR plant illegals inside foreign country, it is done with specific purpose in mind. This is called *napravlennaya missiya*. Maybe best English words for this are *directed mission*."

"Wait a minute," Mongo said. "If we're right, the mission didn't start with Paul and Gloria. It likely started with *their* parents, Timothy's grandparents."

Anya said, "Yes, you are correct, and their *napravlennaya missiya* was likely seizure of Rivet Amber project. I was not yet born when airplane was stolen, but I have seen it."

Suddenly, the interior of the SUV was silent, and everyone appeared to be hanging on Anya's every word.

Disco pointed northwest. "You've seen the Rivet Amber?"

"Yes, I told to you this already. I have seen it many times. You know of Beriev A-Fifty, yes?"

Disco said, "Of course. The Bumble Bee."

"Yes, this is silly name for very serious airplane. Airplane is based on Ilyushin Il-Seventy-Six but is built specifically to be airborne target detection and command-and-control platform. When radar system for Beriev A-Fifty was designed, it was based on radar inside Rivet Amber."

"How do you know?" Disco asked.

Anya shrugged. "Is well known inside Russian government. How is it possible that you do not know?"

Disco said, "Oh, I don't know. Maybe I missed the day they taught that in flight school while the Russians were our enemy and the Cold War was raging."

"This is not important right now," she said. "What is important is that Paul was small boy when all of this happened, and he stayed inside United States after his parents *supposedly* died in Alaska."

"Why is that important?" I said.

"Because after his parents were gone—regardless of what happened to them—Paul was probably taken by his parents' Soviet handler."

"What do you mean? Did the handler kidnap the boy?"

"No, this would not happen, but he probably knew handler and maybe called him Uncle. Is very common."

"So, you're saying the handler adopted Paul."

"No. Adopting him would change his name, and he would not be Taylor any longer, but we know this did not happen. He kept name, but he probably changed bodies."

Gator threw up both hands. "Hold on. Changed bodies?"

"This is terrible phrase for what happened. Is in Russian called *obmen*. This means *exchange* in English. Soviet Union probably made *obmen* and gave to handler new boy when he was teenager. This new boy became Paul Taylor. Gloria was probably also sent to America with Paul."

"This is a convoluted mess," I said. "Can you fast-track it any?"

Anya laid a hand on our sniper's shoulder. "Yes, I am sorry. My story is turning into story like Singer's that goes on and on. I will do better."

"My stories aren't long," Singer said.

That received a collective groan from the team.

Fearing the discussion might turn into a family squabble, I motioned for Disco to get us moving, and he shifted the Suburban into gear and pulled away from the fire.

Anya said, "Where are you going? Are you not going to wait until firemen go inside and find bodies?"

Disco reset the windshield wipers to samurai mode, and I watched them duel it out with the rain. "If you tell me there will be bodies inside that house, I believe you. Tell us more about the exchange."

"Is very simple. Inside Soviet Union in those days, KGB trained many children to speak American English by watching American television. This is how I learned, but I also had English classes in school."

"Don't get sidetracked," Singer said. "This is a tough group."

She continued. "Thank you for advice. When exchange was made, boy who became Paul Taylor was sent to United States to live with handler—"

I said, "Sorry to cut you off, but what happened to the real Paul Taylor during the exchange?"

Anya looked away. "This is not something you truly want to know, so I will continue story. After Paul has been inside United States for some years, he would be trained and educated and placed inside company that Soviet Union wants to know about. In this case, it was Norfolk Naval Shipyard. This is perfect place for spy to work. He would have access and knowledge of inside of every ship in facility being built or refit."

Kodiak grimaced. "You mean the Russians have had copies of the blueprints for every ship we've got?"

"Yes, this is most likely truth, and same is true for Russian ships. United States probably has all of plans, and maybe even pictures and video, of inside of every ship in Russian Navy."

"That's terrifying."

Anya said, "Is only truth."

I asked, "Does that mean Timothy was exchanged, too?"

Anya closed one eye and glanced upward. "Probably not. Since Gloria and Paul were accepted in society, Timothy is probably their real son. He was raised as American but also taught glorious things about Soviet Union."

"Sorry to have interrupted," I said, "I just wanted to make sure I understood the details."

Anya continued. "Is okay. You may ask all questions you want. I will answer if I know. So, after Timothy became adult and went to college, it was plan for many years for him to apply to all of intelligence services in United States."

She hesitated before saying, "This part is frightening, but is true. I believe Kremlin knows exactly what to write on application to make sure person is found to be qualified but not selected on first effort. This is what I think happened. Either Paul or his handler made sure this thing was included on all applications to keep him from being chosen."

"I don't understand," I said. "Why wouldn't they want him to be selected? Don't they want spies inside the intelligence agencies?"

"Yes, of course, this is what Kremlin wants, but they have already plenty inside those agencies. I believe Timothy was intentionally routed to Board, but there is one thing much more important than that." She stopped talking, and everyone froze in anticipation. "I believe Kremlin directed Timothy Martin Taylor intentionally toward this team. This is what Fred and Will told you, yes?"

I said, "No, neither of them said anything about directing him to this team. They said they wanted me to take a look at both trainees for potential assignment to us, but neither said we'd be forced to take either of them."

Anya said, "This is magician's trick of misdirection. Every box was checked to see that you would see Timothy, and you would be interested in taking him. On theory, he is perfect for this team. He is good at everything but not great at anything. You are best in all of world at turning people who are good at things into becoming best at these things. Look at Gator, for example."

I didn't enjoy Anya's punch in my gut, but I couldn't deny that she was on to something. And I wasn't arrogant enough to believe I was a brilliant teacher, but I had enormous confidence in the people around me to take a well-qualified student and turn him into a serious killing machine.

I said, "So, let me get this straight. You think we're the target—the *napravlennaya missiya*—the directed mission."

Anya met my eyes in the mirror. "I am only operator, not planner. But you made embarrassment of Kremlin many times, and I am very good example of this. They would never suspect I would defect to United States. I was very good officer of SVR. It is reasonable to believe Putin would love to have krot—a mole—inside this team, so he can destroy you from inside like cancer."

Before I could respond, my phone chirped, and I punched the speaker button.

"Chase, it's Skipper. I just got a call from a guy named Charles Gordon."

"Am I supposed to know who that is?"

"Apparently, he's a fire chief in Norfolk, and he said you left one of your Secret Service business cards in his vehicle."

"Oh, that guy," I said. "What did he have to say?"

"He called on the Secret Service line on your card, so, of course, I answered as if I were the switchboard operator and told him you were out of the office."

"Nice work. What did he say?"

"He said he needs to talk with you ASAP."

"Did you get a number?"

"Of course I got a number."

She read it off, and I said, "Thanks. I'll call you back after I talk with him."

I dialed the number, and he answered in short order. "Chief Gordon."

"Hello again, Chief. It's Special Agent Fulton with Secret Service. I just got a call from my office saying you needed to talk with me."

"Yes, Agent Fulton. I found the card you left in my vehicle, and I thought you'd like to know what we discovered when the house was finally cool enough to enter."

"Let's hear it."

He cleared his throat. "We discovered the badly burned remains of three adults. We don't have any official identifications made yet, but my guess is that they are Paul, Gloria, and Timothy Taylor. Is that who you were looking for?"

I groaned. "I'm sorry, but I'm not at liberty to release the names I'm looking for. It's a national security issue. I'm sure you understand. Is there enough left for the coroner to identify any of them?"

"Probably not. If anything, maybe they can compare some dental records, but in a fire that hot, sometimes we never officially identify the victims."

"I understand. Did you determine what accelerant was used?"

"Not officially, but I have a lieutenant on the scene who's been through all the arson investigation classes there are, and his first guess is chlorine and maybe diesel."

I glanced into the mirror to see Anya nodding, and I said, "Thanks, Chief. If you'd do me a favor and keep me in the loop when you get an ID on the bodies as well as the accelerant, the Secret Service and I will owe you a big favor."

"Sure, no problem. But it'll be a few days... maybe a couple of weeks."

"That'll be fine. I really appreciate the information, Chief."

"I do what I can to keep you feds happy. I gotta run and see if I can find a wrecker big enough to pull these trucks out of the mud."

I ended the call, and Anya said, "Lieutenant is very smart. In my training, I was taught to repair Sheetrock inside house so I could put chlorine tablets inside plastic bags and put inside walls of house. Diesel fuel is also good with chlorine because it burns slowly and for a long time. If I have to burn house for some reason, when chlorine tablets reach temperature of one hundred fifty degrees Celsius, they can help feed oxygen to fire and also react with diesel. This makes fire burn longer and hotter even when there is foam and water being poured onto flames."

I glanced at Mongo, our resident mastermind, and he nodded, confirming Anya's chemistry lesson.

"I think that does it," I said. "I'm convinced. Although we don't have any concrete, physical evidence of the Taylors being a long line of Soviet and Russian illegal plants in the U.S., our stack of circumstantial evidence could make it to the moon and back."

Heads nodded, and Mongo said, "I'm with you. It's too much to ignore. So, what's next?"

"I think there's only one option for us," I said. "Let's go home and make ourselves easy to find. We're nearly one hundred percent certain that Timothy Taylor is after us, so let's give him a target that shoots back."

Anya said, "No, Chasechka. This is not true. He is not coming for *us*. He is coming for *you*."

Chapter 10
Putin's Dartboard

The storm passed, and blue skies replaced God's fireworks show over Norfolk. We parked the Suburban in the same spot we left it the last time we left Norfolk and then climbed aboard the *Grey Ghost*.

Although I wasn't looking forward to it, I had no choice. A call to Clark was essential, so I settled into my seat in the back of the *Ghost* and dialed his number.

"What's going on, College Boy?"

"You sound like you're in a good mood, but let me warn you up front, I'm about to ruin your day."

"Is anybody dead?" he asked.

"Yes, but none of us."

I briefed him on the fire and Anya's revelation about being trained to destroy American real estate, one house at a time.

"Don't let that surprise you," he said. "The Russians aren't the only ones who like to hide little surprises inside walls. We've been doing that for decades. The key is getting and keeping the fire hot enough and long enough to scare away the firefighters and let everything burn."

"Nobody ever taught me that set of skills," I said.

"There was no need. You're not a safehouse kind of guy. You're an operator, not a spy. So, what's the plan?"

"There's more you need to know before I tell you about my plan."

"Oh, goody."

I said, "Goody, indeed. You need to know about the history of the

Taylor family. Their service to their country is long and distinguished."

"Which country would that be?"

"You're catching on," I said. "Give Skipper a call and have her give you the full briefing."

I took three minutes and briefed him on the Rivet Amber, and to my surprise, he knew every detail of the disappearing airplane. What he didn't know was that the Amber was resting peacefully inside a Russian hangar somewhere.

He said, "When life gives you cookies, don't try to make lemonade."

I shook my head. "I'm sure that's supposed to mean something profound, but I'm too tired to decipher it."

"You know what I mean. Go home, get some rest, and I'll call Skipper."

Disco and Gator had us wheels-up and climbing into the flight levels above the commercial airliners in no time. Having an additional pilot freed me up to do a lot of work I didn't want to do, but there's no way to deny that Gator was becoming more of an asset to our team every day.

As we leveled off at forty-one thousand feet, my phone asked for my attention, so I said, "Hello, this is Chase."

"Hey, College Boy. I just got off the phone with Skipper, and this thing is turning into a bona fide kurfuckle."

I couldn't hold back the laughter. "I'm pretty sure you mean kerfuffle, but you're not wrong."

Clark said, "No, I'm sticking with kurfuckle for this one. Listen, this is just you and me talking, okay?"

"Sure," I said. "I work for you."

He cleared his throat. "No, this isn't a boss-and-underling conversation. This is two old trigger-pullers kicking ideas around. Somebody dropped the ball on Tim Taylor's background check."

"There's no question about that, but it's too late to point fingers. We have to play the hand we've been dealt."

He said, "That doesn't mean we have to keep the same dealer for the next game."

"What are you saying?"

His tone turned conspiratorial. "I've got some concerns about the Board. They haven't exactly been Johnny-on-the-spot with good intelligence lately, and missing the string of events dangling from the Taylor family tree is a serious oversight."

"Think about it from my perspective. These guys may have dedicated a big portion of their lives to developing and deploying a deep-cover operative specifically to hit me."

He said, "This ain't the first time the Russians have done that."

I huffed. "Yeah, but this time, I'm the target."

"How quickly you forget, College Boy. Take a look down the aisle of that airplane you're on 'til you see a headful of long blonde hair attached to the first operator the commies trained and deployed to flip you or kill you."

"But I was just a dumb kid back then."

"That's right, and that should've made you an easy mark, but you weren't quite as gullible as they expected you to be. They certainly didn't expect to lose an operator of Anya's caliber because of you, but that's exactly what happened. You've grown up a little since those days, so you should be a much harder target this time. The Kremlin knows that, but you're still a thorn in their side."

"I still don't get it," I said. "If they gun me down in Walmart, there's a thousand more just like me waiting to take my place."

"Listen to me, Hotshot. Don't ever let yourself believe that. I could handle any team I wanted, and there's nobody I'd rather have answering my phone calls than you. You've got a well-earned reputation in the covert ops community, and take it from me, you can bet your butt that Putin has your face taped to his dartboard."

"It's nice to know he cares. Maybe he'll invite me over for vodka and caviar and we can paint each other's toenails or something."

Clark laughed. "I'll see if I can set that up for you, but you're missing my point."

"I rarely get your points. Are you suggesting we step away from the Board?"

"Slow down. I didn't say that out loud, but the more I think about them dropping the pickle on this one, the more I question their ability to get the details right."

"I'm sure you meant drop the ball, but I do hate a fallen pickle. Let's table this discussion until we get Timothy Taylor in custody. After that, we can talk about our future."

"You got it," he said. "Call me if you need me."

* * *

We touched down in St. Marys with Gator on the controls, and the landing earned him a round of quiet golf claps from the cabin. It was a pleasant change to step from the plane and into air that wasn't pouring waterfalls of rain on the tarmac.

Don Maynard had the *Ghost* refueled and tucked away in her hangar within minutes of our arrival, and I was on my way to the op center.

I passed the thumbprint- and cipher-lock challenge, and the door to the third-floor operation center clicked.

Skipper was exactly where I expected her to be, at the keyboard of her computer, but to my surprise, my wife Penny sat in my chair at the conference table, reading a script.

She tossed the screenplay onto the table, jumped to her feet, and threw her arms around me. "It's nice to have you home, baby."

I returned the hug and offered a kiss that she enthusiastically accepted.

"Would you two get a room?" Skipper said.

Penny giggled. "Technically, this is our room."

I grimaced as Skipper spun in her seat.

She said, "You two can claim every other room in the house, but I think we should all agree that this one is mine."

Penny backed away. "Okay, I guess we can live with those terms. How was the flight?"

I tossed my hat onto the table and slid into Mongo's chair that made me feel like a little kid sitting at the grown-up's table. The big man's chair was designed and built to precisely match the rest of the chairs at the table, with one small exception. It was thirty percent bigger than everyone else's.

I said, "The flight was good, and Gator did a nice job on the landing. It's good to be home."

"Can you tell me what's going on?" Penny asked.

"Technically, no, but I'm going to tell you anyway because this one affects you."

I took her through the details, and her expression grew more concerned by the second.

After she had the background, I said, "I'm trying to decide what to do with you until we catch this guy."

She narrowed her gaze. "What do you mean, catch him? Aren't you going to kill him?"

I took her hand. "I don't start missions with the intention of killing anyone. If it becomes a necessity and there are no other options, we'll pull the trigger, but if we can capture this guy and get him to talk, we stand to gain a whole new understanding of how the modern Russian intelligence service works."

"I get it, but if this Taylor guy is determined to kill you, and he's as good as you say, I don't see an arrest in his future."

"We don't arrest people. We detain them until someone with the authority to arrest them arrives."

"You know what I meant," she said.

"Yes, I do, and you're probably right. If this guy comes hard, we'll push back even harder. It's what we do, but I don't want you to get the impression that I'm swatting a mosquito. If we're right about this guy and his family, they're serious, long-term players, and people like that don't stay alive very long unless they're extremely good at what they do."

Skipper said, "Uh, Chase. I'm sorry to interrupt, but we've got a problem."

I turned in my enormous chair. "What is it?"

She motioned to a screen to the right of her monitor. "The perimeter alarm system says we've got an intruder at the airport."

"Where?"

"North side behind hangar number six."

I dialed Mongo, and he answered on the first ring. "I know, boss. I got the alert on my phone. Shawn, Kodiak, and I are en route. Singer's on his way to high ground for overwatch. Have you talked to Disco or Gator since we landed?"

I said, "No, I think they were doing a postflight brief, but I'll call them. Where are you?"

"We're ten minutes away."

"I'll meet you at the main gate, and we'll move in together."

Mongo said, "I'll see you there. We've got sidearms and M-fours. Do you want me to call the police chief?"

"Not yet. We may not want the cops in the middle of this thing."

When I ended the call, I headed for the door, and Skipper stuck a rifle in my hands. She buzzed the lock, and I collided with Anya only inches outside the door.

She leapt backward. "I am sorry. I did not know you were coming out."

I shoved the rifle toward her. "Protect Skipper and Penny. We've got an intruder at the airport."

I expected an argument, but instead, she press-checked the rifle and stepped around me. Penny may not have loved the idea of being under the protection of the woman who still loved me, but she couldn't be in better hands. Anya had proven more than once that she was willing to make enormous sacrifices for my wife, and I had no doubt she would do everything in her power to keep her alive if Taylor threatened her.

I made a run through the armory for body armor, another rifle, spare magazines, and a satchel of CS grenades just in case I got the chance to smoke out our intruder with tear gas. Mongo, Gator, and Kodiak arrived at the main gate to the airport at the same time I rolled up.

The big man held up his phone. "I've got Disco. He and Gator are at his place. What do you want me to tell them?"

I said, "Get them airborne in the chopper in case we flush somebody out who thinks he can outrun us."

He shoved the phone back to his face and relayed the message.

The gate opened smoothly when I entered the code, and I said, "Give me Kodiak, and we'll circle around from the east."

Kodiak stepped from Mongo's truck and slid onto the passenger seat of my Suburban. "Let's get 'em, boss."

Mongo and Shawn headed across the airport with debris flying from their tires, and I turned right and headed toward the North River. I didn't drive as fast as Mongo, but Kodiak and I didn't waste any time. By the time we reached hangar six, Mongo and Shawn were already on foot and approaching the massive structure. Shawn watched Kodiak and me approach and tapped his hip with an open palm.

We got the signal and activated our sat-coms and bone conduction devices.

When I heard the click, I started the roll call. "One's up."

Everyone checked in except Gator and Disco, so I said, "Skipper, get Disco on the phone, and tell him to come up on the sat-com."

"Roger."

Seconds later, our pilots were on the network, and we had solid comms with the whole team.

Singer's confident baritone filled my head. "Sierra Six is in position on the rotating beacon tower. I've got one hundred percent coverage on the front and about eighty percent of the west side of hangar six. If you flush 'em, send 'em my way."

I said, "Roger, Six. We're checking the perimeter."

Kodiak said, "The fence has been cut back here."

Singer was next to speak. "I've got a scuff mark on the concrete beside the walk-through door on the southwest corner and light around the top of the main hangar door."

I'll never know how our sniper could pick out such small details from a thousand yards away, but he'd never been wrong, so I trusted every word out of his mouth.

I said, "Roger. There shouldn't be any lights on inside, so that means somebody has been or still is in there."

Mongo said, "We'll take that door. We're fifty feet away. Where are you, Chase?"

"Kodiak and I are on the east side at the rear door. Let's breach together."

He said, "We're in position. Call the breach, One."

I gripped the doorknob and looked up at Kodiak. He gave me a nod, and I said, "Execute. Execute. Execute!"

Chapter 11
Rat Killing

The heavy knob should've been frozen in position by the locking mechanism that cost more than my first car, but it spun freely in my palm, and Kodiak plowed through the opening with his rifle at his version of the low ready position. The butt was seated in the pocket of his shoulder, and the muzzle rested only three inches below the horizontal. I cleared the fatal funnel of the three-foot doorway almost as quickly as my partner, but I kept my muzzle high to avoid sweeping him as I scanned.

Shawn led the advance from the other door because Mongo was simply too big to be on point. The familiar sounds of their boots striking the concrete floor in uniform cadence reminded me of the countless hours we'd spent training as a team and learning every detail of our team's instincts, movements, and even their thoughts. It was as if we were all small, interlocking pieces of the same efficient and deadly machine.

The hangar had been a vast open space when we bought the airport, but since then, it had become the redheaded stepchild of our family. We neglected the space more than we should have, and it had become our twenty-thousand-square-foot junk drawer. Piles of airplane parts and discarded projects from Dr. Mankiller's lab lay dying in various states of decay at random intervals across the floor.

Shawn said, "Moving aft along the west wall."

I drew their progress on the scrap paper in my brain and followed Kodiak toward the front of the structure. Ten steps into our progress, a scurry followed by falling glass sounded from the center of the hangar floor.

I spun to face the sound and brought my rifle into position. Uncertain exactly where my teammates were, I left the selector switch on safe as I maneuvered to get a line of sight.

"Say position," I said softly as I sidestepped an overturned bucket that had apparently been someone's seat long before that night.

Shawn said, "We're at the midpoint of the western wall and moving north."

"Stay on that wall," I said. "We're crossing the main door."

Singer said, "Open the big door so I can see."

Kodiak pulled the lever, freeing the lock, and I pressed the switch. The massive electric door began its slow rise, mimicking the look of a massive, yawning beast.

The commotion came again, and more debris fell to the concrete floor.

"Anyone have visual on what's making that racket?"

The door continued its laborious rise, and as it progressed, Singer said, "Contact. Hold positions."

We froze in place and waited for the crack and hiss of our sniper's projectile searing its way through the air. The seconds passed like eons as we waited, but the round never came.

Instead of pressing the trigger, Singer said, "Movement twenty meters deep and thirty meters off the eastern wall. There's an airplane propeller sticking into the air a few meters short of the motion."

I said, "Shawn, Mongo, push them forward. We have the front flanked."

Shawn said, "Moving."

"Singer, call any motion."

"Roger," came the sniper's calm reply.

I called out, "You're surrounded and outgunned. Your only chance of staying alive is to surrender now. Lay down your weapons and kneel with your hands over your heads. Do it now, or we'll carry you out of here."

My threat served to cover the sound of Shawn's and Mongo's approach. I had no belief that whoever was inside our hangar would do anything resembling surrender. Whoever they were, they'd leave the building in body bags.

Singer's reassuring tone sounded. "You're on line, Shawn. Push 'em to me."

Shawn said, "Moving forward."

I contorted my body in a futile effort to spot the rest of my team. Kodiak knelt beside me with his rifle trained across the broad expanse of the open hangar door.

A new commotion rose to my right, and I scanned the depths of the building, praying I'd catch a glimpse of whoever was making their way toward the door I'd come through only moments before. Metal fell and clanged off the floor, glass broke, and movement was evident. What wasn't evident was how many intruders we were facing and where they were.

In desperation, I called Singer. "Anything?"

"Negative. Nothing definitive. I'm seeing small movements, but I don't have a target yet."

Shawn said, "We just passed the center of the hangar, and there's nobody here."

"Keep pushing," Singer said. "You'll flush 'em out."

Mongo and Shawn continued their measured progress, scouring every inch of junk as they came. After a few more strides, Mongo pressed his back to Shawn's, and they continued toward the door.

Shawn's boot appeared below and beside my muzzle, so I lowered my rifle and locked eyes with the former SEAL.

He shook his head. "Nothing."

"Somebody's in here," I said as I held up my satchel of CS grenades.

Shawn grinned, and I tossed a pair to him. He handed them off to Mongo, and I threw two more. Armed with both a new plan and new weaponry, our tactics changed in an instant.

Singer obviously watched the exchange through his scope. "I like where your head's at. We're about to have a rat killing."

That one stumped me, and I instinctively glanced across the airport and to the tower, where our sniper lay taking in every detail. "What does that mean?"

He said, "Where I grew up, we had corn bins, and we used to scare rats out of them and kill them when they tried to get away."

I nodded in his direction. "Yep, that's exactly what we're doing."

We pulled the pins and lobbed the tear gas grenades to strategic positions throughout the hangar. On our way out, we shoved concrete blocks against the two walk-through doors and took our positions by the front. With no breathable air left in the building and only one direction to escape, our bandits were sure to either run from Singer's corn bin or succumb to the noxious gas filling the air.

I watched as the plumes of disgusting white smoke filled the hangar. We were seconds away from pinning our unwelcome guests to the deck while they gagged and coughed.

Singer said, "Movement! East side. Coming forward."

"Don't put them down," I ordered. "Let us intercept them. I'm looking forward to a good old-fashioned enhanced interrogation session with these boys."

I couldn't believe the next sound I heard. It was coming from our sniper, but it wasn't a target call. It was laughter.

"What's going on?" I asked with my rifle still trained into the hangar.

Singer composed himself, caught his breath, and said, "Stand down, boys. It's raccoons, and they're waddling their way into the fresh air."

As if on cue, a pair of fat, disheveled raccoons emerged from the smoke-filled chamber and took in the clean air their lungs so badly wanted. Apparently content to be able to breathe again, the two animals parted ways and wandered toward the fence.

Mongo stood from his kneeling position wearing the same look our sniper was sporting. He laughed and dropped his rifle across his massive chest, letting it come to rest at the ends of his oversized sling. "Well, that was exciting."

Disco's voice joined Mongo's. "Gator and I are at the main gate. It sounds like we missed all the excitement."

I slung my rifle. "Yeah, it was a raccoon invasion."

Singer's voice suddenly turned ominous. "Chase. Those coons didn't turn on the lights, and they didn't cut through the fence, either. Stand fast. There are likely . . ."

If he finished his sentence, I didn't hear him. An earth-shattering explosion rocked the air, and everything in it, as an orange ball of fire rose from what had been our main hangar on the opposite side of the airport. Fifty-million-dollars' worth of airplanes had occupied that hangar in the previous minutes when it had been protected from the elements, but in an instant, it turned into a raging inferno beneath an ever-expanding mushroom cloud, with secondary explosions cooking off by the second.

I yelled over the cacophony of fire, falling debris, and my own heartbeat. "Skipper, get the fire department over here now!"

"They're already en route," she said. "Is anybody hurt?"

"Sound off," I yelled, and one by one, my shooters replied.

Kodiak leaned against me in a wordless report of his status.

Mongo said, "Two is up."

I ran through the team roster. "Sierra Three, Sierra One. Say status, Disco."

Nothing.

I swallowed hard and repeated the call, but still, no answer came.

I called, "Sierra Five, say status."

Just like Disco, Gator's voice never came.

I turned to the spot where the rotating beacon tower had been and prayed Singer was still alive. "Singer! Sierra Six, say status!"

Following protocol, Shawn said, "Seven is up."

I gripped my rifle and bolted into a sprint across the airport. "Singer, Disco, and Gator are down. Skipper, roll the ambulances. Get everything St. Marys has got headed this way. We need everybody! And get a perimeter set for squirters."

My breath came hard and fast as my boots pounded the earth and concrete between me and the fire. With every stride, the heat from the roaring beast strengthened, singeing my hair and baking my skin.

Looking toward the fire destroyed my night vision, but I could still make out shapes of what had been. The SUV at the main gate was on its side and burning. With every bit of my being, I wanted to believe Gator and Disco had escaped the vehicle before it joined everything else in the environment and caught fire.

The tower where Singer was perched lay in pieces on its side, and the shattered glass of the rotating beacon was scattered across the tarmac like flakes of glitter reflecting the dancing flames.

Needing desperately to be in two places at once, my focus darted between the burning SUV and the silhouette of our sniper.

Kodiak said, "I'm going for the gate. You check on Singer."

I ran as fast as my body could propel me and fell to the ground beside my friend, my moral compass, and the best sniper I'd ever know. I slammed a pair of fingers against the flesh of his neck, begging God to let me feel a pulse.

I repositioned my fingers several times, but all I could feel was near panic. Fighting everything inside myself, I battled to control my rage and quash my fury. I pulled my hand from Singer's neck and laid my left ear against his chest. As I pleaded for a heartbeat, I saw a single bubble form in a pool of blood just beneath his nose.

"Singer's alive but unconscious. Where are those paramedics?"

Skipper said, "They're rolling and should be there any minute."

I shot a look across my shoulder toward the main gate, where Disco's Suburban lay on its side, still burning. "Somebody clear that roadway! We have to be able to get the ambulances in here."

Another explosion sounded, and I shielded my face against the light and heat as the fuel truck flew through the air, slinging jagged shards of metal and jet fuel everywhere. I watched in disbelief as if I were living inside a nightmare, and my mind raced.

Jet fuel doesn't explode. That had to be a bomb.

Mongo said, "We got Gator and Disco out of the truck, but they're in bad shape."

"Can you move their vehicle to clear the road?"

The big man said, "No, but I can tear out a section of fence if you want."

I said, "Skipper, tell the lead fire truck driver to plow the fence. I'll pay for a new truck."

Skipper said, "Done. Where do you want the ambulances?"

"Send the first one through the hole in the fence behind the fire truck, and tell him to turn left toward the terminal building. I'll flag him down. I'm here with Singer."

"What about the others?" she asked.

"Stop them at the gate. Is there just one or two?"

She said, "I'm not sure. I'll get back to you."

The sirens came into range, and flashing red lights filled the entrance road to the airport. Just as directed, the driver of the first truck rammed the gate to the right of Disco's SUV and sent the chain link flying like a child's toy. A second fire truck followed the first, and they moved in on the flaming hangar.

The sound of the first ambulance's siren was music to my ears as the driver bounced the truck across the curb and through the gaping wound in the fence. I stood and waved both hands above my head until the ambulance slid to a stop a few feet away.

Before the paramedic's feet hit the ground, he yelled, "Are you okay, sir?"

I pointed toward Singer. "Forget about me. Take care of him!"

I stretched high and squinted against the glare of endless flashing lights to see two more ambulances parked haphazardly alongside the overturned SUV, where the front gate had been only minutes before.

I fought the overwhelming urge to run to Disco and Gator, but nothing I could do or say would change the outcome. Paramedics, police officers, and firemen worked in unison as if they'd practiced the procedure to respond to a hangar bombing, sabotage, critically wounded victims, and a fire raging out of control.

Ire twisted through me as I watched flames climb into the sky and my world crumble at my feet. As medics still labored over Disco and Gator in the distance, the doors of the ambulance closed behind me, and they carried Singer away with lights and sirens screaming into the darkness.

Chapter 12
I Want Anya

Police Chief Bobby Roberts laid an arm across my shoulders and removed his cap. "Why don't you and your men put those rifles back in your trucks? You're making folks nervous."

I brushed his arm from my shoulder. "Look at me, Bobby. Do I look like I care who gets nervous right now? I've got three casualties and an inferno consuming about a million dollars a minute. If I get half a chance at whoever did this, you won't have to worry about my rifle. It'll be out of ammo and smoking."

He ran a hand through what had once been a solid head of hair. "The state police are on it. I talked to Skipper, and she's working on some security camera video."

I turned to the chief and pointed a finger at his chest. "These bastards better hope the state police find them before I do."

He opened his mouth, but I cut him off. "Don't do it, Bobby. Don't give me the vigilante speech. I'm not a vigilante." After catching my breath, I asked, "Where are they taking my men?"

The chief pulled a radio from his back pocket and called the EMS dispatcher.

"Go for dispatch."

Bobby said, "Can you find out where the victims from the airport fire are being taken?"

"Sure, Chief. Stand by."

A few seconds later, the dispatcher said, "They're going to Memorial, Chief, but MedFlight is en route from Jacksonville for one of the victims."

I grabbed his sleeve. "Which one?"

He glared up at me as if I were speaking Dutch, and I said, "Which man are they flying to Jacksonville?"

Bobby spoke with the dispatcher for another minute and said, "We don't know." He groaned. "Call me as soon as we *do* know."

Without another word, I slapped the chief on his back and trotted toward the gate, where I found Mongo sitting on the ground with his back against the top of the overturned SUV.

I said, "You okay?"

He dropped his head. "No. Disco's in bad shape, Chase. Gator's beaten up and burned some, but he's young and tough. I doubt they'll keep him at Memorial. I assume that's where they were going."

"Yeah, they're going to Memorial, but the chief said they're sending MedFlight from Jacksonville for one of them. I guess that's Disco."

The big man sighed. "He's gonna need some good doctors and some even better prayers. Speaking of which, how's Singer?"

"He was alive when they put him on the bus, but he was out cold."

Mongo closed his eyes. "What's going on here, Chase?"

"I don't know yet, but I know this much. We're definitely not dealing with one twenty-something kid. This took a team and some time."

I helped him to his feet, and Shawn sidled up. "That kid from The Ranch couldn't have pulled this off by himself."

I said, "I'm not ready to say he had anything to do with this." I motioned at what remained of our airport. "This could be completely unrelated."

Kodiak wiped the sweat from his brow. "It doesn't really matter if it was him or not. We're down three good men and a bunch of air assets. We're crippled, to say the least."

I turned and took in the destruction and utter chaos still unfolding on the airport. "Let's get back to the op center. We've got a lot of work to do."

Driving away from the scene left me more furious than I'd been in years, and by the time I made it into the op center, everything I thought I knew cascaded from beneath my feet.

Skipper looked even angrier than I did when she looked up from her workstation. "They got the cameras."

I held up a finger as Penny leapt from her chair and ran into my arms. "Chase, I'm so glad you're all right. What happened? How are the others?"

I took a breath. "The main hangar is destroyed, along with everything inside it. Somebody blew it. Singer, Gator, and Disco are hurt, but I don't know how badly yet."

She squeezed me in her arms, and I don't remember a more soothing feeling. I hesitated to pull away, but too many questions remained to let myself continue enjoying the embrace.

"What does that mean, they got the cameras?"

Skipper groaned. "It means they somehow got into the camera network I designed and built. It should've been bulletproof."

"How did they get in?"

"They took over the network and fed data from twenty-four hours ago as if it were live. And the worst part is that I have no idea how they did it."

I planted myself into a chair and rolled toward hers. "When did the old video start playing?"

"It's impossible to tell. When you landed and got off the plane, the video was live, but sometime after that, it flashed back to yesterday's feed. Chase, whoever did this is an electronic mastermind . . . even better than me."

"Don't beat yourself up. I spent twenty minutes and a case of CS grenades clearing a pair of raccoons out of a hangar while somebody was wiring the main hangar with a lot of C-Four."

"That's the other thing that bothers me," she said. "The raccoons were a setup to get you to the airport to see the explosion."

I mentally replayed the events of the evening. "Who would do that and why?"

"I don't know the who, but I have a theory on the why."

"Let's have it."

She pushed away from her computer. "I think they wanted you to watch. I think whoever they are, they're sick, warped, and demented. They don't want to physically hurt you . . . yet. They want to make you pay for some sin you've long forgotten, but they clearly have not."

"Maybe, but we can't be sure of that yet. Any word from the hospital?"

She slid her headset onto one ear and pulled the microphone to her lips. After waiting for whatever happened on the other end of the line, she said, "This is Elizabeth Woodley. Three victims of the explosion at the airport should've arrived by ambulance in the past few minutes. Do you have any updates on their conditions?"

She struck a key, broadcasting the call through the speaker system. "Hello, Ms. Woodley. I was just about to call you. Chief Roberts with St. Marys PD asked me to keep you posted. Mr. Grossmann is in surgery, but I don't have specifics on his injuries yet."

"What about the other two?"

The woman said, "Let's see. Blake Riley is aboard a MedFlight chopper on his way to the Mayo Clinic in Jacksonville."

My brain hit a brick wall, and I whispered, "Who's Blake Riley?"

Skipper threw up her hands and mouthed, "That's Disco. Did you get hit in the head, too?"

I couldn't remember ever hearing anyone say Disco's real name out loud, but I felt terrible for not recognizing it.

The woman on the speaker said, "We do have some good news about Mr. Barrow, who keeps insisting that we call him Gator. But anyway, other than a few cuts and bruises, his condition isn't serious, and we expect to discharge him shortly."

Skipper said, "Thank you, ma'am. Please let us know if anything changes."

"I will, and we'll be praying for your boys."

She ended the call and spun to face me. "What's next?"

"We call Mongo, Kodiak, and Shawn."

Almost before I finished my statement, Mongo's voice rang in my ears. "We're here, boss. We're all still hot on the sat-coms. We did a perimeter sweep and briefed the chief deputy. There's nobody out there."

"I expected as much," I said. "Get over to the hospital and check on Singer. Gator's probably bouncing off the walls, so get him out of there if you can."

"What about Disco?" he asked.

"He's still in the air on his way to Jacksonville. Apparently, he's in critical condition."

Mongo said, "Okay. We're going to shut down the comms, so call us on any of our cells if you need us. I'll call you from the hospital."

I thumbed off my satellite transceiver and leaned back in my chair to let my brain go to work, but Skipper interrupted. "We've got a secure call coming in from Ramstein, Germany."

"Ramstein? Who do we know there?"

She shrugged and activated the line. "Op center."

A series of clicks preceded a highly distorted male voice. "Well, that was exciting. Don't you think?"

"Who is this?" I demanded.

"Careful with your tone, Dr. Fulton. I'm easily offended, and trust me, you don't want to offend me."

"Who are you?"

"That's irrelevant," the voice said. "What is important, though, is the fact that you weren't injured in the unfortunate accident at the airport. One can never be too careful with flammable material around aircraft. Who knows what might happen?"

I gritted my teeth. "What do you want?"

"Have you read the Book of Job in the Bible, Chase? May I call you Chase? Doctor feels so formal, and you and I are well past formality."

"Of course I've read Job, but what does that have to do with any of this?"

The voice laughed. "Remember the rules the Devil had to play by in that story?"

"What are you talking about?"

"Try to keep up, Chase. I'm very disappointed in you. I expected a much more formidable opponent. If you believe the fairy tale in that Bible of yours, God and the Devil made a little wager on Job's devotion. The only rule was that the Devil couldn't kill Job. Is this ringing a bell?"

I growled, "I remember the story, but what is the relevance to this situation?"

He laughed again. "Lucky for you that since the rule was good enough for the Devil, it's good enough for me. I'm not going to kill you, Chase, but I am going to destroy everything you love. We'll see just how far I have to push you to destroy your faith and devotion to the Board you seem to worship."

Skipper rolled an index finger in the air, signaling for me to keep the man talking.

"Tell me what you want, and maybe we can work something out."

"You're funny, Chase. What I want can't be given. It can only be taken away with extreme violence, and that's precisely what I'm going to do."

"Why me? What did I do to you?"

His laughter rang out again. "Oh, Chase . . . naïve little Chasechka. It's not what you did to me. It's what you did to the people I'm loyal to. If I remember the story correctly, Job lost ten children. How many did the Devil take from you tonight?"

I said, "Listen to me—"

He cut me off. "I listen and I talk when it pleases me, so don't tell me what to do. I know what you're doing, by the way, and it won't work. You'll never trace this call, no matter how long you keep me on the phone. Take a look at the point of origin of the call."

Skipper and I shot a look at the monitor, where a column of locations across the globe scrolled down the screen. Skipper's shoulders dropped, and she threw her head back in well-deserved frustration.

The voice said, "Oh, there's one more thing before I go. It's always a shame when a MedFlight helicopter goes down . . . especially with a patient on board."

The speaker fell silent, and the list of locations stopped scrolling. Skipper's fingers flew to the keys, but after several seconds of work, she leaned back with exasperation written all over her face. "It's no use. I can't trace it."

I thought about the things I loved, and I immediately turned to Penny. "We're getting you out of here tonight, and I'm putting three men on you around the clock."

With resolution in her eyes, she said, "I don't want three armed guards . . . I want Anya."

Chapter 13
Everybody Breaks

Instead of immediately reacting to Penny's unbelievable declaration, I begged my brain to prioritize the necessary tasks that followed. "Find out if Disco's MedFlight went down."

Skipper typed as if all of our lives depended on the outcome of her search. When she finally leaned back, she wasn't wearing a look of satisfaction, and her tone was ominous. "A MedFlight went down ten minutes ago near Pearson Island on the Nassau River, just north of Jacksonville."

"Was Disco on that helo?"

"I don't know yet," she said. "But I'm on it."

After two telephone calls and a flurry of keystrokes, Skipper said, "The Navy and Coast Guard are on it, and it was definitely Disco's MedFlight."

After running through a list of options, I settled on dealing with the things immediately under my control and postponing the things I couldn't change. I turned to see the only two women I had ever loved and realized they were the only two women who'd ever loved me.

My eyes finally settled on Penny's, and I said, "You want Anya, but I need her."

The look on my wife's face immediately told me that I had taken the wrong path, so I stumbled through saying what I hoped would get a better reaction. "Protecting you is precisely what I need Anya to do." I reset my gaze on the Russian. "Are you okay with that?"

Anya laced a hand into the crook of Penny's elbow. "Of course. This is exactly what I would choose. If person behind threat is Timothy Taylor, the Russian illegal, I am best person in all of world to protect Penny."

Still tiptoeing on shaky ground, I glanced at Skipper as if she held some magic potion to melt away my discomfort.

She said, "I know if I were in grave danger, I'd want—"

Anya cut her off. "Gator!"

Skipper blushed. "What? No! I mean . . ."

"Is okay," Anya said. "We all know. Is look inside your eyes when he is nearby. Is obvious."

The analyst rolled her eyes. "Maybe for you, but he doesn't seem to be getting the message."

I waved a hand. "Whoa. Cut it out. This isn't the time for whatever this is. We need a plan."

Anya stood and pulled Penny from her seat. "Do you want to know where we are going?"

My ability to think tactically was buried somewhere beneath my heartbreaking fear for my men and the thought of Anya and Penny alone in parts unknown, so I turned, once again, to Skipper. "Do we *want* to know?"

Skipper shook her head as if turning down an invitation from a pit viper. "We do not."

Anya turned into the staff psychologist and couples counselor as she pushed my wife into my arms. "Go downstairs and have moment together, but make this moment short. Is important that I get her away from here quickly."

Penny and I spent ten minutes reassuring each other and doing our best to leave Anya out of the conversation until my wife finally squeezed my hands in hers. "It's important for you to understand why I want Anya to protect me."

"No, I get it. She's the best choice. I'm too close, and I need to run the team. We're down three men, and we don't even know who's attacking us."

"Why don't you want to know where I'm going?"

"You don't want me to answer that question."

"No, I really do."

I took a long breath and braced myself for the blow of one of the unfortunate realities in my world. "Okay, but let me finish before you jump in."

Penny nodded and resituated herself in her seat.

"Sooner or later, everybody breaks. The human mind will only allow the body in which it resides to endure extreme torture to a certain point before giving in."

Penny didn't keep her nonverbal promise of letting me finish. "God, Chase. Are you afraid I'll be captured and tortured?"

I sighed. "No, not at all. I don't think that's even a remote possibility. What purpose would torturing you serve?"

She said, "It would be one way of making you come running."

I closed my eyes. "We're getting way off track here. Nobody's going to capture or torture you. I can't say the same for the team and me. Anya will protect you and kill anybody who even thinks about threatening you. The rest of us don't have that luxury. We may get taken, and if we are taken, we'll be interrogated, even if only for the amusement of our captors. If none of us knows where you are, we can't be forced to divulge your location. Not knowing provides an additional, invisible layer of protection for you."

She stared at the floor. "But what if something happens? I mean, Anya's good and all, but she's not Wonder Woman. Bullets don't bounce off of her. What if something happens that she can't stop, and . . ." She caught a trembling breath and continued. "And they kill me *and* her. If you don't know where we are, you'll never find us."

"That won't happen," I said. "It's not how these things work."

"*These* things? How many times have you been in one of *these* things?"

"Too many to count," I said. "Anya was dispatched to flip me or kill me. She failed at both, and I survived. A deranged sniper tried to destroy the team, and—"

She raised an eyebrow. "Yeah, I remember. We lost Tony and Hunter."

"We lost Tony, yes, but Hunter is alive."

She said, "But he's not part of the team anymore, so in a way, we lost him to the sniper, too."

"I get your point. I do. But we're going to be hypervigilant and keep everyone alive—at least the good guys."

She leaned against me and squeezed. "I'm scared, Chase."

I held her tightly. "I know, and that's perfectly rational. You're in very good hands, though. Other than Mongo, no one has ever protected me better than Anya has. She saved my life on more occasions than I can remember, and she'll do the same for you."

She leaned back, took my hand, and placed it on her stomach. "Yeah, I know. I'm alive today because I've got part of her liver inside me."

Words would've only cheapened the moment, so I sat staring into the eyes of the woman I wanted to spend the rest of my life with. Her smile said she understood, and she kissed me like only Penny Fulton could. The kiss may have lasted only seconds—or perhaps a thousand years—but when it was over, she gently pushed me away. "Go. Do what you do, and I'll take Anya to L.A."

I savored the moment but said, "You're not taking her to L.A. She's taking you somewhere, and if I know her at all, you will have never heard of the place you land."

* * *

Back upstairs in the op center, Anya whispered something into Penny's ear, and my wife nodded.

Anya stepped beside me, placed both hands on my left shoulder, and pulled me toward her lips. She whispered, "I promise I will keep her safe, and I will bring her home to you when this is over." Then, she did something I doubted Penny had approved. She kissed me on the cheek and said, "You will come home safely as well, yes?"

I stepped back. "Yes. I certainly plan to."

I watched Penny and Anya walk through the secure doorway of the op center, and both turned back for one more look before disappearing into whatever lay beyond the confines of Bonaventure.

With their departure, the mood inside the room changed as if someone flipped a switch.

Skipper said, "That's taken care of. So, what's next?"

"What's the status of the rescue effort?"

She ran a finger down a screen of text. "The pilot's dead, but the flight nurse and Disco are alive and on a Coast Guard MH-Sixty-Five Dolphin."

"Disco's alive?"

She tapped the screen. "That's what it says."

Although the words didn't leave my mouth, I sent up a resounding prayer of thanks. "What brought down the chopper?"

"We don't know yet. It went down in the river, and it's pretty remote out there, so it'll be morning before they can start the investigation."

"What about Singer and Gator?"

"Nothing yet, but we should call them."

I dialed Mongo, and he answered on the first ring. "I was just picking up the phone to call you. Singer's out of surgery. He's in serious but stable condition for now, and they have him in a medically induced coma."

"Sounds like a head injury," I said.

"Yeah, that's the big one. He has a massive concussion and serious swelling. They put in an EVD. Do you know what that is?"

"Sure. It's a temporary drain to allow excess cerebrospinal fluid to escape and relieve the pressure inside the skull."

"That's right," he said. "The surgeon told us the EVD is to buy the medical team some time while they monitor Singer's condition. They'll come up with a plan for a more permanent solution tomorrow."

"How about Gator?" I asked.

"He's on his way back with Shawn. I thought I'd stay here with

Singer until you need me elsewhere. Have you heard anything about Disco?"

I briefed him on what little we knew about our chief pilot and the mysterious crash following the telephone warning from our attacker.

"Did Skipper trace the call?"

"She tried, but whatever technology they were using is superior to ours."

"Superior to ours? How? I thought we were state-of-the-art."

I said, "That's what we thought, too, but someone came up with a way to stump us."

"So, what's the plan moving forward?" Mongo asked.

I said, "Stay with Singer, and try to get some rest if you can. We'll hit the ground running when the sun comes up."

"You got it, boss. Keep me posted, and I'll let you know if anything changes here."

I ended the call and said, "It's time to wake up Clark."

It took two solid minutes to draw the retired Green Beret out of his slumber and back into the realm of consciousness. Once I was convinced that he was capable of digesting my words, I started the briefing.

A few minutes later, I finished pouring out everything I knew, and he said, "So much for going back to sleep. What do you need?"

That wasn't the question I expected, but it was definitely the right one.

"I'll be honest," I said, "I don't know who we're fighting or what to expect next. I'm certain we'll need some trigger-pullers and air assets. We lost the Bell Four-Twelve, the Gulfstream, and the Mustang."

"Let's not focus on what we don't have," Clark said. "Give me an asset list."

I drew out the inventory from my head. "We've still got the One-Eighty-Two, but it doesn't have much value in a fight like this. The Twin Otter is still alive, but I've not flown it in months. I don't even know if it's airworthy."

"What about the PBY?"

"It's here, but I'm still not confident in the cockpit."

"I suggest getting confident, College Boy. What about the guy you bought it from? Is he available?"

"I didn't buy it. Penny did. And the guy's an attorney. Do you really think it's a good idea to bring a civilian into this mess?"

He said, "I don't know yet. We'll make that decision when I get there. I'll bring the King Air. Is the runway safe?"

"As far as I know, it is. The explosion was limited to the main hangar, but the camera system is dead. We still don't know how that happened."

Clark said, "All right. Send somebody out there to take a look at the runway. If it's damaged, let me know, and I'll divert somewhere. I'll order up a small army for security, and I'll let the Board know this is now a full-blown counter-aggression op. They'll hand us a blank check, so work on your wish list. I'll see you in a few hours. Oh, and College Boy . . . stay alive 'til I get there, will you?"

Chapter 14
The Necessity of Defense

Skipper buzzed the door, and Shawn and Gator came ambling in. Our youngest hard-charger wasn't quite as well as he led us to believe. His left arm rested in a sophisticated-looking sling. A single crutch was in his right hand, and a patch covered one of his eyes.

I attempted to lighten the mood. "Argh, matey! Thar be a pirate among us."

Gator reached out with his crutch and tapped my prosthetic leg. "I'm not the one with a peg leg, Captain Sparrow." After mocking me, he turned to Skipper, who sat staring up at the hardcore operator he had become. Noticing the concern weighing heavily on her face, he gave her a wink and said, "Hey."

She smiled but didn't speak, and Gator took a step in her direction. "Don't worry about me. I'm good. It's just a few scrubs and scrapes."

"It looks a little more serious than that," Skipper said.

It must've taken enormous willpower to make it happen, but he turned away from the analyst and back to me. "My kit was in the hangar, so I need to build out another set, if you don't mind."

"You're in no shape for a kit," I said. "Get some rest, and we'll see how you're doing in a couple of days."

He lowered his chin. "How I'm doing is pissed off. This sling and the crutch will be history in twenty-four hours, but whatever this is isn't going away without some lead in the air. I'm still in the fight. I just need a good set of tools to take that fight to the bad guys. Do we know who they are yet?"

I said, "Not yet, but we're working on it. Go on down to the armory and kit up. I like your grit, kid, but don't kill yourself trying to muscle through this."

He stuck a hand into his pocket and produced a folded sheet of paper, then dropped it on Skipper's desk.

"What's this?" she asked.

Gator turned for the door. "It's just some things I want you to know. You can read it later when things calm down, or you can throw it away. It's up to you."

She slipped the paper from the desk and tucked it beneath her leg. "Go build your kit. You're the closest thing we've got left to a sniper, and we're going to need you."

I liked her tactical mindset, but I hadn't let the idea of being without a sniper enter my head yet.

Shawn propped himself against the edge of the conference table. "So, tell me about this threatening phone call."

Skipper said, "I can do better than that. I can play it for you."

She cued it up and let the audio play as the former SEAL took in every word.

While Shawn chewed on the contents of the call, I motioned toward the note still tucked beneath Skipper's leg. "Shouldn't you read that?"

She pulled the paper from beneath her leg and rubbed her fingers across its surface several times. "Fine. I'll read it, but not out loud."

Skipper unfolded the paper and scanned the typed page of instructions. She shook the sheet and groaned. "It's about how to care for a victim of a concussion."

"Turn it over, Goofy."

She flipped the page to find Gator's handwritten note. I could see that the first several lines were in slowly failing blue ink. When that pen died, he obviously found a black version somewhere. When she finished, she folded the paper in half and sat in silence for a long moment.

"What does it say?" I asked.

She mumbled. "I guess he did notice after all."

"What?"

She waved the folded sheet a few times as if trying to decide whether to burn it or read it again. Finally, she held it out toward me.

I reached for the note, but I was timid. "Are you sure?"

"Yeah, I'm sure. You need to read it. It's about the mindset of one of your shooters, and you should know."

I unfolded the page and read quickly.

Elizabeth,

When I was trapped inside the SUV and in and out of consciousness, every time I closed my eyes, I saw your face. Every time I thought I might die, I ached because I was never brave enough to tell you how I felt. We shouldn't live our lives in such a way that we might die with regrets. So, after today, I won't have to wonder if you know. I've admired everything about you for a long time. You're the smartest person I've ever met, and in my opinion, you're the most beautiful woman I've ever seen. I'm sometimes brave enough — or maybe stupid enough — to believe you might feel something for me. If I'm wrong about that, I guess I'm pretty embarrassed right now, but at least now you know.

Clint

I handed the sheet back to her. "I guess Anya was right again."

She threw the note onto the desk. "I don't have time to deal with that right now. We've got work to do."

I let her get away with the misdirection. "Try not to let this affect your—"

She scolded me without hesitation. "Do I ever let anything affect my work?"

"Point taken," I said. "When was the last time you slept?"

"I'll sleep when I'm tired."

The secure line rang, and she brought it up on speaker. "Op center."

Clark said, "Did anybody check the runway yet?"

"Give me two minutes," I said as I yanked my phone from my pocket.

Chief Roberts answered after several rings. "How are you doing, Chase?"

"I need a favor. Can you have one of your officers sweep the runway to make sure there's nothing that would make it unsafe to use?"

"Sure. Can you give me ten minutes?"

I said, "Call me back as soon as you get someone to take a look."

He hung up, and Clark said, "Well?"

"One of the St. Marys PD officers is checking it as we speak."

"Great. What's the word on Disco?"

Skipper fielded that one. "I'm still working on finding him."

"Finding him? I thought you said he and the nurse were alive."

"That's the last thing we know," she said, "but I'm digging for more. I'm not even sure where they took them yet."

My phone rang, and I grabbed it. "This is Chase."

"Chase, it's Corporal Brewer with the St. Marys PD. I just checked your runway, and it's clear. There's some debris on the parallel taxiway, but it's small enough for me to clean up. I'll take care of that for you if you need me to."

"That would be great," I said. "Thank you. I've got a King Air and probably at least one other airplane arriving soon."

"How soon?"

"It'll be at least two hours."

"Oh, good. That'll give me plenty of time to clean off the taxiway."

I hung up and turned back to the speakerphone. "Runway is clear, and the taxiway will be clean when you get here."

"Nice work, College Boy. I'll be airborne in ten. I've got at least twenty well-trained, highly disciplined gun toters en route. Use them as you see fit if they get there before me, but they're not operational."

"What does that mean?" I asked.

"Don't take them hunting with you. Just find something for them to guard."

"Got it. Listen, I'm working on the beginnings of a plan. Do you have time to talk about it?"

"Not on this line," he said. "How about getting beyond the beginning stages, and we'll discuss it when I get there?"

"Good enough. I'll see you in a couple of hours."

When I hung up, Skipper was on another call, and she said, "Just a minute. I'm putting you on speaker. Can you start again, please?"

She hit the button, and a man's voice filled the room. "I'm Dr. Arturo, and I'm one of the neurosurgeons on the trauma team here at the Mayo Clinic. I understand you're the next of kin for Mr. Blake Riley. Is that correct?"

"It is," she said. "What is his condition?"

"He's critical and declining, but the team is working to stabilize him. He has several fractured vertebrae, serious internal bleeding, and limited neurological activity."

"What's the prognosis?" I asked.

Dr. Arturo took a long breath. "It's bleak at the moment, but we'll know more in the coming hours. He's in very good hands, and we're doing everything in our power to keep him alive."

Skipper said, "Thank you, Doctor. He should've had an insurance card in his wallet, but please don't worry. We'll cover any expenses."

The sound he made was almost a chopped laugh. "Don't worry about that right now. Our job is to save your brother's life. We'll worry about the details later. Is this the best number to reach you?"

"It is," Skipper said. "And please keep us informed of any changes. Do you know anything about the flight nurse who was in the crash with Disco . . . I mean, Blake?"

"I don't know anything at all about the nurse, but unless she's a neurosurgical candidate, I wouldn't have any reason to know her."

"She's not one of ours, but she was on the MedFlight with Blake."

"Do you want me to inquire about her and have someone call you back?"

Skipper said, "No, that's not necessary, but we're going to request security for Blake. Who should I call to coordinate their arrival?"

"I'm sorry, but I don't know. I've never dealt with that, but I can give you the number to the nurse's station in the neuro ICU."

He rattled off the number, and Skipper jotted it down. "Thank you, Doctor. Is there anything else we need to know?"

He said, "No, but I'd like to know why Mr. Riley needs security. Is he in some sort of trouble?"

Skipper said, "No, other than his medical condition, he's not in any trouble. We're just being cautious. We're private security contractors, and our guys sometimes get a little undeserved attention when they end up in hospitals. We like to ensure they remain undisturbed as much as possible. I'm sure you understand."

"I'm sure I don't," he said. "But that's outside my realm. Work with the nurses. They'll give you the information you need."

"Thanks again, Dr. Arturo."

Without consulting me, Skipper ended the call and dialed the Jacksonville Police Department. In minutes, she had a commitment from the desk sergeant that he'd keep an officer on Disco's door until our private security officers arrived.

She spun her chair and tossed a legal pad onto my lap. "Write down everything you love. It's time to do a good old-fashioned risk assessment."

Tracing the lines on the yellow sheets, I slid my fingertips across the paper and closed my eyes. I'm the last person on Earth who'll ever claim to be in possession of a healthy human mind, but one of the characteristics of such a mind is that it tends to drift to the place it wants to be when it has nothing else to think about. Often, when I lie in bed, just before falling asleep, I often find myself at sea, beneath billowing white sails, with Penny lying in my arms and no one else within a hundred miles. So began my list.

Penny
The team
Our home
Freedom
God
The boats
The airplanes
My health and the health of those I love

Scrolling through the list with both my eyes and heart, I felt a sense of shame and disappointment that I listed material things on a tally of what I love, but the purpose of the exercise was to evaluate the probability of attack and the necessity of defense. Nothing was more important than protecting the people I loved.

Chapter 15
Michael's Purpose

Skipper laid a finger against the tablet and let it glide down the list. "I could've made this list for you. It's exactly what I expected you to write."

"I guess I'm glad I didn't disappoint you, but I must admit I'm ashamed of the order the list fell out of my head."

She said, "I'm a little surprised Anya isn't on the list. Is that intentional, or did she really not come to mind?"

I motioned toward the pad. "Take a look at number two."

She smiled. "Nice cop-out. Now, let's go through these. Penny is taken care of unless you think she needs more security than Anya can provide."

"What do you think?"

She shrugged. "Look at it this way. Is a one-person security detail enough for around-the-clock protection?"

I grimaced. "That's not exactly what's happening. She's not just an armed guard. Anya's taking Penny to some place no one would ever think they would go. That alone has a great deal of security value."

"Okay. If you're good with it, so am I. That brings us to the team, but we'll come back to that one. Let's talk about Bonaventure first."

I said, "Clark is sending twenty well-trained security professionals to take care of the airport and the house. By extension, that covers the boats and remaining airplanes. And that reminds me . . . Did you ever figure out how they were able to steal your camera feed from the airport?"

She let out an exasperated sigh. "Yes, I figured it out, and I'm an idiot. It was a crazy, low-tech approach that I hadn't considered. I can explain it to you if you really want to know."

"As long as you understand it and you can keep it from happening again, I don't need to know the details."

The look on her face said she was happy to have the subject changed. "Good. That brings us down to freedom. That's a little vague. Are you worried about going to prison for killing this guy?"

"It's both bigger and much smaller than that. When I wrote it down, I was thinking about the freedom to walk across the yard and sit in the gazebo without looking over my shoulder, but what I really meant was for that feeling to extend to all of us, not just me."

She wiggled her nose as if conjuring a spell of some sort. "I'm afraid that's a little abstract, and the only way to make it possible is to find the person or people who are behind all of this, and either put them in a pine box or a prison cell."

"I think you're right, and I doubt they're the kind of people who end up in prison. If they are what I suspect them to be, they'll fight until either all of them or all of us are left in a steaming heap of dead bodies."

She said, "I agree, so the way to deal with that line item is to be prepared to duke it out with these guys and make them pay."

I nodded in wordless agreement, and she said, "Let's see. That leaves the boats and planes, but we wrapped them into our home. Let me deal with the God question by saying this. I'm not the right person for that discussion. That one's on Singer. You'll have to wake him up and get him to take you down that path."

"Singer's not the only option," I said. "If we can find Hunter, he'll have the answers I need."

"Finding Hunter isn't a problem. I can have him on the phone in thirty seconds."

"Good. We'll make that call when we finish this conversation."

She huffed. "The health thing falls under the team, so I guess it's time to do that one. We're running out of teammates, and whether we want to admit it or not, we're likely to lose more in the coming days. I know this sucks to say out loud, but Disco is probably done, even if he survives."

That punch landed solidly in my gut and robbed me of my breath. "I don't like it, but you're probably right. Singer is in a similar situation."

She groaned. "As hard as it is, we have to look at this from a tactical standpoint and leave the emotion out of it. We have to assume both of them are out of the fight, and we have to move on without them."

Separating heart from head was never easy for me. My team has never been made up of nameless, faceless fighters. We were brothers first, and brothers-in-arms second.

"You're right, and I hate everything about it."

"How are we going to find these people, Chase? We have to assume it's a network and not an individual, right?"

"Absolutely. There's no way one person could pull this off. It has to be a coordinated effort."

"Okay, so how do we catch them?"

I leaned back in my chair and studied the ceiling. "If we look at it in textbook fashion, we start with known associates and try to diagram the network. Even if we can't find the key players right away, we can take out enough low-level guys to slow them down. And, with any luck, at least one of those low-level dudes will be willing to tell us everything he knows about the operation . . . with a little encouragement, of course."

She raised an eyebrow. "Sounds like you're looking forward to *encouraging* them to spill their guts."

"I'm trying to stay professional, but it won't hurt my feelings to drive these people into the ground if I have to."

She turned away. "Then I'll get to work on known and suspected associates. But if it's driven by the Kremlin, I won't have a lot of luck."

"Just stick your head in the cave and see what growls at you."

"That sounds like fun," she said. "Do I get a spear and a torch?"

"You can have anything you want. Where does that leave us on the list?"

She slid her finger down the page again. "All that's left is calling Hunter or waking Singer up."

"I think it's best if we let Singer have his rest, but I could use a good conversation with Hunter."

She said, "Give me thirty seconds."

Stone W. Hunter was a medically retired Air Force Combat Controller and a tough-as-nails warrior when the bullets started flying. He had been an invaluable member of the tactical team and remained a dear friend after a sniper's bullet demolished most of his shoulder a few years before. Instead of lying down and spending the rest of his life licking his wounds, he changed teams. After completing a seminary degree, he became a missionary in the far-flung corners of the world. Having his counsel would go a long way toward easing my mind about the fight to come.

Skipper glanced across her shoulder. "Speaker or headset?"

"Speaker," I said.

She hit a button, and the overhead speakers clicked.

Instinctually, I looked up as if I'd be able to see his face. "You there, Hunter?"

"I'm here," he said. "How's it going? I didn't expect to hear from you at this hour."

I gasped. "I'm sorry. I didn't realize how late it was. We can talk tomorrow."

He laughed. "It's only late where you are. The sun is still shining where I am. What's up?"

Skipper and I spent several minutes briefing him on everything we knew, suspected, or guessed.

He let out a low whistle. "Book me a flight, Skipper. I can be there in less than twenty-four hours."

I said, "No. Wait a minute. That's not what this call is about."

He huffed. "Regardless of what it's about, you're under fire and down two good men. I'm on my way, even if I have to book my own flight."

"Stay where you are for now," I said. "It's your wisdom I need, not your trigger finger."

He laughed. "I don't have much of that to give, but I'll do my best. What's eating you?"

"You know the situation, but there's a spiritual element I'm struggling with. Don't let me hurt your feelings. I would've gone to Singer, but as I told you, he's a bit indisposed."

Hunter said, "You'll never hurt my feelings by reminding me what a godly man Singer is. I can't promise to do as well as he would've, but I'll tell you what I know. What's on your mind?"

I took a long breath and braced myself. "I told you about the list, and I talked through it with Skipper, but I'm concerned about what made me put God on the list."

Hunter cut in. "Let me guess. You don't like the fact that your faith isn't strong enough to turn it all over to Him."

I said, "I'm even more ashamed to admit that I hadn't thought of that."

He said, "Everything and everybody else on the list is something or someone you don't want to lose. Is that what you're thinking about?"

"Maybe," I admitted. "Honestly, I'm not sure why I wrote His name on the list in the first place."

"That's pretty obvious. It doesn't take Singer to make that diagnosis."

I felt an instant of relief, and he kept talking.

"It's clear the list is all about stuff and people you don't want to lose. That's perfectly rational, but it falls apart when it comes to God. He isn't something you can possibly lose."

"I'm not so sure that's true," I said. "What about turning the other cheek and loving my enemy?"

Hunter chuckled. "Do you think God expected David to turn the other cheek when the Philistines sent Goliath out to do battle? Were

Lot and his wife supposed to love the enemies of God in Sodom and Gomorrah and take them with them when they fled on God's command?"

I sat in silence, contemplating the point of his questions, until he continued.

"Battle is a necessity at times. The Bible is clear on that. Ever heard of Michael the Archangel?"

"Of course I've heard of Michael."

He said, "I was just checking to see if you were still with me."

"I'm still here. Keep talking."

He cleared his throat. "I don't have my Bible in my hand, so I'm working from memory. Don't kill me if I miss something. What is Michael's purpose?"

I sighed. "I don't know for sure, but I think I remember him being the leader of the Army of Angels who threw Satan out of Heaven."

"Do you think he did that by turning the other cheek or loving on the Devil?"

I tried to stifle the laughter I felt rising. "I doubt it."

Hunter let me get away with the chuckle without rebuke. "You're on the right path with our—or at least my—favorite Angel. He's mentioned in only three books of the Bible—Daniel, Jude, and Revelation—and believe it or not, if I remember correctly, he's only called by name in five verses in the whole Bible. Every time he's mentioned, he's fighting somebody or something. We can't know for sure, but from what little evidence we have, it appears that Michael was created for only one reason . . . to whoop somebody's butt when they needed it."

That unlocked the gate to my exhausted sense of humor, and I laughed out loud.

Hunter reined me in. "Okay, okay, calm down. I just wanted to get your attention."

"You've done it, my friend."

He said, "I made a bit of a joke, but think about what we know about Michael. If battle were truly forbidden, would God have made an Archangel especially for that purpose? And that leads us to an even bigger question. If God created Michael uniquely for the purpose of battling evil, don't you think he might've created a few of us humans for precisely the same purpose?"

I wanted to answer, but I was frozen, paralyzed by the thought of having been created uniquely for the thing I did best, but also the thing I hated the most.

Hunter sighed. "Perfect. That's exactly the reaction I was hoping for. Now, I want to leave you with one more thought before I get on the plane. People, especially truly evil people, are capable of taking away everything on the list you made, except for God. Nobody, not even the Archangel, can take God away from you. Only you can take yourself away from Him. Don't let that happen, Chase. Do what's right and necessary, and I'll be there by your side. And so will God."

Chapter 16
Nothing to Fear

I didn't have to ask if Skipper booked a flight for Hunter. My gut and my heart knew he was on his way from some godforsaken corner of the world to go to war by my side, and although I felt sickened that he was leaving the mission field for me, I was glad my brother would be watching my six and laying down suppressive fire when I needed it most.

The brilliant analyst a few feet away held out a bottle of water. "You look like you could use a drink."

"Is that bourbon?"

She tossed the bottle into my waiting hand and smiled. "Not exactly, but close."

I drained the bottle, crushed it, and tossed it into the recycle bin. "Do you think the city really recycles the stuff we put in the blue cans?"

Skipper furrowed her brow. "You worry about the strangest things. How should I know what they do with the garbage?"

"How's that known-associates list coming along?"

She turned back to her monitor and brought up the window in which the search was running, driven by the supercomputer she built with her own hands—and my checkbook.

"I don't see any names on there yet."

She said, "It takes some time, but it'll produce results. Just be patient."

I yawned. "Patience isn't one of my strong suits."

"Oh, trust me, I know. How are you feeling?"

"Feeling?" I asked. "What do you mean?"

That was the very moment the world in front of me fell out of focus, and my eyelids weighed more than I could support. I stared at the plastic water bottle protruding from the recycle bin. "What did you do?"

"You have to sleep, Chase. If you don't, you'll crash, and we need you at your best. Get some rest, and we'll reconvene when you're refreshed."

As badly as I wanted to yell at her for dosing me, she was right, and I was seconds away from perfect slumber.

* * *

With an eight-hour nap in my wake, I showered, put on clothes that didn't smell like death, and poured a cup of coffee down my throat. When I stepped through the door to the op center, the reality of the world I'd left eight hours before slapped me squarely in the face.

What remained of my team sat in their chosen chairs, a grim expression on every face.

I closed the door behind me. "Nothing about this looks good."

Clark stood and pulled me in for a long-overdue brotherly hug. "Hey, College Boy. I'm glad you got some rest. It's good to see you. Are you ready to get to work?"

I returned his hug and stepped back. "We need to talk . . . privately."

My handler said, "Come on. Anything you can say to me, you can say to all of us."

"It's not that kind of talk," I said. "Let's go down to the library."

He followed me down the stairs, limping every step. "You do know you have an elevator, right?"

I shot him a look across my shoulder. "Yeah, but it's for old, crippled . . . Oh, never mind."

"I'll show you old and crippled."

I said, "You're doing a pretty good job of showing me already."

We settled into the wingbacks in my favorite room of the house. The century-old glass in the windows showed the world as I often saw it with my own eyes—wavy, out of focus, and constantly in motion.

"So, what's on your mind?" Clark asked as he pulled an ottoman into position to relieve some of the stress in his left leg.

"Are you okay?" I asked.

"Yeah. It's just been bugging me a little lately. I need to have somebody take a look at it, I guess."

I tapped on my prosthetic. "I know somebody who can make you a new one."

He laughed. "No, thanks. The original doesn't hurt bad enough to chop it off yet."

I picked at a brad in the leather arm of my chair. "We've been friends a long time."

Clark grimaced. "I don't like conversations that start like that."

"I know, and you're not going to like this one, either. In fact, I should probably be having it with Singer."

He checked his watch. "Speaking of Singer, he's having another procedure in a couple of hours."

"What kind of procedure?"

"I don't know. Skipper said something about another port to help drain fluid out of his skull."

I wondered if the greatest sniper I'd ever known was aware of what was happening around him. I'd never known him to miss a single detail in any environment, but in a coma, he was little more than part of the environment.

I asked, "What about Disco? Any word from the Mayo Clinic?"

"I don't know, but last I heard, it's not looking good. We're getting off track, though. What did you want to talk about?"

My mouth suddenly felt like I hadn't had anything to drink in days. "I'm scared."

He kicked away the ottoman and leaned toward me. "You're scared? What do you mean?"

I sighed. "I've been doing this a long time, and I've been in a lot of situations that should've scared me, but they didn't. This is different."

"What are you afraid of?"

I watched the world quiver through the windowpane. "I'm scared of losing everything and everybody I love."

He reclaimed the ottoman. "Two things. First, you're right. You should've been scared a thousand times all over the world. The fact that you weren't worries me more than the fact that you're finally feeling it."

"I can't help it. We don't choose fear. It either happens, or it doesn't."

"Is that something you read in one of those college books, or is it something you just made up?"

"I didn't make it up," I said. "It's a lot more complicated than that, but essentially, it boils down to how my brain deals with threats."

He waved a hand. "Let's not get in the weeds about endorphins or dolphins or whatever else you've got swimming around up there. You're scared. Believe it or not, that's a good thing. I've been scared since the first time anybody shot at me, but I've never been in the situation you're in right now."

He stood and pulled two bottles of water from the small refrigerator beneath the bar. He offered one to me, but I reached for the one he was holding back for himself. I'd been roofied once already, and I wasn't interested in a second episode of the same show.

He unscrewed the cap and drank half the water. "You're the smart one here. You know all that clinical stuff about the brain, but I know a thing or two about fear. What you're feeling ain't really fear."

"This oughta be good."

"Seriously. It's not fear. It's something else entirely. It's the feeling of not having control of the things you want most to control."

I squinted. "What are you talking about?"

"Maybe *control* isn't exactly the right word. Maybe it's *protect*. That's a verb, right?"

It was my turn to drink from the plastic bottle that would likely never be recycled. With the lid back on, I said, "Yeah, protect is a verb, but I'm still not tracking."

"It's simple," Clark said. "You're a natural-born protector. When you were catching baseball, what did you do when a batter threatened your pitcher?"

"I kicked his ass."

"Exactly. You protected him. There's nothing different about this except the number of pitchers and threatening batters. The people you love need protection right now—probably more than any other time in their lives—and you're worried that you can't do that."

I leaned back in my chair and let his wisdom wash over me. "And you don't think that qualifies as fear?"

"Who knows? And who cares what label you put on it? It's a feeling, and you're feeling it, College Boy. Let me tell you a story."

Clark's stories rarely had any connection with coherent logic, but I couldn't wait to see where he was taking me.

He said, "Remember when you pulled me off the top of that mountain in Afghanistan?"

"Sure, I do. You were a mess."

"Yeah, I was, and I would've died a mess if you hadn't shown up. The whole time I was lying in that cave with my back broke, I was trying to come up with a way to hold a rifle and keep the rest of the team alive. I didn't care that I was gonna die because I always knew it would happen in a place like that. I cared that the people around me—the people I was responsible for—were going to die, and there was nothing I could do about it."

"So, you've been where I am," I said. "What did you do to get through it?"

"Nothing. There wasn't anything I could do. I had a broken back and a fever of a hundred and five, but the pain my body was in couldn't touch the hell my brain was going through. I couldn't do nothing, but that's the difference between you and me, Chase. You *can* do something, and you've got what may be the finest team in the world to help you do it."

I'd never understand how so much common sense could live inside one man's head. "Maybe *you* should've been the psychologist."

He laughed. "Yeah, right. I can't even spell it. I'm just an old, worn-out shooter and door-kicker. You've lost your pilot and your sniper. Tactically, that doesn't matter."

His statement was a nasty little sucker punch, and I said, "Wait a minute. How can you say—"

He held up both hands. "I'm not talking about either one of them dying here. I'm talking about their tactical necessity. Your airplanes are a smoldering heap of ashes, so what good is a pilot?"

I didn't like it, but he was right, as usual.

Clark pointed toward the op center two floors above our heads. "You've got Gator. Sure, he's beat up a little, but he'll be all right. Singer's been teaching and preaching to that boy for two years. He may not be able to sing, but he can darn well shoot. We've both seen it. You don't need a sniper. You've already got one, and he's been trained by one of the best."

I still didn't like it, but I couldn't argue with his reasoning.

He said, "Now that we've got that behind us, let's talk about our adversary. He's well supported, well trained, and obviously dangerous. Name one enemy we've ever faced who didn't have the same résumé."

"It's never been like this," I said.

"Sure, it has. It's always like this. Somebody wants to do something terrible to somebody else, and you stop him. It's the basic recipe for what you do. The names change, but the evil never does. That's how you've got to look at this. There is no other way. Give everything you have for everybody you care about, and leave every ounce of everything you've got on the field."

He let that admonishment hang in the air before continuing. "I've seen the old tapes of you playing ball. You were the best there was, and you proved it on every play. That was just a game, though. The thing about you that's impressed me since the day we met is your tenacity in battle. Nobody works harder than you when the lead starts flying. Nobody sacrifices more for his team than you. Nobody will ever fight harder than you do. I want you to think about that for a minute. I've seen the greatest warriors on Earth stand toe to toe and beat each other into the ground for over thirty years, and I've never seen one single man who fought harder than you."

I'd had a lot of locker room pep talks, but I'd never had one like that. Clark was right. I wasn't feeling fear. I was feeling helplessness, and I was about to crush that feeling beneath my boot.

Before I could put my attitude adjustment into words, Kodiak opened the door and stuck his head in without knocking. "You guys need to come back to the op center. Penny's house in L.A. is on fire."

Chapter 17
Splitting Cells

I leapt from my wingback. "Were they there? Are they okay?"

Kodiak said, "According to Skipper, there was no one in the house, and as far as we know, Penny and Anya are fine, wherever they are."

I followed him up the stairs, and Clark took the elevator. We beat him to the third floor by more than a comfortable margin, but he showed up just before our analyst began the briefing.

Skipper said, "The house is insured, and I'm certain no one was home when the fire started."

I jumped in. "Wait a minute. How can you be sure?"

"Like I told you earlier, I figured out how those guys got into the security network, so I have control of the cameras again."

"You've not plugged the hole yet, have you?"

"Not yet. I thought we could use it to our advantage somehow."

"Great minds think alike," I said. "Tell me about the fire."

She punched a few keys, and a live feed appeared of a burning house in the Hollywood Hills.

Seeing it burn sickened me, but I swallowed the bile in my throat. "That's definitely Penny's house."

"Yeah, I know. It's not like I have cameras trained on every house in California. The security system turns on the cameras anytime a motion detector is set off. That's how I know nobody was in the house. They pulled the same stunt with the camera system out there as they did here at the airport, but I was able to uncover the live feeds and ignore the video they wanted us to see."

I reached out with the toe of my boot and turned Skipper's chair to face me. "Look at me and tell me if you know where they are."

Her shoulders dropped. "I honestly don't know where they are, but I think I know where they're going."

"So, spit it out."

"I think they're going to Switzerland. Bern, to be exact."

"How do you know?"

Before she could answer, Gator said, "Hey! If you can get the hidden video from L.A., doesn't that mean you can do the same at the airport?"

Skipper's eyes turned to saucers, and she spun to her keyboard. After several minutes of every eye in the room being trained on the monitor in front of her, she leaned back and said, "Ta-da!"

Video from the eighteen cameras at the airport filled four monitors, and no one could look away. The faces of five men appeared as clearly as a portrait, and in the instant, the fear—or helplessness—inside me melted away, and the manhunt was on.

"Get me some names," I ordered.

"Already on it," Skipper said. "It shouldn't take long."

I checked the time and turned to Clark. "What time is your twenty-man army supposed to arrive?"

"They should already be here. I'll check on them."

Clark stepped from the op center to make some calls, and Skipper said, "Told you it wouldn't take long."

Skipper brought up a close-up picture of a man in his thirties. He looked like everybody and nobody. She said, "This is Brian Kinkaid from St. Louis." A second face filled another monitor, and she said, "This one is Kelly Brannon from Houston, Texas." Still, a third man's face showed up in sharp focus on monitor number three. "This friendly-looking character is Perry Furgeson from Spokane."

She paused, and I asked, "What about the other two?"

"Still working on them. Keep your shirt on."

It took several minutes, which felt like decades, but she finally said, "Here's number four. He's William Carpenter from Colorado Springs. And finally, here's their fearless leader, Timothy Martin Taylor, whose last known address was Camp Peary, Virginia."

Mongo rapped his knuckles on the table. "Split cells."

I studied the faces on the screens and nodded. "Yep. A whole team of nasty little Russian nationals with American names, scattered across the country until it's time to rock and roll."

Skipper said, "I'm sure their names are covered, as well as Taylor's, but I'll dig for some details and see what I can find."

I said, "The most important piece of information we need is where they are now."

She said, "They're obviously not far from L.A. and the fire they set. Look what I found."

We watched as the same five faces appeared on the perimeter cameras from Penny's security fence.

I pounded my fist into my thigh. "Yes! I need to know how they're traveling, where they're sleeping, and how much money they have."

Without looking up, Skipper said, "You don't want much, do you?"

"There's one more thing I need. Tell me where they're heading next."

Doing her best genie in a bottle impression, Skipper said, "Yes, Master. I'll get right on that. Is there anything else?"

I ignored her except to say, "I'm sorry. I didn't mean to sound so demanding. This is the first break we've had, and we can't let it slip away."

She nodded but didn't answer.

I spun to face the team. "Gator. Tell me the truth. How operational are you?"

The crutch he'd carried with him the previous day was nowhere in sight, and he said, "I won't be fast on my feet for a few days, but I can shoot, and I can fly."

"Pain meds?"

He shook his head. "I had a cocktail before bed sometime late last night, or maybe this morning. That's all."

Clark said, "The security contingent is half an hour out."

I said, "Great. How about you? Do you feel like chasing some bad guys with us?"

He subconsciously glanced at his aching knee. "Put me in the same category as the kid, except I can do both shooting and flying a lot better than him. I don't have a kit, though."

"That's not an issue," I said. "You know where the armory is, and you can take anybody with you who needs to resupply."

I didn't expect the whole team to stand, but that's what happened. Seconds later, I was alone in the op center with the woman I'd always see as my baby sister.

She watched them leave. "Looks like it's just us."

"Happens a lot."

She looked up at me. "I hope it always does."

"Me, too. Listen, we need to talk about your security."

She said, "I've been thinking about that. It seems that these guys are firebugs, and you've already rebuilt this house once."

"When we assess the guys Clark rounded up, I'll put the best four on the house and two on you."

"Thank you. Can I confess something?"

"I'm no priest, but I'll always listen."

She looked away. "As much as I hate to admit it, this one scares me a little bit."

I stood and rested my hands on her shoulders. "I know how you feel, kiddo, but things are falling into place, and we're getting closer to catching these guys by the minute."

"I know. I just don't like that it took me so long to figure out the back door into the camera system. I let you down, and it cost us a hangar and some irreplaceable airplanes."

"Like Clark said, let's focus on what we do have, not what we've lost.

I do want to know about Bern, though. What makes you think that's where Anya's taking Penny?"

She put on a sheepish grin. "You know that everything I do is to protect you, right?"

"Sure. Where's this going?"

She let out a breath. "I keep an eye on Anya when she's not with us. You know, just so we can call her up if we need her, and stuff like that."

"Okay, but what's that got to do with Bern?"

"I made her Citation disappear from the FAA's database so she couldn't be tracked, but I can still see where the plane is."

I said, "Come on, give it up."

"So, she's flown into and out of Bern, Switzerland, eleven times in the past twelve months. There's something there she likes. Maybe she's got a house or something, I don't know. But something keeps her going back."

I said, "So, just because she's been there eleven times this year, what makes you think she's headed there now?"

"Because she made the same fuel purchase from the same FBO in Nova Scotia that she makes every time she takes the North Atlantic route to Europe."

"But wouldn't she also make that same purchase no matter where she was heading in Europe?"

Skipper said, "Probably, but people are creatures of habit."

"Not Anya. If she habitually goes to Bern, there's no way she'd lead these guys straight to her place. She may want them to think that's where she's headed, but she's too smart to repeat a pattern in a situation like this."

Skipper shrugged. "Okay, you know her better than I do, and you've got the scars to prove it. I just wanted you to know my theory."

"Keep an eye on them if you can. Part of me wants to know where they are, but the tactical sector of my brain understands the necessity for ignorance in this situation."

A telephone rang, and I couldn't remember hearing that particular tone in the op center.

Skipper obviously wasn't surprised and lifted the receiver from its cradle. "Op center." She listened for a moment and then turned her attention to me. "It's Don Maynard from the airport. Are we expecting a C-One-Thirty to land?"

"I'm not expecting one, unless that's Clark's team." I rolled to the console beside her and pressed the intercom for the armory. "Hey, Clark. There's a C-One-Thirty on final approach to our airport. Do you want Don to shoot them down or let them land?"

Clark, no doubt, looked up for the disembodied voice and said, "That would be our security contingent and a little gift from the Board."

I nodded at Skipper, and she spoke into the receiver. "They're friendlies, Don. There should be twenty or so. Fuel up the plane, and tell their boss we'll be there ASAP."

I spoke into the intercom. "Do you want to go meet them, or should I?"

"Let's both do it," he said. "They need to meet their commander."

"That would be you."

"Not hardly, College Boy. I just placed the order. They work for you. I'll meet you in the driveway."

I laid a hand on Skipper's arm and asked, "You good?"

"I'm fine. Go."

When I slipped onto the driver's seat of the VW Microbus, my knees hit the steering column. I jumped from the seat and took several running strides away from the vehicle.

Clark recoiled from the passenger seat. "What's wrong with you?"

"The seat's been moved. Somebody's been in the bus. Get out of there. It might blow."

Instead of dismounting the vehicle, he held up something invisible between his fingers and laughed. "I think we're safe, Jumpy McJumperson. This looks a lot like a long blonde Russian hair."

The absurdity of the moment left me lost to laughter, and I adjusted the seat before climbing back in. "Well, that makes me feel like an idiot."

Clark offered the single strand of hair. "Do you want to keep this as a souvenir?"

I swatted his hand away. "Stop that. This is serious."

He caught his breath. "If Penny discovered that hair on you, it would be serious."

We pulled into the airport through the gate Don had obviously repaired in the previous few hours, and a gray C-130 Hercules rested on the ramp with the hose from our fuel truck hanging from the fuselage. A dozen men milled about in the shade of the left wing, but our approach seemed to make them nervous. The group dispersed, taking cover and concealment behind the massive airplane with their weapons drawn.

Don noticed the commotion and waved them off. "Relax, boys. That's the boss. He's no threat . . . unless you do something stupid."

The weapons returned to their holsters and slings, and the men seemed to relax as Clark and I stepped from the Microbus. Soon, Clark was holding court in the same shade the squad had been enjoying before we arrived.

Introductions were made and hands shaken.

A rugged-looking man, who could've been thirty or sixty, stuck his hand in mine. "Name's Digger. Nice to meet you, Mr. Fulton."

"Please, just call me Chase. We don't stand on formality around here. Thanks for coming, Digger. May I assume these are your men and you know them well?"

"You might say that. I've been shot at with each and every one of them, but I'd be glad to have any of them in the foxhole with me when it happens again."

"That's high praise from a man in your position."

He closed one eye against the glaring sun. "It ain't praise. It's honesty."

I said, "That's good enough for me. When you're ready, I'll talk you through the details."

He looked over his shoulder. "I think Mr. Johnson wants to introduce you to the crew first, if that's all right with you."

"Sure, but don't go far. We've got a lot to cover."

Clark approached with three men in green flight suits. "Hey, College Boy, you need to meet these guys. This is Gordo, Tubbs, and Slider."

I shook each man's hand. "I'm Chase Fulton. I work for Clark, who you seem to already know."

Gordo said, "Yeah, we know that crusty old paratrooper. He's stepped out of more airplanes we've flown than anybody I know. I think he's got something against landings."

"He does that," I said.

The second man, Tubbs, said, "Nice to meet you, Chase. I'm surprised we haven't met before today."

His comment left me wondering who those guys really were. They wore no rank insignia and no branch or unit affiliation. The insignia on the first two nameplates boasted Command Pilot Badges above their call signs, with no other identifying markings.

Slider shook my hand and motioned toward the charred remains of hangar number one. "Is that why we're here?"

"It is," I said. "Forgive me, but I don't recognize the wings you're wearing."

He patted his nameplate. "Oh, they don't mean anything. I'm the engineer and loadmaster. That basically makes me the errand boy."

Gordo gave the younger man a shove. "Don't let him fool you, Chase. He can do anything we can do on that airplane, but neither of us is smart enough to do any of the stuff he can do."

Slider said, "They try to flatter me since I don't make as much money as they do. They've got the executive seats up front with a windshield. I'm stuck in the dark with no view of anything. Congratulations on scoring the Herk. She'll do anything you ask except go fast."

Tubbs grabbed his chest. "That's hurtful. We may be slow, but at least we're ugly."

I motioned toward what had been the FBO before the municipal airport closed and became an asset of the Bonaventure Trust. "Make yourselves at home. There's a shower and some fresh coffee in there if you need either. If you're planning to stay overnight, we'll be glad to put you up at the house."

That comment seemed to confound the three men, and Gordo

said, "We're staying as long as you need us. They told us the plane and crew are yours indefinitely."

I turned to Clark in disbelief, and he put on that crooked grin of his. "Merry Christmas, College Boy. She ain't no Gulfstream, but she's the best I could do on short notice."

Chapter 18
Something Less than an Airport

I stared up at the workhorse with wings. "Are you serious?"

Clark kept grinning. "She's all yours . . . for now, at least. She's a highly-modified J-model with a few tricks up her sleeve."

At that point in my life, I knew very little about the Herk, but something about that big, lumbering flying machine gave me a degree of confidence I lost when I watched our hangar and the *Grey Ghost* burn to the ground.

When the shock of our new accessory waned, I assembled the team of what turned out to be twenty-*four* well-armed commandos and laid out the situation for them. They listened intently, and no one stuck a hand in the air, even after I opened the door for questions.

I said, "We're going to break you up into squads and send you on a tour of the properties you'll be protecting." I motioned to my team. "These guys will show you around, and they'll have answers for your questions if they come up."

Digger, the team commander, stepped beside me. "Before we get too far into this thing, it'd probably be a good idea to go over the ROE."

I turned back to the gathered team. "Digger brought up an excellent point, so I'd like to cover it before we disperse."

The crowd huddled up, and I said, "Digger asked about the rules of engagement. They're extremely simple for this mission. We're under brutal attack by a well-organized team of operators. Our analyst will see that each of you gets photographs of five of the people who are determined to destroy us. If any of those people are spotted, proceed with extreme caution. They are to be considered hostile and extremely violent. Do not try to subdue any one of them alone. Always work in teams of at least two. Defend yourselves if it becomes necessary, but do not shoot unprovoked."

Someone yelled, "Do you want these guys in body bags or flex-cuffs?"

I took a breath. "Protect personnel with deadly force and material assets with physical aggression and apprehension. Does that answer your question?"

He said, "Yes, sir. Body bags, it is."

I let it go because I spent my adult life living and working with warriors just like those guys, and I instinctually understood their ability to use force only as long as necessary.

We broke up into squads, and the tours began. Skipper collected email addresses and cell phone numbers, and we issued handheld radios to every man.

With the administrative work behind us and the security teams in place, Skipper pulled me aside. "Who do we know in Lubbock, Texas?"

I ran through my mental Rolodex and came up empty. "I don't know anybody in Lubbock. Why?"

She said, "I think that's where Taylor and his guys are headed."

"What makes you think that's where they're going?"

She groaned. "Just trust me. They're heading for Lubbock. I need you to . . ." She froze, and recognition overcame her. "Oh, my God, Chase. Lubbock is just south of Plainview."

"I'm still not following."

"Plainview, Texas, is where Penny's parents live."

I growled. "Get them on the phone now, and do whatever you have to do to get them out of there. As soon as you've done that, send the team to the airport with complete kits for a week."

She snatched her phone and typed frantically while I ran for the

Microbus. I did everything in my power to stomp the accelerator through the floorboard as I begged the old bus to go faster.

When I came to a stop inside the airport gate, Gordo and his crew were strolling from the former FBO. I piled out of the bus and sprinted toward them. "Hey! We need to be in Lubbock, Texas, right now."

Gordo shot Tubbs a look and said, "Don't expect the Herk to do anything fast, but we'll get you there. What's it, maybe a thousand miles to Lubbock?"

"Yeah, just over a thousand nautical miles," I said.

Gordo didn't need a calculator. "Three hours. How much cargo and how many bodies?"

Before I could answer, the sound of a helicopter approaching from the south caught my attention, and I turned to watch it grow larger and more ominous with every passing second.

I grabbed Gordo's flight suit. "Find a rifle or find some cover. I don't know who that is."

As if appearing out of thin air, six of the twenty-four commandos materialized in full battle rattle with their eyes on the same target as mine.

I slipped my M4 from beneath the seat of the Microbus and called Skipper. "Ops, Sierra One."

"Go for ops," she said instantly.

"We've got an unknown chopper approaching from the south. I've got six shooters plus me. Are we expecting company?"

"Not that I know of. What do you want me to do?"

I looked back up to see the chopper still coming. "Get the local PD rolling. I don't like where this is going."

She said, "The team is en route. Should I call them off?"

"Negative. Keep them coming. We may need all the guns we can find if that bird starts shooting."

She was silent for several seconds before saying, "Cops are rolling."

"I'm going to open-channel comms. Get the team up on channel two."

As the chopper continued directly for the field, I kept him in sight and moved to the corner of the nearest building to put anything I could between him and me.

The roar of an engine sounded from behind me, and I glanced back only long enough to see a Toyota Hilux come screaming down the ramp of the C-130 with Tubbs behind the wheel and Slider on the Ma Deuce fifty-cal in the bed. They hit the concrete parking apron and accelerated away from the Herk.

I spotted the incoming bandit again, and he was still coming. As much as I wanted to keep my eyes on the chopper, I couldn't resist the draw of the technical with Slider on the fifty. Tubbs slid the truck to a stop with the tailgate facing the approaching chopper, and Slider raised the armored shield in front of the M2 machine gun, protecting both himself and Tubbs from incoming small-arms fire.

No matter what weapons system they had aboard the chopper, we had them outmanned and outgunned. Two black-and-white St. Marys PD cruisers poured through the gate and slid to a stop between me and the burnt hangar. The officers stepped from their cars and eyed the six shooters with rifles trained on the helicopter. I recognized one of the officers from the night of the fire, so I ran from my position to his side and took cover behind his car.

He popped his trunk as I knelt beside him, and he pulled an AR from its mount. "What's happening here, and why are we aiming rifles at a helicopter?"

I said, "Because we don't know who they are, and this is a private airport."

"Good enough for me." Then, he gasped. "Is that a fifty-cal on a technical?"

"It is," I said. "And I'm glad to have it on our team."

The officer said, "Is the military here?"

"Not exactly, but they're definitely the good guys."

The tiny transceiver glued to my jawbone beneath the skin sent its bone conduction message to my ears, and Shawn's voice rang out.

"Sierra One, this is Sierra Team. We're sixty seconds out. Say condition."

"I've got two local cops, six of Digger's men, and a fifty-cal technical. If that chopper opens fire, we'll put him in the dirt. I want you to stop short of the airport as a quick reaction force in case this thing gets out of hand."

"Roger, boss. We'll hold at the entrance road, and we do have the chopper in sight."

I yelled to Slider on the fifty-cal. "Have you got tracer rounds in that thing?"

"Affirmative, sir!"

I yelled, "When I tell you, I want you to put two to three seconds' worth across his bow."

"Yes, sir."

I refocused my attention on the chopper that was now within two thousand feet of the airport. I didn't recognize the paint scheme, but nothing about it looked threatening except its unannounced approach. As I watched and considered the fallout from shooting down an innocent helicopter pilot, the chopper came to a hover, and it's landing light flashed several times.

My phone vibrated and chirped inside my pocket, but nothing on that ringing phone line was as important as what was playing out in front of me.

"What's he doing?" one of the police officers asked.

"No idea," I said, "but he could be setting up for a shot."

"Are you seriously going to put three seconds' worth of fifty-cal rounds in the air?"

"I hope not, but I'm not willing to—"

Skipper's voice interrupted in my ear. "Chase! Don't shoot! It's Hunter in the helo."

"How do you know?"

"I'm on the phone with him since you didn't answer when he called you."

I said, "All Sierra elements stand down. Inbound is a friendly."

I waved to Tubbs and yelled, "Hold your fire and stand down."

He lowered the Ma Deuce and relaxed. "Standing down."

The chopper nosed over and continued for the field. The pilot touched down on the ramp near the fuel tanks, and Stone W. Hunter stepped from inside. He jogged across the ramp, and I hugged him as if I hadn't seen him in years.

"Thanks for not gunning us down. Why doesn't anybody have an airband radio at this airport?"

"As you can see, we've had a little chaos around here lately, so our electronics aren't exactly at their best. It's good to see you, old man. Welcome home."

He looked over the remains of what had been hangar number one. "I can't say I like what you've done with the place."

The rest of the team pulled up in a pair of Suburbans and dismounted for a hardy round of homecoming hospitality with our brother.

When the handshaking and backslapping ended, Hunter squinted against the sun and asked, "Have you got a kit for me?"

"Build your own," I said. "You know where the armory is. It's good to have you back."

"It's good to be back, but I wish it could be under more pleasant circumstances."

I took a step closer. "Me, too. And thanks for coming. It means more than you know."

He pointed southward. "Remember that thing in the jungle when you pulled my butt out of a rather nasty jam? That's what brothers do. We come running when we're needed."

The rotor blades of the chopper behind us slowly came to a stop. To my surprise, a kid who looked barely old enough to drive stepped from the front seat wearing flip-flops, shorts, and a Grateful Dead T-shirt.

"That's your pilot?" I asked, and Hunter laughed.

The pilot ambled up. "What is this place?"

"It used to be an airport," I said. "Now it's a . . . well, something a little less than an airport."

Hunter said, "Forgive my lack of manners. Chase, this is Bip. He flies tourists over Jacksonville Beach. Skipper booked me into JAX, but she forgot to book the final leg here to Bonaventure, so I recruited Bip."

I shook the pilot's hand. "Nice to meet you, Bip. That's an interesting name. Is it short for something?"

"It's a long story, but anyway, Mr. Hunter said I could fuel up when we got here, so if you don't mind . . ."

I motioned toward the pump. "Help yourself. Jet fuel is on the left. The other pump is avgas, and you don't want that."

He hesitated. "Thanks, but there's one more thing."

Hunter patted his pockets. "Oh, yeah. I almost forgot. I don't have any cash. Would you mind paying him, and I'll get you back?"

I stuck a few bills in the man's hand. "Thanks for dragging my broke brother all the way up here."

He pocketed the money without counting and nodded without another word.

Hunter pointed at the C-130. "New toy?"

"Temporarily," I said. "It'll have to do until we can find a replacement for the *Grey Ghost*."

"Nice. How soon are we moving out?"

I checked my watch. "As soon as you get back from the armory with your new kit."

Chapter 19
I Don't Know

While Hunter was building his kit, the rest of the team loaded gear onto the Herk, and Slider had a few more tricks up his sleeve. I watched him secure the Toyota technical to the deck. He moved effortlessly as if he'd completed the task a million times.

When he finished with the tie-downs, he looked up. "I've got something else to show you."

Slider pulled a tarp from two pallets, revealing a pair of highly-modified desert patrol vehicles. Each of the dune buggy–type vehicles boasted seating for four trigger-pullers and a fifty-caliber Ma Deuce, just like the one on the technical.

I slid my hand across the smooth surface of the rails. "What made you bring these?"

He said, "We didn't load them for you. We just came back from a training exercise, and we never unloaded the DPVs or the technical."

I kicked a tire. "I ran one of these across a river on the border between Kazakhstan and Russia one time."

Slider tossed the tarp back over the buggies. "Yep, these things will take you anywhere you want to go and bring you back with a smile on your face."

"You're just full of surprises," I said.

"It's not me. It's the gear. I just take care of it. Come on, I'll show you a couple more features you might like."

"Give me three minutes," I said. "I need to make a call."

I settled into one of the net seats along the side of the cargo bay and dialed the op center.

Skipper said, "I'm glad that worked out."

"Me, too. I guess I'm just a little jumpy."

"You've got every right to be. Did you need something?"

"I'm calling to check on Penny's folks. Did you get in touch with them?"

She said, "Of course I did, and I booked them a nice private charter to parts unknown. They'll be aboard in minutes."

"So, they're already gone from the house?"

"Yes. You said get them out of there."

"I know. I just wish I could've talked to them before they left. I'd like to have some lights and televisions left on in the house to give the impression somebody's home."

Skipper said, "Come on. Give me a little credit. I've been doing this almost as long as you. I know what you want before you want it. The house will look and sound like it's life as usual, and that's not all. When you had their house built, I specified an electrical system that would allow them to control lights, heat, AC, and televisions remotely from their phones. I have control of that system now, so we can do whatever we want with the house."

"What would I do without you?"

She laughed. "We've had this talk. You'd be broke and coaching a middle school baseball team somewhere."

"Right now, that doesn't sound so bad. Nobody attacks baseball coaches."

"You'd be bored out of your mind. Oh, and Hunter just left with his kit. He should be there in a couple of minutes."

"Sounds like it's time to rock and roll. I need you to keep me posted on anything that happens in Texas. If you can grab a couple of satellites, that would be great."

She said, "Way ahead of you again. I've got two birds already painting pretty pictures. As long as the weather stays good, you'll have live feeds on your phones and tablets."

"You're the best. Are you still tracking Taylor and his guys?"

"I'm not exactly tracking them," she said. "I'm pulling a bunch of sources together and interpolating what they're doing and where they're going."

I said, "I don't need to understand it. I just need to know you're right. You are right . . . aren't you?"

"I am. Now, get in the air. You'll need to hurry to beat them there."

Hunter pulled up and ran up the C-130's ramp with two hundred pounds of gear hanging off of him.

Mongo said, "Did you get enough stuff? You know I'm not going to help you carry that mess."

Hunter patted his gear. "Oh, this isn't everything. I've got six more bags in the truck."

I motioned for Slider to close the ramp. "I hope you're kidding. Now, sit down so we can get airborne."

Slider worked his magic, and the massive ramp closed, sealing us inside the Herk's cavernous cargo bay.

I wanted to be in the cockpit, but I had too much work to do with my team to enjoy a field trip up front. Once we were airborne and cruising, we unstrapped from our seats and set about sorting and arranging gear.

As Shawn checked the edge on his knife, he asked, "So, what's the plan, boss?"

"It's simple," I said. "We get there first, wait for them to show up, and drive 'em into the ground when they do."

"That's what I call the Naval Special Warfare kiss. Keep It Simple, SEAL."

"I'm not saying it'll be simple or easy, but if we can get in place in time, we should be able to make short work of them."

The SEAL sheathed his blade and patted the deck next to him. "Sit down a minute. I want to tell you a story."

Shawn had never been much of a conversationalist, but when he spoke, it was profound, and that day was no exception.

I got comfortable on the deck beside him, and he began. "When I was with the Teams, we had a simple little mission to pick up two guys who were running the financial side of a small-time warlord's nasty operation. These guys were bankers or something. They weren't a physical threat, so we watched them for a while and then set up an ambush behind a crappy restaurant they liked to meet at on Tuesday nights."

He paused as if to check my attention span, and I said, "Don't stop now. I'm intrigued."

He said, "We didn't do a workup. We didn't do a threat assessment. And we only took three guys. It was a driver, another SEAL, and me. The whole ordeal should've taken ten minutes. We just roll up these bean counters and move out. Nothing to it."

I said, "Let me guess. They weren't bean counters after all?"

He shook his head. "Oh, no. They were. We pegged them perfectly. They were university-educated MBA types."

"So, where's this story going?"

To my surprise, Shawn crossed his arms, grabbed the bottom of his T-shirt, and pulled it over his head. He could bench-press a school bus, so I'd never consider pulling off my shirt next to him.

He pointed to a horizontal scar about two inches long beneath his arm. "See that?"

"That's a knife wound," I said. "I've got a few of those."

"I like to call them experience reminders."

I chuckled. "I'll go along with that."

He pulled his shirt back on. "Anyway, we hit the two guys as they were walking to their car after cocktails and a dinner no self-respecting Muslim should eat. My partner locked his guy up a second before I grabbed my dude, and that tiny instant gave my target time to draw the switchblade he liked to carry and spin to face me."

"I don't like where this is going."

"Me neither," he said. "But I was in it up to my ears, and all of a sudden, it was a knife fight. You know me well enough to know that I don't back away from a fight, so I stepped into the guy. A knife in the hands of an untrained fighter is a bigger threat to him than me. My training and experience gave me the confidence to strip the guy of his knife and have him in the van before he knew what hit him."

"So, what went wrong?"

He rubbed the scar through his shirt. "I got no idea. I went for his wrist, and the next thing I knew, I was waking up in sick bay aboard a ship, and my buddy was covered in my blood."

"What?"

He huffed. "Oh, yeah. The whole op went to crap, and both bankers got away. I became a victim of my own overconfidence, and my partner became the only person in the country who could keep me alive. How he got me back to the boat, I'll never know, but they tell me I lost over half the blood in my body."

"Seriously?"

"Dead serious. The tip of his switchblade nicked the superior vena cava taking blood back to my heart. I should've died, but my buddy wouldn't let me."

He took a minute, as if reliving the moment. "I learned something that night. There's no such thing as an easy or simple op. They're all potentially deadly and should be given the respect they deserve."

I took a long breath and let it out. "You're saying we don't have enough intel on this group to hit them, aren't you?"

"Nope. I'm not saying anything like that. All I'm saying is don't let your confidence talk you into writing a check your butt can't cash."

He was right, and I was disappointed in myself. We were up against an enemy we knew little about, and I believed we could waltz in ahead of them and cut them off at the knees because they'd never know we were there.

He cocked his head. "How many are there?"

"I don't know."

"What is their weapons loadout?"

"I don't know."

He never took his eyes from mine. "How well trained are they at hand-to-hand?"

I sighed. "I don't know."

"Do they have an overwatch sniper?"

I wasn't willing to make my confession out loud again, so I sat on the aluminum deck of that C-130, shaking my head.

Shawn slapped me on the back and leaned in. "I'm not suggesting we don't go in. I'm just trying to tell you to stay on your toes like a short guy at a urinal. Are we cool?"

I said, "That's why this team works. We have a relationship that allows us to get each other's minds right when we start to slip. Thanks for checking me."

He reached out and took a handful of my shirt in his hammer fist. "Don't lose your confidence. Just temper it. We'll get these guys, and we'll take everybody home in one piece."

I looked up to see Slider standing a few feet away.

He said, "Sorry to interrupt, but we need to talk about the insertion plan."

I pulled out my tablet and brought up a map of the desert-like terrain northeast of Plainview. My finger landed on the forty-acre plot of land Penny's parents owned. "That's our ultimate objective."

"Got it," Slider said. "How far away do you want to get out?"

"What's the range on your DPVs?"

"Two hundred miles or so, depending on how aggressively you drive them."

"We're nothing if not aggressive, so plot us a track that'll put our boots—and your buggies—on the ground twenty miles northeast of the objective."

He studied the map for a long moment. "You got it. We'll be in position in less than half an hour. You boys better gear up. I've got the DPVs rigged to go. Do you want the technical?"

I turned and admired the Toyota Hilux with that big, beautiful fifty-cal in the bed. "As much as I'd love to take it, we can't spray that kind of lead all over Texas and not kill a good guy. We'll stick to the buggies and small arms."

"Whatever you say." He checked his watch. "Twenty-five minutes."

I hopped to my feet and called for the team to huddle up. "We've got a little over twenty minutes. Suit up."

Minutes later, everyone had their gear slung onto their bodies, and they were conducting pre-jump checks on each other's parachutes.

Slider held up two fingers, and I yelled. "Two minutes! Clear the ramp!"

Chapter 20
Princess Buttercup

Slider moved like a machine inside the cargo bay of the C-130 Hercules. He obviously knew every inch of the airplane as if it were part of his body. Stepping between the two sticks of commandos perched and ready to fly, he said, "Gentlemen, or whatever, we're at seventeen-five, and the desert down there is at thirty-four hundred above sea level."

Each of us set our altimeters and our automatic opening devices that would pull the pilot chute for us if we happened to miss our opening altitude or, God forbid, we became unconscious or injured and unable to pull for ourselves.

He said, "I'll depressurize, open the ramp, send the desert patrol vehicles, and you'll follow. The cargo chutes will open on a static line, so you'll pass the buggies on the way down. Please don't get beneath them. They're heavy, and you don't want them to land on you."

Each of us gave the thumbs-up, and Slider pulled on an oxygen mask. Above twelve thousand feet, the air tends to get a little thin, and our brains don't function well without twenty-one percent oxygen in every breath. The team and I would fall through the high altitude too fast to worry about oxygen, but Slider had work to do.

The massive cargo ramp began its yawn, giving us our first view of the world outside. When it reached its max open position, Slider yelled, "Stand clear! Cargo moving!"

Each of us moved to the front of the cargo bay to remain clear of the desert patrol vehicles that would exit the airplane first. If anything we owned got snagged on that cargo, it would rip us from the airplane and make for quite the unpleasant day. We watched the pallets carrying the DPVs slide away and gain speed with every inch.

When the two pallets cleared the ramp, Slider held his tether and peered over the edge. An instant later, he turned to us and yelled, "Four good chutes. Go, go, go!"

We left the airplane like a pair of caterpillars and began our acceleration to terminal velocity in free fall. We fell in formation, flying our bodies like living wings. At eight thousand feet, I waved off and turned from the formation. The team followed suit, and we flew away until everyone was clear of other jumpers and our chutes became billowing black clouds, growing over our heads, until each of us was suspended beneath a good canopy and descending slowly enough to survive contact with Mother Earth.

A glimpse upward showed me four cargo chutes above the DPVs. I steered my canopy upwind of the pallets and kept the ten thousand pounds of cargo in sight. The desert spread out beneath us, and I struggled to find the plot of land that would become our battlefield if the mission played out the way I envisioned it. Finding one forty-acre plot from a mile above the ground, in an endless world of sand-irrigated fields that all looked the same, was a fool's pursuit, so I directed my attention to a landing site.

A quick inventory of my gear confirmed that everything I left the airplane with was still on my body, but that was a temporary condition. As the ground rushed upward in the final two hundred feet of my jump, I pulled the pin holding the tether to my gear. When the pin was clear, my rucksack and front-loaded gear bag fell away until it reached the end of its nylon tether some twenty feet beneath me.

The gear hit the ground in a mighty cloud of sand and dust and stopped my forward motion. Unlike the cargo chutes over the DPVs, I had brakes. I pulled both toggles from well above my head all the way to my knees the instant before my left foot—my only remaining real foot—touched the rocky ground.

I wasn't the first of my team to find terra firma. Mongo beat me to earth by thirty seconds or more. One by one, each of us touched down like seasoned jumpers until Gator, the boy wonder, came soaring from the sky with his gear still firmly attached to his body.

Clark yelled up at him, "Jettison your gear! Cut the gear!"

Gator worked frantically to free his packs before colliding with the planet, but it was no use. They weren't moving, and he was committed to a trainwreck I didn't want to watch but couldn't look away from. The coming event was the last thing the youngest member of our team needed in his life. He was still wounded from the explosion at the airport, and practically no one could survive the crash he was about to endure without breaking a few bones.

Twenty feet above the ground, he pulled the toggles with every drop of strength he could muster, and the end cells of his Ram-Air parachute curled downward, increasing lift and slowing both his vertical and horizontal motion. Gator hit the ground harder than the DPVs would sixty seconds later. He attempted a parachute landing fall, but the bulky gear stopped him the instant it hit the dirt, and he let out a mighty groan like a dying beast as he disappeared inside a brown cloud.

I shucked off my parachute and ran to his side, fearing what I would find when the dust finally cleared. As I slid to a stop beside my teammate, I found him pounding on his front-loading gear bag with a thundering fist. "You piece of—"

"Easy," I said. "Are you hurt?"

"No, I'm just mad. My cutaway tether is fouled, but I'm okay."

I dusted him off. "Let's get you on your feet and make sure you're still in one piece."

Before I could offer a hand to help Gator stand, two massive hands seized him beneath his armpits and hoisted him to his feet.

Mongo said, "That didn't look like much fun. Are you okay?"

Gator took a few steps, wiggled his fingers, and stretched out his arms. "I think I'm all right."

I thought, *Man, I miss being young.*

The two pallets carrying the desert patrol vehicles found the ground and sent two more enormous clouds of dust into the air. We waited for the wind to clear it up before moving in, but we didn't waste any time once the visibility returned. The buggies started on the first effort, and we split up into two teams. I took the vehicle commander's seat in the DPV with Clark and Mongo while Gator, Kodiak, Hunter, and Shawn boarded the second buggy.

Once on the move to the southwest, I watched the sun kiss the western horizon in a brilliant light show that would've been the perfect final sunset of my life. I prayed it wouldn't be, but if I never saw another, that one was good enough for eternity.

We crossed several semi-paved roads that were little more than hard-packed sand, but we couldn't use the roads as the thoroughfare they were intended to be. I didn't need the local sheriff asking questions about our automatic weapons and grenades. Those would be hard to explain, even in Texas.

It took almost an hour to cover the twenty miles separating us from our objective, but the property came into sight just as darkness consumed the western plains.

"There she is," I called over the open-channel comms. "Let's move within two hundred yards of the house and hold."

We continued cautiously until we made the point I called and then brought the DPVs to a halt.

Dismounted, I said, "I want Mongo and Gator on the vehicles for two reasons. I don't want any Texans driving away in our new toys, and we need a quick reaction force in case we get pinned down."

The rest of us advanced on the house with our rifles at low ready, and the motion of the television screens inside was already obvious through the parted drapes and shades.

I said, "Hunter, you're with me and Clark. We'll take the north side. Shawn and Kodiak, I want you to take the south and meet on the opposite side. We're looking for any signs of ingress or movement."

The slow perimeter patrol left us easy pickings for the horde of blood-thirsty mosquitoes, but our focus on the house left no time for swatting. We completed the circuit with no signs of life and took a knee in front of the house.

I asked, "Did anyone see anything interesting?"

Heads shook, but no one spoke up.

"I want Shawn and Kodiak to make entry and build a couple of dummies. Set the lighting to sell it, and we'll see if we can get Taylor and his team to bite. While you two are working on that, the rest of us will set a perimeter."

Mongo and Gator brought the DPVs in and stashed them beneath a cluster of the ugliest trees I'd ever seen. They looked like something that might grow in Hell or another planet, but they certainly didn't belong in Texas.

The SEAL and the former Green Beret moved in on the house and made entry through the back door.

When they emerged, Kodiak said, "It won't pass close-up inspection, but they look pretty good from the windows, don't you think?"

The two bodies they built out of pillows and laundry looked lifelike from fifty yards, and we established a solid perimeter nobody could penetrate without detection.

"It's time to call home," I said.

Skipper answered quickly. "Hey, Chase. I've been listening on the open-channel comms. It sounds like everything is going smoothly so far."

"Your boyfriend took a bad fall from three miles high, but he's not smart enough to know he's hurt."

She growled. "Don't get him hurt any worse than he already is. I don't want prosthetics and electronic ears on him. He's too pretty for that."

I laughed. "Yes, he is, but let's talk business. Are Taylor and his gang still headed this way?"

"They are. In fact, they landed in Lubbock twenty-six minutes ago."

"Can you track them on the ground?"

"I wish. The best I can do is live satellite imagery, but neither of the cameras on the birds is good enough to identify faces. I'll tell you when somebody's approaching, but I won't be able to name them."

"That's good enough," I said. "Nobody should approach the house other than the bad guys so we're ready when they come."

She said, "I'll be on live comms, so you don't have to call back."

"Sounds good. Have you heard from Anya and Penny?"

She sighed. "No, Chase, and I'm not going to. It's a little thing called operational security. Ever heard of it?"

"Yeah, yeah, I get it. I just thought—"

"Well, stop doing that. Thinking is too much for you. Just catch the bad guys, will you?"

"As you wish, Princess Buttercup."

She chuckled. "I guess that makes you the Dread Pirate Roberts, huh?"

"Not me," I said. "You don't hide a face as good as mine behind a mask."

Before she could shoot back with something snappy, my phone beeped, and I checked the screen. What I saw left me quivering in my boots. "Earl's calling. I'm putting her on three-way." I pressed the button. "Earl. Is everything all right?"

Her tear-filled voice drove daggers through my heart. "No, Chase. They've got Kenny."

Chapter 21
Battlefield Sins

My heart broke, and I wanted to kick myself in the face for not including Earl at the End and Kenny LePine on the list of things I love. Now, I was a thousand miles away and practically powerless to keep them alive. I fought desperately to calm my fear and self-loathing long enough to handle a situation I never considered until that moment.

I said, "Try to stay calm, and tell me where you are."

Earl gasped. "I'm on the floor in the kitchen. They tied me to a chair, but they didn't take my phone."

"Where's Kenny?"

"They took him and said they'd be back for me."

"Okay. How many were there?"

"Three."

"How long ago did this happen?"

Her breathing was slowing enough to almost speak clearly. "I don't know. Maybe five minutes ago. Chase, I'm scared. Please do something."

I took a long breath to avoid having panic slip into my voice. "Skipper, are you with us?"

The analyst said, "I'm here."

"Good. Get a team of at least five of the security contingent over there now."

"It's already done. Six men are on their way. Do you want me to call the police?"

I considered her question, but Earl beat me to the answer. "No! No police. This ain't the kind of thing the cops are good at. These people aren't..."

She faded, and I said, "Earl! Earl, are you there?"

The quivering voice returned, and she said, "They're back. I can hear them outside. Chase, please get over here."

"I'm sending a team, Earl. I'm in Texas, but the guys I'm sending can handle whatever this is. They should be there any minute."

A commotion arose and sounded as if someone was tearing down the house around Earl. I listened closely, trying to pick up on anything that might identify the men inside her home. The next sound I heard chilled me to my spine.

"*Ubey etu suku!*"

"They're speaking Russian, Skipper. Where's that team?"

She said, "They're on scene now and moving in. Earl, if you can hear me, stay down. Help is coming through the door."

The next sound I heard was even more ominous than the aggressors speaking Russian. It was the sound of silence.

"Earl! Earline! Are you there?"

Nothing.

"Skipper?"

She said, "Yeah, I'm here."

"Do you have comms with the team?"

"Just cell phones."

"Get somebody on the phone. I have to know what's happening over there."

"I'm on it," she said, "but nobody's answering."

As the rage inside me boiled, my phone vibrated in my hand, and I checked the screen. "Hang on a minute, Skipper. I'm getting a call from Kenny's phone."

I pressed the button to add the new call to ours. "Yeah."

"Hello der, Chase. Dis here be yo ditch-diggin' friend, ol' Kenny LePine. Can you hears me good 'nuff?"

"You're loud and clear, Kenny. What's going on over there?"

"Well, I gots me two dead bodies and one mo' das fixin' to be dead, me. Plus I gots six peoples who say dey be workin' fo you, but ol' Kenny ain't never seen none of dem 'fore. I gots to get dis here straightened out."

"Are you and Earl okay?" I asked.

"Earline be still skeert, but she ain't be hurt, hers ain't. I can't say da same fo dese other fellas. Do dey really be workin' fo you?"

I said, "The three who hit you initially are not mine, but the six who showed up to help are ours. Please don't shoot any of them."

"It be a little too late for dat kinda talks. I done kilt two of dem first tree. I done knocked out da one dat be trying to hurt Earline, me."

Maybe it was the stress or the relief I felt knowing the situation was under control, but I actually laughed. "That's good, Kenny. One of the six should have a phone ringing in his pocket."

Kenny apparently pulled the phone away from his mouth. "Which one of you done gots a ringing phone in dey pocket, huh?"

A few seconds later, he came back on the line. "One of 'em gots one of dem ringin' phones."

I said, "Have him answer it. It'll be Skipper."

"If you says so, Chase. You knows how much I truss you, me."

After a few clicks, a man's voice came on the line. "Mr. Fulton, this is TD. I'm the team lead, and this Cajun won't put down his shotgun."

I said, "Kenny, are you still with me?"

"Yes, sir, me is."

"You can relax and put down the shotgun. They're the good guys. Take care of Earl, and I'll deal with the rest."

He said, "What's you be wantin' me to do wiff dem dead bodies? I can bury dem, me. Dat ain't no problem."

"Don't bury them," I said. "Let TD take care of it, and surrender the one surviving member of the trio to him as well. I've got something special planned for him."

"Consider it done did."

I said, "All right, TD. The scene is yours. Do something with the dead guys, and roll up the prisoner."

"Yes, sir. We've got a solid interrogator with us if you'd like us to warm up the prisoner for you."

"I like that idea," I said. "I've got my hands full out here in Texas right now, but if all goes well, we'll be back in St. Marys within a couple of days. Keep him alive and unhappy until I get there. Can you do that?"

"No problem, sir."

I said, "It's all yours, Skipper. Let's put a few guys on Earl and Kenny, and anybody else you can think of that these guys might want to hit."

"I'll take care of it," she said. "Let me know what else you need."

"Those satellite feeds would be nice."

"Oh, I'm sorry. I thought I already did that."

"We're not receiving them on our end."

Her fingers on the keyboard rattled through the phone. "Okay, you should have them now."

I turned to Mongo. "Check your tablet for satellite feeds."

He slipped the thin device from his pack and dimmed the screen. "Yep, I've got 'em. Nice work."

"We're receiving them now," I said. "Thanks."

Clark spoke just above a whisper into his comms. "Contact northbound on the street."

I said, "I'm going to hang up, but you're still on sat-coms, right?"

"Absolutely," she said. "And Chase . . . be careful."

"I'm always careful," I said just before hanging up. I craned my neck to see around the house, and a four-door sedan cruised by at no more than ten miles per hour. "Do you think that's our guy?"

Clark said, "That's the second time they've come by, but they didn't slow down the first time."

I watched the car accelerate. "Skipper, mark the car that just passed and keep track of it. It could be our boy."

"Got it," she said.

Gator asked, "Does anybody else hear a buzz?"

No one answered, so I asked, "What do you think it is?"

He said, "Oh, I know what it is. I just saw it, and it probably saw me. It's a drone."

I said, "All Sierra elements, move to cover. We've got an active drone."

Although I couldn't see everyone in our perimeter positions, I believed everyone was making themselves as small and as hard to see as possible.

I said, "Is there anything you can do about that drone, Skipper?"

She said, "No, I can't do anything from here. Can't you shoot it down?"

I said, "Gator, do you still have visual on the drone?"

"Affirmative."

"You're running a suppressor on your M4, right?"

"Affirmative."

"Kill the drone," I ordered.

It may have already been too late, but I couldn't risk that flying camera seeing the rest of us.

A few seconds later, I heard the hiss of a suppressed rifle round, and Gator said, "Dead drone."

Shawn said, "Contact front. Single male approaching the house on foot."

"On foot?" I asked. "Where did he come from?"

"Unknown," Shawn said. "Maybe that slow-moving car let him out. Do you want me to take him down?"

"Not yet. Let's see what he does. Can you see him clearly enough to tell if it's Taylor?"

"It's not him," he said. "This guy's over six feet, and Taylor can't be more than five ten."

"Do you see any trailers?"

"I'm looking, but he appears to be a true single."

"He's a probe," I said. "He's going to ring the doorbell and tell some story about his car breaking down and that he needs to use the phone."

Mongo spoke up. "I think you're right. What's the play?"

I said, "Shawn and I will move in from his five and seven o'clock to pin him down. The rest of you, cover us. Gator, I want you to stay on the rear in case he's a frontal diversion."

"Roger," Gator said. "I've got the back door."

The rest of the team moved into position to cover Shawn and me, and I gave the order. "Ready, Shawn?"

"Affirmative."

"Let's roll," I said.

Shawn and I moved silently across the rocky ground with our night vision in place and our rifles at the ready. As we drew closer, the man stopped in his tracks and turned as if he'd heard one of us. We froze. Without night vision, the man would never see us as long as we were silent and still.

Our target scanned the darkness, hesitating at first but finally turning to continue his approach. Shawn and I moved in unison with him, ensuring that our boots hit the ground at the same time his did to mask our sound signature.

Skipper's voice came. "The vehicle is returning."

"How far out?" Mongo asked.

"Maybe a quarter of a mile."

He's definitely a probe, I thought. *Or bait.*

The same thought must've hit Mongo at the same instant. "He's not a probe. He's bait, and we just swallowed the hook. Gator, get on that roof double-quick. We're going to need the overwatch. This thing is about to turn into a fireworks show."

The man stopped again, turned, and ran back for the street.

I said, "We're made. Hit him, Shawn."

Our resident fireplug of a man leapt to his feet and charged the runner. Just as I hoped, the man heard Shawn and made a right turn to build distance between him and the rapidly approaching SEAL. The redirection sent him sprinting directly toward me, and my heart picked up the pace in anticipation.

That old, familiar feeling of a runner charging home from third base rang in my chest, and I couldn't wait for the coming trainwreck.

Shawn adjusted his angle and continued his thundering run toward his target, and the runner changed course again. The crash was no longer imminent, so I hopped to my feet and joined the chase. I had the angle, and he was ours.

Gator said, "Overwatch is in position. I've got the runner and the approaching car."

With the element of surprise abolished, I said, "If the runner gets past us, kill the car."

Gator said, "Roger."

The situation continued developing faster by the second, and the runner was obviously trying to make it back to the vehicle. I was determined to keep him from making it.

I maneuvered to cut him off and picked up my pace. When we were less than ten yards apart, the runner drew a pistol from his waistband and brought it to bear directly on me.

In my haste to intercept and tackle him, I let my rifle lay tightly against my body on its sling. There was no way I had time to bring up the muzzle and get off a round before he could put two in my face, so I ordered, "Kill him, Gator!"

The instant I made the call, the runner pressed the switch on his pistol, flooding my night vision with a couple thousand lumens of brilliant, white light. His plan was perfect, and his execution was brilliant.

I was suddenly blind, but the sniper I had just unleashed was not. Gator squeezed off four rounds in rapid succession, and my mind lost all comprehension of the situation.

Why would he send four rounds downrange so quickly to take out one man on the run?

That's when the whole scene turned into a massive gunfight, but I wasn't invited.

Mongo said, "They're out of the car and shooting. Chase, are you hit?"

"Negative. I'm just blind from the runner's light. I'm out of the fight. I can't see anything."

I heard the action around me and tried to create a mental picture. Gator had killed the car instead of the runner, and that was tantamount to kicking a hornets' nest . . . if the hornets had automatic weapons.

Shawn leapt across me and took a prone position, returning fire. "Are you okay, Chase?"

"I'm fine, just blind from the light."

He said, "I've got you covered. Just stay down, and keep those eyes closed. You'll get your vision back."

The fight raged, and I wanted nothing more than to crawl beside Shawn and lay down fire with him. Instead, I fed him magazines every time his fell empty.

Skipper said, "You've got another inbound. I can't tell what kind of vehicle it is, but it's doing at least a hundred miles an hour from the south."

The incoming fire continued, and we had no choice but to eat it. We had no cover and very little concealment if the shooters had nods. I had put us in an unsurvivable situation, and that was an unforgivable battlefield sin.

"The vehicle just left the road," Skipper said. "He's crossing the field on the opposite side of the road."

I looked up, even though I couldn't see our sniper. "Gator, do you have eyes on the vehicle in the field?"

"I'm looking."

A few seconds later, he said, "I've got him, but I don't have enough rifle to make that shot. All I've got is a three hundred Blackout."

Not bringing a heavy gun for our only remaining sniper was sin number two.

Mongo said, "They're running for the vehicle."

I ordered, "Mow 'em down, boys."

The incoming fire slowed, but the outgoing did not. We were still filling the air with lead.

Skipper said, "The vehicle slowed, but it's accelerating again and headed north fast."

The fight had to come to an end, and all we had to show for it were empty shell casings scattered over the property with our fingerprints all over them.

Chapter 22
Golden Bullet

Every cell of my body wanted to climb back into the desert patrol vehicles and chase our foe all the way to the north pole, if that's what it took, but they had at least a two-mile head start, and the DPVs couldn't make more than sixty miles per hour with the weight of the team on board. I was left with only one real option.

"Skipper, I need you to track that vehicle to the moon if necessary, but whatever you do, don't lose it. Those are our guys, and we have to catch them."

She said, "I'm on it, but I can't promise I can stay with them. The satellites are geosynchronous, so I can't really move them. I can track the vehicle as long as I can see it, but after that, I'm at a loss."

"How were you tracking them when they left L.A. and headed for Texas?"

"That's a little piece of software Dr. Mankiller built for me. It's not perfect yet, but it's pretty good."

"Can you use it to track them on the ground?"

She said, "Maybe. I'm trying, but they have an airplane on deck at Lubbock. My guess is that they'll eventually make their way back there. How do you feel about staking out the airport?"

"Stakeouts aren't our kind of ops, but I've got an idea."

"Send it," she said.

"Do you know if Penny's father is a hunter?"

"A hunter? Like a deer hunter?"

"Hopefully something bigger than deer."

"I have no idea. Why?"

I said, "In that case, I think I'll commit another felony tonight."

"What are you talking about?"

"I'll let you know if we get lucky."

She wanted to argue, but I didn't have time.

I called over the sat-com. "All Sierra elements rally on me."

The team collapsed and took a knee in a semicircle where I stood. "Shawn, Kodiak, did you see a safe or a gun cabinet when you went into the house?"

Shawn nodded. "There was a safe in one of the bedrooms."

I pointed to Gator, the closest thing we had to a sniper. "I need to commandeer the heaviest rifle we can find for him. We've got a little demolition work to do."

Mongo spoke up. "Was it digital, or did it have a dial?"

Shawn closed one eye and thought about the question. "I'm pretty sure it had a keypad."

I grimaced. "We could sure use Anya's safecracking skills right about now."

Clark said, "We don't need no stinkin' Russian." He wiggled his fingers. "We've got these."

I ducked my chin. "Are you saying you can crack the safe?"

He kissed the tips of several fingers. "I can't defeat the keypad, but I'll bet dollars to duck eggs there's a keyhole behind the electronic pad, and I know for sure I can pick that."

I said, "Take Kodiak with you, and make it happen. We're looking for the longest, strongest rifle we can find." I turned to Gator. "That reminds me. How did you stop the car with that light rifle of yours?"

He shrugged. "One in each of the left-side tires, and two in the windshield. I figured if the tires didn't do it, maybe not being able to see through the glass might get them to hit the brakes."

"That's pretty good logic, but you missed the actual command I gave. I told you to kill him.'"

He recoiled. "Are you sure? I could swear you said to kill *it*."

"I've got an idea," I said. "From now on, when any of us is issuing kill orders, name the target instead of *him* or *it*."

Heads nodded, and I said, "Hunter and Shawn, grab our buggies and move them in. Mongo, Gator, and I will check the shot-up car for anything useful."

When we reached the car, we discovered Gator's call was spot-on. Both left-side tires were demolished, and the windshield looked like a thousand overlapping spiderwebs.

"Nice shooting," Mongo said.

Gator rubbed a finger over the impact point of the first bullet against the windshield. "Ah, this one's about three inches lower than I intended. I can do better."

"You were shooting two hundred fifty yards with three hundred Blackout. Even Singer couldn't do any better."

Gator huffed. "Singer could've taken the tip off the antenna with a slingshot from that range. I'll never be as good as him."

The mention of our beloved sniper sent lightning bolts down my spine. "Ops, Sierra One."

Skipper said, "Go for ops."

"Do we have any updates on Singer and Disco?"

She said, "Negative, but I'll make some calls after the sun comes up."

"Roger. Thanks."

We opened all four car doors with our fingertips wrapped in our T-shirts to prevent the forensic evidence of our presence, even though every shell casing in the yard was covered with our prints.

Mongo said, "Back seat's clear. Nothing at all back here."

I planted a knee on the driver's seat and leaned in. "Same up here. It's clean."

Gator said, "They're thorough if nothing else."

I said, "Oh, they're a lot of things, and thorough is just one of them. Get pictures of the VIN and the license plate, then get it out of the road and torch it."

The DPVs pulled up with Shawn and Hunter at the wheels and Kodiak and Clark on board.

"Any luck finding a rifle?" I asked.

Clark said. "You could say that."

He held up a rifle with a massive scope. "This one is a three hundred Win Mag, but her big brother is the real find."

"She's got a big brother?"

He slapped a heavy plastic case on the seat beside him. "This is a little thing called a Barrett fifty-cal."

"I could kiss you," I said.

"Oh, no you don't, College Boy. I'm not falling for that one again."

I chuckled. "There wasn't a car in the garage by any chance, was there?"

Clark nodded. "There's a crew cab F-One-Fifty and a John Deere."

"I think we'll take the Ford. With any luck, the keys will be in it."

He said, "Nope. The keys are on a hook in the mudroom, but that's almost as good."

With the sedan in flames and our DPVs tucked away inside the garage, we climbed into the truck and headed for Lubbock.

I said, "Please tell me you grabbed some ammo with the rifles."

Clark snapped his fingers. "I knew we were forgetting something."

Kodiak held up two green ammo cans and gave them a shake. Based on the sound, the cans clearly weren't full, but if things went our way, we'd only need a single golden bullet.

Gator drummed his fingertips together. "I assume you want me to employ one or both of those rifles, right?"

I said, "Just the fifty-cal."

He said, "Yeah . . . about that. I have no idea if the scope is zeroed, and even if it is, I don't know the DOPE on that gun."

Clark gave Kodiak a wink. "Tell him."

Kodiak said, "There just happens to be a DOPE card taped to the stock, and it says the scope is zeroed at two hundred yards."

Gator wagged a finger. "That whole thing about not knowing the zero or the DOPE . . . You can forget I ever mentioned it."

Clark checked them in the mirror. "Sounds like you're flying under a lucky star, Sniper Junior."

Gator shook his head. "Sniper Junior? That's what we're going with?"

"It seems appropriate."

It took almost an hour to drive to Lubbock, and another twenty minutes to find anything resembling high ground. We discovered an abandoned construction site just northeast of the airport, and Clark, our overqualified driver, parked with the tailgate facing the flightline.

We climbed out, and Gator put on an enormous smile.

"What's that grin about?" I asked.

"You want me to kill their airplane, don't you?"

"It's almost like you're reading my mind."

He pulled the enormous weapon from its case and pressed five rounds into the magazine. "I need a file, or at least something harder than this barrel that'll slide into the muzzle."

Clark patted his pockets. "Where did I put that pesky file?"

I said, "I like where your head's at, sniper, but don't worry about ballistics. We've got a replacement barrel for that thing in the armory at home. We'll melt that one down or drop it in the ocean. Either way, nobody needs to worry about matching your bullet to that rifle."

Gator lowered the tailgate and climbed into the bed of the truck. "Did anybody think to bring a range finder?"

I opened my pack, pulled out the handheld device, and tossed it to Gator.

He sighted on the airport. "Wow! That's sixteen hundred yards."

"Can you do it?" Clark asked.

He nodded. "Sure I can, but if you want to take the shot, I'll surrender the gun."

Clark's crooked grin showed up. "With that rifle, I could take a cigarette out of your mouth at a mile."

"Is that so, old man?"

Clark grabbed his chest, "Oh! That stings. But next time you see Singer, ask him who taught him to shoot when he was a sniveling little Army corporal."

Gator eyed my handler and considered his words before laughing out loud. "You almost had me there for a minute. You're a funny guy."

Clark said, "Laugh it up, kid. Just don't botch the shot."

Gator sidled up behind the rifle, flipped open the scope covers, and focused. "Which one is theirs?"

"Sierra Ops, Sierra One. Which airplane is Taylor's?"

She rattled off the tail number, and I relayed it to our sniper.

He said, "In sight. Where do you want the impact?"

"Can you hit an engine?" I asked.

He sighed and nestled in until he was in the perfect position to take the shot. "Get back. I don't want the muzzle blast to hit you."

We stepped back, and I pulled my small binoculars from a pocket. With the airplane in clear focus, I said, "Send it when ready."

Almost before I finished talking, the mighty weapon roared and bucked in front of Gator. It was impossible not to flinch at the report of the rifle, but I didn't close my eyes. My resilience was rewarded by the sight of fiberglass and metal flying from the starboard engine.

I tossed the binoculars to Clark, and he focused on the plane. "Not bad for a cold-bore shot, kid. I'm not impressed, but you did all right. Let's wake up our flight crew, wherever they are."

* * *

Skipper said, "I've got Gordo on the phone. The Herk is on deck at Lubbock Executive. Do you want to meet them there or someplace else?"

"Have him meet us in Plainview," I said. "We've got a truck to return and a couple buggies I don't want to abandon out there."

"Consider it done."

I checked my watch. "We'll be there in ninety minutes if everything goes smoothly."

"I'll pass it along," Skipper said. "Are you coming home?"

"That depends on your answer to my next question. Are you tracking Taylor?"

"I lost him, but I've got a contact in Amarillo who can put eyes on their airplane and let us know when anybody shows up to fly it away."

I said, "Make that happen."

* * *

Just as I predicted, we pulled onto the parking ramp at the Plainview–Hale County Airport an hour and a half later. Slider had the DPVs strapped down and ready to fly in no time.

Gordo came down the four metal steps leading from the flight deck. "How'd it go?"

I waggled a hand. "Not great, but we're all alive and fit to fight another day."

He ran a hand through his hair. "From what I've seen so far, I'd say there's a better than good chance of that fight happening as soon as the sun comes up."

I settled onto the net seats and slipped off my boots. "I hope you're wrong. We could use some rest, but if the fight comes, we'll be more than happy to pass out free lead at three thousand feet per second."

Chapter 23
Good Cop/Bad Cop

The cargo bay of a C-130 is an interesting combination of noise, rattles, and discomfort, but after the night we had, it was the perfect atmosphere to catch three hours of sleep on our way back to the East Coast.

I slept through the landing and didn't come to life until the engines were shut down and Slider opened the ramp. After pulling my boots back on, I stretched and climbed to my feet. Don showed up at the foot of the ramp with the forklift and motioned toward the desert patrol vehicles.

When I shot Slider a look, he shrugged and said, "They're not mine. As far as I know, they belong to that organization you work for."

I waved Don off and told Slider, "Let's keep them on board for now. This thing is a long way from over, and I'd rather have them loaded and ready to fly."

"Sounds good to me," he said. "I'll refuel and inspect them for damage. I'm no mechanic, but I can tighten bolts and change a tire if necessary. Did you notice anything they needed?"

"They were perfect for us."

I followed the rest of the team down the ramp and onto the tarmac. My body wasn't finished sleeping, but my mind wouldn't stop spinning. I wanted to be in the op center, planning our next assault, or counterassault, but across the airport stood an empty hangar with one very uncomfortable Russian who was on the verge of telling me everything I wanted to know. If he wasn't excited about spilling his guts, I was more than willing to spill a great deal of his blood.

I grabbed a handful of Gator's shirt. "How's your stomach?"

He cocked his head. "Uh . . . fine. Why?"

"Good. You're coming with me, and I don't want you to puke in front of our guest."

"What are you talking about?"

"You'll see."

We rode across the runway in Dr. Richter's ancient Microbus, and I thumbed the code on the cipher lock. When the door swung open, the scene inside took me by surprise. One of the security troops Clark delivered was standing beside an upside-down naked man who was suspended by his feet from a rope attached to the steel trusses overhead. The upright man held a green plastic watering can designed to provide life-giving water to somebody's plants, but he had obviously discovered a secondary use for the implement.

Gator paused. "Wow, I wasn't expecting that."

"Neither was I."

The man with the watering can gave us a wave. "Oh, look. The bad cop is here."

I tried to remain stoic. "So, the good cop routine didn't get it done, huh?"

He watered the flowers inside our guest's nostrils one more time for good measure and placed the can on the floor.

We crossed the concrete floor, and the man stuck out his hand before yanking it backward. "Sorry, I'd shake, but I've got something on my hands. I think it's the first layer of that guy's resolve. I'm Kennon."

"No problem," I said. "We'll probably get a little on us as well. How long have you been working on him?"

He leaned close. "Let's go have a little talk."

Gator and I followed Kennon from the hangar and onto the concrete pad outside the door, where he drew a knife and a pouch from his pocket. He cut off a plug of chewing tobacco and tucked it into his mouth.

He spat once and said, "Sorry. I know it's a nasty habit, but . . ."

Gator said, "Dude, you were just pouring water up a guy's nose while he's hanging upside down. After that, you can do whatever you want."

Kennon chuckled. "He's new, huh?"

I said, "Not new, but we've not done the advanced interrogation class yet."

"There's no time like the present," Kennon said. "And we've got what you might call a captive audience in there."

Gator looked as if he'd fallen into the deep end wearing lead boots. He said, "I don't think this is the time to be messing around. You can train me another day. We need to get that guy to talk."

I patted him on the back. "Don't worry. You'll do fine. Just establish the expectations up front and be willing to change tactics when necessary."

"Tactics? What tactics? I don't know anything about interrogation."

"Use your imagination and have fun," I said. "Make him understand that you're the only person who can give him what he wants, and the only way to get it is by first giving you what *you* want."

"All right," Gator said. "But don't let me screw it up."

"I have faith. Let's get to it, but I want you to use all the tools at your disposal."

He turned for the door, but Kennon took his arm. "I'm one of those tools, so use me."

Gator glanced at me as if asking for direction, but I clammed up, and he sighed.

After a moment of thought, Gator asked, "Have you found anything that works on this guy?"

Kennon said, "Well done, young man. That's exactly the right question. I guess you're not as green as you look. I haven't found his weakness yet, but that's on me. I like to take it slow and let these things drag out. It makes the experience more memorable for them."

"Memorable?" Gator said. "I don't think he's going to forget the water up the nose trick very soon."

"Oh, that?" Kennon said. "That's not the lesson I want him to take away from this little adventure he got himself into. I want him, and everybody I interrogate, to remember my patience and willingness to put in the hours."

"I'll try to remember that, but I'm not sure that'll be my approach."

"Do what feels right, and Chase and I will be here to back you up if you hit a wall."

We marched back inside the hangar to find Mr. Inverted with his arms hanging to the floor and his face as red as a beet.

Gator checked the man's pulse and breathing. "Let him down."

Kennon pulled the rope from a cleat on the wall and lowered the man to the concrete floor. Gator helped lay him on his side as he descended.

Once on the floor, Gator slapped the man's face several times, increasing the intensity with every blow. Our prisoner gasped and jerked awake.

Gator said, "Welcome back. We missed you. Did you miss us?"

The man growled, *"Da poshol ty! YA ub'yu tebya prezhde, chem eto zakonchitsya."*

"Sorry, I don't speak Klingon. Try that in English, and watch the tone."

The man spat in Gator's face, but he didn't flinch. "That's not very nice. I'm here to help you, and you're being disrespectful."

"Da poshol ty!"

Gator threw an abbreviated punch to the man's throat, leaving him coughing and gasping. "Don't make me play rough. You wouldn't like that game with me. Now, let's start with something simple. What's your name?"

The man let out another tirade in Russian, and Gator said, "I told you already. I don't speak whatever that is. English! Got it?"

While none of us on the team could compete with Mongo's size, Gator wasn't a boy. His height and muscular bulk made him an imposing figure, towering over the bound man lying at his feet. He unbuckled his belt and yanked it through the beltloops of his cargo pants. The bullwhip crack that followed shocked even me, and I made a mental note to practice that move when nobody was watching.

Gator looped the belt around the man's ankles. "Let's go for a little stroll. What do you say?" He dragged the man a few feet and stopped. "I'm sorry, I forgot to turn you over. This is a lot more fun for everybody if you're facedown."

He rolled the man onto his belly and continued dragging him across the smooth floor. "Not bad, huh? It's nice and slick in here, but it's a little less comfortable when we take this show on the road."

He pointed to the massive hangar door and motioned for us to open it. I hit the switch, and the door rose almost silently. When it was seven feet above the floor, he dragged the Russian from the hangar and onto the waiting tarmac.

The sound that came out of the man was sickening, and I believed the prisoner wished he were still upside down and drinking through his nose.

To my disbelief and enormous pride, Gator took a knee beside the Microbus. He opened the side door and then closed it again with his belt stuck in the hinge side of the metal slab Volkswagen calls a door.

He leaned down and whispered, "Tell me your name, and this stops before it gets started." The man spat again, and our tactical savant patted him on his head. "Okay. I guess that means you'd like to go for a ride."

Gator hopped into the bus and dragged the man a few feet across the rough asphalt.

Kennon said, "I've never seen that approach, but I don't hate it."

I said, "He probably saw it in a movie. I certainly didn't teach him that one."

After a minute or so of being dragged beside the bus, the man screamed out in broken English. "Okay! Stop! Name Bogdan. Please stop."

"Impressive," Kennon said.

"Beginner's luck," I said. "You softened him up. Gator just delivered the knockout punch."

The roughriding came to a halt, and Gator stepped from the bus. "What was that? English?"

The man panted like an overheated, exhausted dog. "Bogdan. I am Bogdan."

"Nice," Gator said. "I've never met anyone named Bogdan. Now, give me the hit list."

Bogdan furrowed his brow. "I do not know this word, *hit list*."

"Who are you planning to attack? I want the list."

"I do not know. I am, uh . . . small. No, this is not word. I am maybe not important."

Gator checked the knots holding Bogdan's ankles and wrists. "So, you don't know anything. Is that right?"

"I do not know. I do only when told. This is all."

Gator rolled his eyes. "Oh, Bogdan. I don't believe you. I think you know a lot more than just your name. Let's change things up a little and see if that improves your memory."

He opened the door and removed the belt from around Bogdan's ankles, then he made a show of dropping the loop across the Russian's head until the belt became a noose. My young teammate slammed the other end of the belt in the door again and dusted off his hands.

He stared down at Bogdan. "I've never had anyone survive this treat for more than three minutes. Are you interested in trying for the record?"

Bogdan's eyes filled with terror. "I do not understand. I am, uh . . . not understand."

I wanted Gator to rock him around a little and *make* him understand, but instead, he glanced at me as if asking for help.

I took a knee beside Bogdan and spoke in Russian. "He's going to drag you to death by your neck. You might bleed to death as your skin comes off, but more likely, it'll break your neck or suffocate you."

The terror in his eyes doubled, and I drew my pistol. "If you prefer, I can shoot you in the head right now."

He stared into the muzzle of my Glock as if actually contemplating taking me up on the offer, but he finally said, "Please stop."

I holstered my pistol. "Okay, I'll stop. Hit it, Gator."

He pressed the accelerator, and the bus lunged forward twenty feet. After hopping out to check the belt, he said, "It looks like it's going to hold, so we can go for a nice, long joyride this time."

The man caught his breath. "I do not understand!"

Gator knelt beside him. "Understand this, Bogdan. I will drag you to your death and play in your blood. Just try me."

He climbed behind the wheel and revved the engine. Normally, there's nothing intimidating about the sound of a Volkswagen engine. It sounds more like an electric hair clipper than a car, but to our new friend, Bogdan, I doubt if he'd ever heard a more terrifying sound.

Gator let out the clutch, and the bus accelerated away.

Kennon said, "He does know that he's not supposed to kill the guy yet, right?"

"Maybe," I said. "But if he's going to talk, who cares if he's alive or dead? It's a teaching moment."

After a spin around the parking apron in front of the hangar, Gator brought the bus to a stop in front of us. Bogdan was still conscious, but barely. The damage to his skin from the asphalt made it look as if he had the worst case of poison ivy in the world.

Gator shut down the bus and slid from the seat. "How's he doing?"

"Still alive," I said. "Maybe you should go around one more time. I think he's about ready to break."

Bogdan begged, "Please, no. I cannot do again. Please."

Gator spoke in a calm, relaxed tone. "I told you how to make it stop. You simply have to answer our questions truthfully and completely."

Bogdan looked up at me, begging for a translation, and I gave him one.

He replied in Russian, "What do you want to know?"

"Have you not been listening?" I asked. "We already told you we want the hit list—in chronological order."

I screwed up the Russian word for *chronological*, but I think he got the point.

He bucked against the belt around his neck, and I opened the door, releasing the tension. He collapsed in a bloody heap with his tongue hanging from his mouth.

Gator asked, "Does this mean you're ready to talk?"

Bogdan sobbed and nodded.

Kennon hefted the Russian across his shoulder in a modified fireman's carry and hauled him back inside the hangar. He deposited him on a long-abandoned couch in the corner. "Are you thirsty? Do you want some water?"

Bogdan nodded, and Kennon returned with his watering can. The cascading liquid across his body sent the Russian into fits of pain he thought were finished.

Kennon laughed. "What's wrong? I thought you said you wanted water."

The man licked his lips, and the original interrogator forced open Bogdan's mouth. He poured more water than anyone could swallow efficiently, but the badly injured man seemed to find solace in the momentary kindness.

After swallowing all he could get down, Bogdan closed his eyes and spoke in Russian. "We are supposed to be in Miami tomorrow to kill the chef."

Chapter 24
Kislota

The instant Bogdan said Miami, I drew my phone and dialed Clark.

"Hey, College Boy. How's the game of twenty questions going over there?"

I said, "It's over, and Maebelle is their next target."

I expected to hear him drop the phone, but instead, he laughed.

"Why is that funny?"

Clark said, "Because finding my wife would be like finding a popsicle in Hell. I've got her so tucked away that even I forgot where I put her."

"That's an enormous relief," I said. "And for once, your metaphor was appropriate."

"What's a metaphor?"

"Never mind. What should we do with this information?"

He said, "Let's talk about that face-to-face. Should I come to you or verse vices?"

I shuddered. "What?"

He said, "Forget it. I'm coming to you."

Clark showed up a few minutes later and walked into a scene that no one wants to witness. "Whoa! What's with the skinless bloody dude?"

I shot a thumb toward Gator. "That's all him, and it's one of the things I want to talk about with you."

He couldn't seem to look away. "How did that happen?"

"We'll get to that," I said. "But first, we need to talk about Miami."

"All right. Let's hear it."

"These guys were supposed to hit Earl and Kenny and move on to Miami to hit the chef, but that didn't work out quite the way they planned."

Clark huffed. "Yeah, it looks like he's having a pretty bad day."

"They weren't expecting our Cajun friend to fight back quite as hard as he did. So, how are we going to use this little morsel of intel?"

He scratched his chin. "I'm sure the team lead was supposed to check in after hitting Earl and Kenny to report their success. Have you thought about having Mr. No Skin over there do that?"

"No way," I said. "He'd pass a code in the conversation, and we'd be burnt."

Clark grimaced. "You're probably right. To be honest, though, I don't think the information about Miami and Maebelle being next on the list has any real value to us. She's safe. I made sure of that before I jumped into this mud puddle with you."

As badly as I wanted to believe the intel was valuable, Clark wasn't wrong. I said, "So, what do we need him to tell us?"

"We need to know where the other team—the one Taylor's running—is going next. That's the goods."

"What if he doesn't know?"

Clark's patented half-grin made its appearance again. "I'll be right back."

He jogged out of the hangar and returned a few minutes later with a syringe in one hand and a bottle of bleach in the other. "We're going to play a nice little game of *Let's Make a Deal*. How's his English?"

"Not great, but my Russian is good enough."

"Mine's a little rusty," Clark said.

"Yours has been rusty for twenty years. I'll do the talking, and you can be Vanna White."

"I'm way prettier than her," he said.

I couldn't resist chuckling. "Yes, you are. Let's go."

We crossed the floor, and I took a knee in front of Bogdan. If he had looked bad from across the hangar, he was ground beef up close.

I cleared my throat and kicked off the conversation in my best Russian. "How are you feeling, comrade?"

He scowled back at me but didn't speak.

"I thought you'd had enough and you were ready to talk."

Bogdan said, "I told you what I know."

"We'll see about that. Take a look at my friend behind me. He's got a syringe full of morphine in one hand and a bottle of bleach in the other."

I couldn't remember the Russian word for *bleach*, so I called it *kislota*, which I hoped meant *acid* in the language of the Rodina.

Doing the best I could, I continued. "You get to choose which one you get. If you tell me everything—absolutely everything—I want to know, you get the morphine, but if I don't get what I want, you still win a prize. And that prize is *kislota*."

If possible, the lingering agony on his face worsened exponentially. "I told you what I know."

I said, "I have a theory that most people know far more than they realize until remembering becomes essential for staying alive." I looked up at Clark. "Pour me a capful, please. I'd like to test my theory."

Clark obliged, and I held the one-ounce shot of *kislota* in front of our guest. "Let's start with an easy one. I want the full names of the two men who didn't survive the encounter with my friend, Kenny."

He hesitated, but I did not. The next sound out of his mouth was one of the most horrific noises I've heard a human make and could've been the death throes of an ancient dragon.

I leaned close as his bellowing turned to sobbing. "That was about thirty milliliters, my friend. The bottle holds almost four liters. I need the names of your two teammates, and you've got three seconds. Go."

Clark lifted the plastic cap from my hand and threw it across the hangar in a brilliant display of psychological warfare.

Bogdan suddenly remembered a pair of names, and Gator jotted them down in his notebook.

I said, "See? That wasn't so hard. Now, I need the passcode to your cell phone. I'd like to call your boss and tell him what a good little soldier you are."

The hesitance returned to his eyes, so I said, "Gator, hold his hand nice and tight. Since he's not interested in telling us the code, we'll take his thumbprint."

Gator followed the order and pinned Bogdan's hand to the concrete. I drew my switchblade and thumbed the button. An instant before my blade would've severed his thumb, he whimpered. "*Shest' dva shest' chetyre.*"

I closed the knife. "He said six-two-six-four. Try it."

Kennon typed the code, and the Russian's phone came to life. He studied the screen and tossed it to me. "It's in Cyrillic."

"Not for long," I said.

It took only a few seconds to scroll through the settings and change the language to good ol' American English. I searched the phone, but like any good operator, Bogdan had wiped the phone clean of recent calls, text messages, and contacts.

I tossed the phone to Clark and took the bottle of bleach from his hand. "I want Timothy Taylor's number right now. I gave you three seconds last time, but I'm losing my patience."

I slowly tilted the bottle toward Bogdan and waited for the bleach to flow from the opening.

The Russian looked up at me through pleading eyes. "*Pozhaluysta, ubey menya.*"

Clark leaned toward Gator and whispered, "He just said, 'Please kill me.'"

I let a teaspoon of bleach land on his bloody chest. "That's what I'm doing. I'm just taking my time."

He howled again, but this time, his outburst contained nine numbers that Clark typed into the phone.

I placed the bottle on the floor and reached for the phone. "You better hope he answers."

Bogdan wallowed in unimaginable pain while I listened to the phone ring.

I said, "Shut him up, would you? I'm trying to make a phone call."

I turned my back on the man while Gator stuck a boot heel in his mouth.

A voice I'd heard before came on the line. "*Da.*"

"Let's go with English, Timothy. Chase Fulton here. I've got some bad news for you. Two of the three boys you dispatched to take out my friends didn't survive the encounter. Fortunately for me, though, your little buddy Bogdan came out alive, and boy, oh boy is he ever talkative."

Taylor said, "You are lying."

"Hold on just a second. I'll send you a selfie with your boy."

I opened the camera app, crouched near the bloody Russian, and snapped a picture. "Check your texts."

The line went silent for several seconds before he said, "Remember when I told you that I would not kill you? I have changed my mind. I think you will now die, but only after I've killed everyone you care about."

"I love it," I said. "Determination is such an admirable attribute in a leader. I'll bet your men practically worship you."

I glanced down at my prisoner. "Well, maybe not Bogdan. He just spent an hour in Hell because of you. But hey, we expect some sacrifices from those beneath us, don't we?"

His tone sharpened. "You're quite the arrogant one, aren't you, Mr. Fulton?"

"That's Doctor Fulton to you, you piece of Russian trash. Have fun hiding like a coward until I find you and tear out your communist throat."

Taylor remained stoic. "You have a great deal of faith in yourself and in a team that couldn't land a single round on any of us in Texas. You're a laughingstock, *pretend* Doctor Fulton."

"Keep it up. I love it when my enemy underestimates me and my team. I'm crawling around in your head right now, and very soon, I'll be crawling up your back to slit your throat."

Taylor said, "You should really stop. You're embarrassing yourself. By the way, the man you cornered in Texas could've cut you down with one press of the trigger, but he's a highly disciplined professional, and he obeys my orders to the letter. You have been under the protection of my no-kill order, but now that you've upped the stakes, I'll call your bet and remove that order. You're now my target, but first, I'll pull your beloved little world right out from under you while you watch. Then, you and I will have a little one-on-one time when I can do to you what your treasonous little bitch should've done years ago before she deserted the country that made her."

Clark started working his fingers in a circle, and I stayed on the line.

I said, "You still have an opportunity to get out of this alive. Surrender, and I'll see that you're given a fair trial for the murders you've already committed."

"Oh, yeah," he said. "I almost forgot about that. I'm sorry to hear about your wife's house in Tinseltown, where you were naïve enough to think she'd be safe. What a shame."

"That's exactly why I'm giving you one, and only one, opportunity to surrender. Take it now, or the offer is off the table, and I'll hunt you down and drive you into the dirt."

"Idle threats, you foolish, weak American."

Clark gave the okay sign, and I ended the call.

"Did she get it?" I asked.

Clark nodded. "She did, and it's a rock-solid position fix. You've got him, Chase. All that's left is for us to go collect our bounty."

With the assurance of Skipper's phone-tracing skills behind me, I stared down at Bogdan. "I'm sorry you had to be the one to survive, but I've got a deal for you. I can call the FBI, and they'll haul you out of here and get you the medical treatment you need, or I can dump you in that alligator-infested river out there and let you take your chances. What'll it be, comrade?"

He stared up at me, but he was a million miles away, lost in an agony so horrific that his mind couldn't comprehend the pain his body was enduring.

I said, "Put him out of his misery."

Chapter 25
A Man of Peace

Clark buried the hypodermic needle in Bogdan's thigh and pumped him full of morphine that would temporarily end his suffering, but the feds would wake him up soon enough, and he would be their problem.

We reconvened in the op center on the third floor at Bonaventure, and Skipper pointed to a map of Northwest Texas. "He's in Ransom Canyon."

"Never heard of it," I said.

She zoomed in on what looked like a peaceful community around a placid lake. "That's Ransom Canyon Lake. I don't know for sure why he's there, but it could have something to do with a fifty-cal bullet hole in his airplane."

"That's possible. Compliments of our very own Sniper."

She looked over her shoulder and gave Gator a wink and part of a smile. "Nice shot."

He tipped his imaginary cap. "Why, thank you, ma'am. I do what I can."

I pointed to a chair. "Speaking of doing what you can, why don't you have a seat? We need to talk about that interrogation sequence."

He grimaced and planted himself on the chair. "Yeah, I know I took it a little too far. I don't know what came over me. It was working, and I didn't want to stop until we could drag everything out of that guy's head."

I settled onto my seat. "That's not what this talk is about. I'm not going to scold you. I'm commending you."

Disbelief flashed in his eyes. "Are you serious?"

"Yeah, I'm dead serious. I expected you to pull a tooth and maybe break a finger or two. I never thought you'd drag him by his neck behind the bus—naked, nonetheless."

Skipper jolted in her seat. "You were naked?"

Clark was prone to fits of laughter when stress levels went through the roof and somebody cracked a good joke. Skipper's question sent him over the edge, laughing until he couldn't catch his breath. When he finally got himself under control, he said, "Oh, yeah. Your boyfriend was naked as a jaybird and dragging that other naked guy all over the airport. You should've seen it."

Skipper looked the young sniper-turned-interrogator up and down. "I hate that I missed that show."

Gator blushed. "I wasn't naked. The Russian was."

Skipper rolled her eyes. "Oh, in that case, I'm not interested. Carry on."

"Thanks for the permission," I said. "Now, let's talk about what happened out there."

Gator drew imaginary circles on the conference table with his fingertip. "I just got carried away, I guess."

I leaned toward him. "I'm going to play battlefield psychologist for a minute. You did not get carried away. You revealed the man inside you."

"What does that mean?"

"It means you're now a man of peace."

"Peace? Nothing about that was peaceful. Just ask the Russian."

"I'm not saying what you did was peaceful. You're right, it certainly was not. But let's run a little experiment."

His posture softened. "Okay. What kind of experiment?"

I said, "Tell Skipper she's beautiful."

"She is beautiful."

I shook my head. "Don't tell me. Tell her."

He suddenly looked like he was watching a professional Ping-Pong match as his eyes darted back and forth between the analyst and me. "I don't . . . I mean . . ."

"Just tell her," I said.

He threw up his hands. "Okay, okay. Elizabeth . . ."

She turned to face him and put on a smile no man could resist.

"You're very beautiful."

It was her turn to blush, and she did. "Thank you."

I pointed directly at his face. "See? That is the man of peace. Most men believe they're peaceful when what they really are is weak. They claim to be sensitive and caring, just like you were when you told Skipper you loved her."

"Whoa! I didn't tell her that. I said she's beautiful."

I leaned back in my chair. "Yeah, I know, but what you meant was . . ."

He looked away, and I said, "I'm sorry to embarrass you, but it's true. You looked at her, and you melted in that seat. That's not the behavior of a man who dragged a naked Russian nearly to death behind a fifty-year-old Microbus."

"What is it, then?"

"It's the action of a true man of peace, not a man who's weak and unable to commit necessary violence. What we do is ugly and deadly and sickening to most civilized people, but it's necessary for the protection of those same people who lack the stomach, will, and ability to protect themselves."

I let the lesson hang in the air for a moment before continuing. "When a man can be both of those things, then he is truly a man of peace, like you. What Clark and I witnessed out there tonight was gruesome and grotesque, but it probably saved the lives of people we love, like Skipper."

His eyes met mine. "To be honest, I didn't know I was capable of what I did out there."

I said, "Most people think they'll be heroic and rise to the occasion when evil rears its ugly head, but most of those people are wrong. They would cower and withdraw in mortal fear. That's the difference between warriors like us and soft men like them."

Clark collapsed onto his chair. "You showed us something out there we've been hoping to see for a long time. You're not the rookie anymore. You're truly and completely one of us now."

Gator bit his lip. "I don't know what to say."

"That's the beauty of this," Clark said. "You don't have to say anything. You just wear your scars and learn to dance with the demons in your skull. Taking a life is one thing, but pushing another man to the point where he begs you to kill him is quite another. Good work out there, man."

I stood. "Go get some rest, and get ready to deal with a few of those demons Clark mentioned. They'll be breakdancing in your head all night."

He stood and offered his hand. I didn't fully understand the reasoning behind the gesture, but I shook it anyway and said, "Keep one thing in mind. If the demons don't come, I need to know that."

He laid the hand I'd shaken on Skipper's shoulder. "And you really are beautiful. I don't say things I don't mean, even when Chase orders me to say them."

She kissed the knuckles he'd been dragging. "You're sweet. Get some rest."

When the door closed behind Gator, Clark said, "I remember having that same talk with you a few years ago. The kid done good, didn't he?"

"He did, but he's not going to have a good night after that."

Clark said, "Nobody does, College Boy. Nobody does."

"So, what's next?" I asked.

Clark grunted. "I'm glad that decision isn't up to me."

I ignored his jab. "Do we chase him or set another trap?"

"He knows the Miami op is a bust. He knows he failed in Plainview. And he knows he accomplished nothing except getting three men killed at Earl and Kenny's place."

I sighed. "All of that's true, but he also knows he succeeded at destroying several million dollars' worth of hardware at the airport. He knows he survived a gunfight with us. And he believes he killed Penny in the house fire."

Clark chewed on a pencil. "Yep, all of that's true, too. So, what do you think he'll do next?"

"I don't know, but he's down three men, and his airplane is useless. He's not going anywhere fast, and he'll have to either deploy more men or cut his operational tempo in half."

"What would Anya do?" Clark asked.

Skipper said, "She'd gut everybody like pig."

I said, "Indeed, she would."

"Then there's your answer," Clark said. "The same schools that taught her to be what she is taught Taylor the same things. He's been waiting his whole life for them to flip the switch and turn him loose."

I reclaimed my seat and let my head recline over the top. "I wish she were here."

Clark said, "Who? Anya?"

"Yeah. She could probably predict what Taylor will do next."

Clark extended his boot and spun Skipper's chair to face us. "Can you get her on the phone?"

"I can, but I won't. Protecting Penny is more important than knowing what Taylor will do next."

I turned to Clark. "Where did you hide Maebelle?"

"She's on a cruise ship on some ocean somewhere in the world, under the name of Mary Bell, and she's a redhead now."

"Nice choice."

He said, "What, the hair or the cruise?"

"Both."

"That's because I don't make bad decisions. You should've learned that by now."

I propped my real foot on the conference table. "I've watched you make some terrible decisions."

"Name one."

"Just one? Let's start with Tiffany and Tammy in Virginia Beach."

He jabbed a finger toward me. "Hey! They were twins, and that means it doesn't count."

"All right, then. How about investing in that company in Costa Rica?"

He narrowed his gaze. "The escort service? That one wasn't my fault. I was misled about what they were selling. I thought they were escorting tourists into the rainforest on some kind of eco-tour."

"My point exactly. Now, put on your good-decision-making hat and tell me what we're doing next."

"I already told you I don't know. What do you have in mind?"

I spoke just above a whisper. "This doesn't leave the op center, but I don't have any idea what to do next."

Skipper stuck a finger in the air. "I've got an idea."

"Let's have it," Clark said.

She pulled off her glasses and slid them onto the console beside the keyboard. "We know a lot we didn't know a couple of days ago. We know who and what he wants to hit. Now, we know he wants you dead and not just defeated. That's new. And the big one is that I now have access to his satellite phone."

"I like it," I said. "Well, maybe not the part about him wanting me dead, but keep talking."

She said, "Since you and Clint made it personal, Taylor is now emotionally involved, and not just driven by the orders of the Kremlin."

Clark furrowed his brow. "Who's Clint?"

I shoved his chair with my robot foot. "That's Gator, you dummy. Try to keep up."

He repositioned his seat. "I knew that."

Skipper huffed. "Anyway, I think we can use his emotional state and wait for him to screw up. They always make mistakes when they react out of emotion."

"They're not the only ones," I said. "We do it, too. That's why I'm trying to keep this purely tactical. That doesn't mean I won't beat him to death with my bare hands when we catch him, but I plan to be devoid of emotion when I do it."

"Would you two shut up and listen to my idea?"

Clark and I threw up our hands.

I said, "Sorry. Please continue."

She said, "Thank you. Taylor and his crew aren't far from the middle of the country. From Northwest Texas, in a good airplane, they can be anywhere in the country in two and a half hours. Unfortunately, we don't have a good airplane anymore."

I cut her off. "The Herk is a fine airplane."

She groaned. "Yes, it is, if you don't mind doing half the speed of the *Grey Ghost* and burning four times as much fuel."

I said, "We're not concerned with expenses on this one."

"That's not the point," she said. "We can't chase anybody at three hundred miles per hour and expect to catch them, let alone sneak up on them in that big, noisy thing."

"So quit stalling and get to the point," Clark said.

"I'm trying, if you two would stop interrupting. I say we reposition somewhere in the middle of the country and watch what he does. If he moves, we move with him. If he stays, we close in a little at a time until we're standing right in front of him."

I said, "There's only one problem with your plan. Not only do you have access to his sat-phone, but he also has access to mine."

After opening a drawer with the toe of her shoe, she pulled a box from inside and tossed it onto the table. "Go ahead. Open it up."

I pulled the flap and found eight shiny new satellite phones. "These are great, but if he can track the one I've had for years, what's to stop him from tracking these?"

Skipper put on her mischievous grin. "Because those are all clones of your old one, and they're about to take the ride of their lives."

"What are you talking about?"

"Dr. Mankiller built each of those herself, and there's a little bit of tradecraft magic in every one of them. The second you get on that big, dumpy airplane, each of these will begin a never-ending journey around the world. Some of them will travel by FedEx, some by UPS, a few via USPS, and the rest by any other carrier I can think of."

"That's great," I said, "but they're limited by battery life, and when they die, the only one still active will be my original. With a little patience, he can just wait us out."

She rolled her eyes again. "Were you not listening when I said Dr. Mankiller built these with her own two hands? Each of them has a one-thousand-hour battery, and for those of you who are arithmetically challenged, that's over forty-one days of battery life. If Timothy Taylor isn't dead or in prison in forty-one days, we've got a lot bigger problems than just dead sat-phone batteries."

Chapter 26
Pretty Good Coon Hunters

Skipper's idea was a good one, and it was certainly better than anything my brain seemed to be capable of coming up with. Clark agreed, so he assembled the team for a briefing while I took a short drive to Kenny and Earl's place.

"Get in here, Baby Boy. Where have you been?"

I could always count on Earline for a little over-the-top energy, no matter the circumstance.

I wrapped her in a bear hug. "Are you okay?"

She pulled away. "Oh, I'm fine, baby. My big strong hunk of a man over there took care of business."

I shook Kenny's hand. "How about you? Are you doing all right?"

"Who was dem boys, dem? They done bites off more than dey can swallow of ol' Kenny. I showed dem boys fourteen or four tings 'bout gettin' sideways wiff an old man like me."

Never completely certain what Kenny said, I listened, nodded, and said, "I don't think they'll be back any time soon."

He laughed. "At least dem two dead ones ain't gonna be back 'round here, dem."

"The third guy won't be back, either. Gator dragged him behind our bus until he looked like shredded cheese."

Kenny let out a whoop. "Ooh wee! I done knowed I liked dat Gator boy da firs' time I done mets him. He sho'nuff be one mo' handful. Ol' Kenny can see dat in dem eyes o' his. He be serious bidness, dat boy is."

"He did all right," I said.

It took ten minutes to bring my old friends up to speed on what was happening, and they listened until they couldn't restrain themselves any longer.

"Who dem boys is what come and took da other ones away from here?"

I explained the security team, and Earl perked up. "Did you say your Mustang was in that hangar they blew up?"

I sighed. "I'm afraid so. That's the one material thing I'll never be able to replace."

She closed one eye and seemed to study the ceiling with the other. "Are you sure?"

"I've not sorted through the rubble yet, but the Mustang was in there."

She shook her phone at me. "Hang on a minute, Baby Boy. Let's give Cotton a call."

Cotton Jackson was Earl's brother and, in my opinion, the greatest aircraft mechanic on Earth. No one besides Cotton touched our flying machines with a wrench.

Earl said, "Hey, it's your sister. I'm putting you on speaker." She pressed the button and laid the phone on the table. "Chase is here with me."

Cotton said, "Howdy, Chase. How's it going?"

"I've had better weeks, but things could be worse. I don't know why Earl wanted us to talk, but she insisted."

He laughed. "Don't try to figure out my baby sister. It'll just make your brain hurt. Say, listen . . . We've got a little problem with the propeller. It's blowing a little oil, and I don't like it. Would you rather rebuild it or replace it?"

"You'll have to forgive me," I said. "Which airplane are we talking about?"

"The Mustang. That's the only one of yours I've got in the shop. You know the annual inspection is due at the end of the month."

My jaw hit the floor. "What? You've got the Mustang?"

He seemed even more confused than I was. "Well, yeah, of course I've got it. Where else would it be?"

I deposited myself onto a barstool. "You've got the airplane?"

"What's wrong with you, Chase? Are you okay?"

"Cotton, if you were here, I'd kiss you squarely on the mouth. You just made my day!"

"I'm glad I could help, but I'll have to pass on making out with you. You ain't my type, and I'm partial to the old girl I've got at home."

I told the abbreviated version of the hangar explosion, and he said, "Now it makes sense. I thought you were having some kind of mental breakdown or something. Did anybody get hurt?"

"Yeah, Disco and Singer are still in the hospital."

"You're going after whoever did it, ain't you?"

I said, "We surely are, and it shouldn't take long for us to have them by the tail."

He said, "I know you're good at what you do, but be careful out there. You're my best customer and a great friend."

"Careful isn't always possible, but we'll do our best. Let's talk about that prop. If it were yours, what would you do?"

"I'd rebuild it. Nobody's really making a direct replacement for it these days. There's not much demand for props on seventy-year-old airplanes. If we replace the one you've got, it'll be rebuilt."

Without hesitation, I said, "Treat her like she's yours. I'd rather have your hands on it than anyone else's."

"I was going to rebuild it anyway so you'd have a spare if we bought another one."

"That sounds good. Do both, and I'm going to send a couple of guys down to keep an eye on your shop, just in case."

He said, "All right, my friend. Anything else?"

"That does it unless there's anything else you need to tell me about the Mustang."

"Fly her more often. She needs to stretch her legs. She's a thoroughbred, not a stable queen. Let her run."

"You got it. Thanks for everything, Cotton. We'll see you soon."

* * *

The next item on my to-do list for the day put me on I-95 South and deposited me at the Mayo Clinic. I lifted the telephone from the wall outside the double oak doors leading to the neuro ICU, and a tired voice answered.

"Nurses' station."

"I'm Chase Fulton. I'd like to see Disco."

The tired voice became exasperated. "Sir, this line is for patients and family only."

"I'm sorry. I'm here to see Blake Riley."

Without another word from the nurse, who'd obviously reached her limit of dealing with idiots like me for the day, the door buzzed, and I stepped through. Disco's room was at the end of the long corridor, and the door was slightly ajar.

An armed guard—one of the men Clark delivered—stood when I approached. "Good afternoon, Mr. Fulton. He's still unconscious."

"Thanks for doing this," I said. "I know it's the most boring duty you could dream up, but I really appreciate it."

"It's my job, sir."

"Don't call me sir. I'm just Chase."

I tapped lightly, and movement came from inside. I was ecstatic believing Disco was awake, but my elation fell when Ronda No-H pulled open the door.

Our CFO, the woman who adored our chief pilot, threw her arms around me. "Oh, Chase. Thank you for coming. It's bad . . . really bad."

I stepped inside and leaned against the bed. The sight before me sickened me to my very core. The collection of equipment connected to my friend and brother-in-arms was overwhelming and reduced me to little more than a man trying to hold back the tears.

Ronda stepped beside me and laced her arm around me. "I don't know if he's in there, Chase. I've never seen anybody in this condition before. It's . . ."

She sobbed and leaned against me as if I were the only thing in the world that could keep her on her feet. I squeezed her, and we stood beside a man we both loved for very different reasons.

"What are the doctors saying?" I asked.

She grimaced, fighting hard to hold back the tears. "The swelling is too bad to do surgery, so we're just waiting for the fluid to drain. They're not optimistic."

I stepped from beside the bed and into the hallway outside. The guard looked up expectantly, but I shook my head and pulled out my phone.

A passing nurse said, "I'm sorry, sir, but there's no cell phone use permitted in the hall. You can step outside or back into your friend's room to make a call."

I chose the room, and Skipper answered quickly. "Op center."

"I need you to find the best neurosurgeon on the planet. I don't care how much it costs. I want him here in twenty-four hours."

"That's a big ask, but I'm on it. Based on that, I assume Disco's not doing well."

"No, he's in bad shape. Ronda's here with him, and we've got good men on the door. We just need somebody to put him back together."

She asked, "Is he—"

"Just find the surgeon."

"I'll take care of it. Are you coming home?"

I checked my watch. "I'm going to see Singer on the way, but I'll be there in a couple of hours."

"Good. Clark has the team building kits for the deployment, and he wants to leave at first light tomorrow morning. Is that good with you?"

"Absolutely," I said. "Have you picked a spot yet?"

"McConnell Air Force Base."

"Where's that?"

She said, "Don't get too excited. It's in Wichita, Kansas."

"Sounds like a rip-roaring place."

"I wouldn't know," she said. "But it's an Air Force Base, so how bad can it be? At least you'll have a little security."

"Good point. I assume you've worked out all the PPR."

"What's that?"

I said, "It's the prior permission request to land a civilian airplane at a military airfield."

"Oh, that. It's not a problem. The Board gave us a blanket authorization for anything we need anywhere on Earth. They're taking care of everything."

"That's new, and I like it. Is that everything?"

The sound of rustling papers wafted through the phone. "That covers the important stuff. We'll go over the rest when you get home."

I said, "Find that neurosurgeon."

* * *

The drive from Jacksonville to Memorial in St Marys was uneventful and filled with unforgettable memories with Disco and Singer. The thought of losing either or both of them was too agonizing to endure. There were no telephones on the wall or locked doors between me and Singer.

The man standing guard outside his door rose and held up a hand before quickly lowering it again. "I'm sorry, Mr. Fulton. I didn't recognize you at first."

"No worries. How's he doing?"

The man shrugged. "I don't know. One of the doctors is in there with him now."

I stepped into the room to see a woman in a long white lab coat and two more wearing scrubs. "May I come in?"

The woman in the lab coat turned. "That depends on who you are."

"I'm his brother."

The doctor looked back at Singer and then at me. "I'm not seeing the family resemblance, but I know who you are. You're Chase Fulton, right?"

"That's right, but you'll have to forgive me. I don't remember meeting you."

She laughed. "That's not surprising. I took care of you after your boating accident with the shrimp boat, and you spent most of that time unconscious."

"Of course," I said. "It's nice to see Singer in good hands."

She frowned. "Singer?"

"That's what we call him. He's got quite a set of pipes."

She said, "I'll have to remember to ask for a concert before we release him."

"Release him? Is he okay?"

She said, "He will be. We're about to wake him up. You're welcome to stay if you'd like, but I have to warn you—patients say some crazy things sometimes. You'll have to overlook any nonsense he spits out, and I'll need you to stay still and quiet."

"I can do that. I'll stay over here, out of the way."

She nodded to one of the other two women in the room, and she injected a hypodermic needle into a port on one of Singer's IV lines. In seconds, the monitor showed his heart rate increasing and his breathing quickening. I wanted to ask a thousand questions, but I forced myself into silent stillness and prayer for my brother.

Singer took a long, deep breath, and his eyelids shuddered. When fully open, his eyes fell on one of the nurses—a beautiful young lady in her twenties with dark eyes and a brilliant smile. He seemed to stare into her soul. "Rose? Is that you, Rose?"

She took his hand, and a tear escaped his eye.

"Rose..."

She squeezed. "I'm Tiffany, not Rose. How are you feeling?"

"Is this Heaven? I didn't expect..."

"It's okay, Mr. Grossmann. I'm afraid you'll have to wait a little longer to see Heaven. This is the neurology unit at Memorial Medical Center."

Lab Coat said, "I'm Dr. Plumber, Mr. Grossmann. How do you feel?"

"Like I've been asleep for a hundred years. What am I doing in the hospital?"

She pulled a penlight from her pocket and examined Singer's eyes. "You had a little accident, but we're taking very good care of you."

The nurse who Singer had called Rose motioned for me to come closer, and I didn't hesitate. Seeing Singer's eyes open was an unimaginable relief, but seeing him smile when my face came into focus was priceless.

"Chase. Are you okay?"

"I'm fine, buddy."

He blinked several times. "How about everybody else? What happened?"

I cocked my head. "You don't remember the explosion?"

He tried to shake his head, but that effort didn't work out so well. "No, I don't remember an explosion. The last thing I remember was something about a raccoon."

I chuckled, and Dr. Plumber said, "I warned you, but don't worry. It's common for people to be a little confused and say odd things when they first wake up."

I said, "He's right. There was a raccoon."

She said, "In that case, that's very good news. His memory is intact."

He released the nurse's hand and reached for mine. I took it, and he asked again, "What about the rest of the team? Is anybody else..."

Dr. Plumber looked concerned, so I said, "Don't worry about anybody else right now, okay?"

Singer said, "No, that's not okay. I'm the overwatch."

All three women contorted their faces, and Dr. Plumber said, "Overwatch? Does that make sense to you?"

I nodded. "Yes, it makes perfect sense." Turning back to Singer, I said, "Disco is in the Mayo Clinic in Jacksonville. He got a little banged up, too."

"I'll pray for him," Singer said. "Did the raccoon get him, too?"

"Something like that. Just relax and let these folks take care of you."

He seemed to drift off for a moment until his eyes landed on Tiffany again. "Are you sure you're not Rose?"

She pointed to her name tag. "I'm sure, Mr. Grossmann. I'm Tiffany."

Dr. Plumber said, "We're going to help you go back to sleep now. Don't worry. You're in very good hands."

He smiled. "I'm in Rose's hands, so I'm going to be just fine."

The other nurse injected the IV with another syringe, and Singer's eyelids began their fall. Through his grogginess, he mumbled, "Did you catch them?"

I said, "Not yet, but we will. We're pretty good coon hunters."

Chapter 27
The Honey Bucket

Perhaps it was the relief I felt over Singer's condition, but more likely, it was the sheer exhaustion that gave me the best night's sleep I'd had in weeks. The whole team and I were up at daybreak, and we had the Herk loaded in no time.

Slider double- and triple-checked the cargo netting and straps holding our gear on the pallet and to the deck of the cargo bay. Gordo and Tubbs walked up the ramp and gave the load a cursory glance.

Gordo asked, "Is everything good to go, Slider?"

"Yes, sir. We're ready to fly."

Their informal nature didn't mean they weren't meticulous in their operation. I liked believing our team was exactly the same. We could have fun together without jeopardizing our missions. The civilian in me wanted to believe Disco would be back in the cockpit by the end of the month, but the operator and realist inside my head thought the flight crew in front of me wouldn't make bad additions to the team.

I said, "Tell me about your call signs."

Tubbs said, "Mine's pretty simple. When I was on active duty, I flew with a guy named Sonny Crockett, just like Don Johnson in *Miami Vice*. He and I became Crocket and Tubbs."

I said, "That's pretty boring. I was hoping for something dramatic. How about you, Gordo?"

The senior pilot said, "Mine's even more boring. I got a crappy haircut in Korea that turned into a flattop, so the guys in the squadron started calling me Gordo because they apparently thought I looked like Gordo Cooper, the astronaut."

I was a little disappointed, but I still had one more crewman to go, and I had my fingers crossed that the story would be better than the pilots'. "All right, Slider. Your turn."

The loadmaster stood with his arms crossed and shaking his head.

Before he could speak, Gordo said, "Oh, I've got this one. Please let me tell it."

Slider sighed, still shaking his head, and said, "You'll tell it regardless of my answer, so go ahead."

Gordo said, "Follow me."

He led me to the side door where the paratroopers would get out if they were on a jump mission, and he pointed to a funnel-shaped contraption by the door. "Do you know what this is?"

I shrugged, and he said, "It's a urinal of sorts. Since we don't have a real lav aboard, this has to do. It dumps outside the airplane. I don't like thinking about folks getting sprinkled from above, but that's how we do it."

I said, "This doesn't feel like it's getting us any closer to Slider's call sign."

"We're getting there, I promise. Just try to keep up."

He pulled a second contraption from the fuselage that resembled a five-gallon bucket with a garbage bag inside.

I said, "Trash can?"

The three aviators laughed, and Gordo said, "Not exactly. This is our high-speed, low-drag Porta Potty for those long flights and moments when you just can't hold it any longer."

"You're messing with me. Is that really what it's for?"

All three nodded, and he said, "Oh, yeah. That's really what it's for. We call it the honey bucket, and there's one rule for the honey bucket. If you use it, you carry it off, no exceptions."

I laughed, and he continued. "We were working a classified mission in South America—in Paraguay or Uruguay or one of those -guays.

Tubbs had the beef, and I had the chicken. It's kind of a rule. Both pilots rarely eat the same thing in case one of the dishes doesn't sit well with our stomachs."

I said, "I think I see where this is going."

Gordo held up a hand. "Don't jump ahead. Stay with me. About two hours into the nine-hour flight, my belly started rumbling, and there was no doubt I had the Paraguayan Calamity happening. I barely made it to the honey bucket the first time, but that's another story completely."

I was already laughing, so Gordo gave me a minute before continuing.

"To make a long story longer, I chose to tie up the bag but leave it in the bucket because there was no doubt in my mind that the chicken wasn't finished having its way with my digestive system. I didn't know how many bags we had on the airplane, so I didn't want to exhaust our supply. So, anyway, after my seventh or eighth trip to the honey bucket, the bag was nearing its limits, and I was on the brink of dehydration."

Tubbs broke in. "Keep in mind that the Herk is a handful with two well-qualified pilots up front, but with Gordo in the back with the bucket, I was all alone up there. Normally, there would've been a navigator and a flight engineer up there with me, but for some reason on that mission, it was just Gordo, Scotty, and me."

"Who's Scotty?" I asked.

Slider raised his hand. "That was my name prior to that fateful flight."

Gordo claimed the floor again. "I'm trying to wrap it up, but I love this story so much. We were out over the Atlantic somewhere, and Slider and I were discussing whether we could throw the bag overboard since there probably wasn't anybody down there for it to hit. Ultimately, we talked ourselves into doing it, and this is where the story gets good."

By that time, the whole team had gathered around the pilot and was hanging on his every word.

He kept going. "We decided we couldn't throw it out the side door because the bag would probably burst and cover the side of the aft section of the plane with my chicken dinner. So, Slider—or Scotty, back then—handed me the harness and tether before he opened the ramp. I don't know why, but for some reason, we only had one harness, so Scotty rigged a Swiss seat and tied himself to the interior of the airplane so neither of us could, or would, fall out."

Gordo got tickled and had to take a moment to gather himself before finishing the story. When he was once again composed, he said, "So, here's the scene. Scotty is tied to the airplane with a piece of green rope he got from somewhere. I was harnessed and tethered. The ramp is open, and it's as dark as outer space behind us. Just as I lifted the bag from the bucket, we hit a massive pocket of turbulence, which isn't rare in that part of the world, but the severity was worse than anything I'd ever encountered."

He paused again and took a sip of water. "I know it's a long story, but I'm wrapping it up, I promise. In the turbulence, I lost control of the bag, and our concern about getting the contents splattered on the outside of the plane was completely gone because the interior of the Herk was covered with it. The turbulence persisted, and I guess Tubbs decided to climb out of it. When he brought the nose up, gravity took control, and Slider looked like he was trying to learn to ice-skate in the cargo bay. He was trucking toward the ramp, slipping and sliding every inch by filthy inch. By the time he reached the end of his homemade rope tether, he was outside the airplane and hanging upside down over the ramp. I thought he was gone until I skated to the edge and saw him flapping like a shot goose out there. By some miracle, I hauled him back in, and just like Saul became Paul, Scotty became Slider."

The entire team collapsed in laughter.

When I finally caught my breath, I said, "That is, hands down, the best story I've ever heard. And that was exactly the break from reality we needed."

Gordo slapped Slider on the back. "Sorry about that, pal, but it was too good not to tell."

* * *

Slider sealed up the airplane, and we were airborne twenty minutes later. The flight was uneventful except for a two-minute wrestling match with some turbulence somewhere over Louisiana that made everyone on board cackle again.

We touched down at the Air Force base, and a pair of crew vans pulled behind the airplane.

A tall, broad man with a closely shaven head said, "Welcome to McConnell, sir. I'm Master Sergeant Washington."

I shook his hand. "Thanks. It's good to be here. Do we need to post a watch for the night?"

"No, sir. The flight line is well guarded by bright young men just itching to throw somebody to the ground if they get too close. We've got you covered."

The vans carried us first to what the driver called the "chow hall," but it was nothing like any chow hall I'd ever seen. Apparently, life in the Air Force isn't so bad because the place looked more like a high-end cafeteria than a military chow hall. Our next stop was lodging, and if possible, it was even nicer.

Kodiak elbowed Clark. "We joined the wrong branch, brother. If I had known about this, I would've been an Air Force lifer."

Clark shoved him. "No, you wouldn't. You love bullets, blood, and guts. You would've lost your mind if you didn't get to paint your face green and kill folks who needed killing."

"You're probably right, but these are some pretty nice digs."

We settled in and assembled in my room for a call to Skipper.

She said, "I was just about to call you guys. Taylor's on the move."

"In his airplane?" I asked.

"No, a Citation jet showed up an hour ago, and they're already outbound. They're headed north, but I'm still working on a destination."

Mongo said, "They're going after Irina and Tatiana!"

"Where did you put them?" I asked.

"They're in a little place on Mackinac Island. Some friends of Irina's own it."

Skipper said, "How could Taylor possibly know that?"

"I don't know," I said, "but we've got to get there. We're already behind if they're in a Citation."

Gordo said, "We're ready, and the airplane is fully fueled."

I said, "Keep 'em in your sights, Skipper. We'll be airborne and giving chase in less than half an hour."

Chapter 28
Blonde Will Have to Do

With our stay at McConnell cut short, we blasted off in the Herk and stuck her four fans of freedom in the wind. A telephone call inside the cargo bay would be little more than a screaming match and a waste of time, so I opted for text messages with Skipper.

We're heading for Pellston Regional in Emmet County, Michigan. We need a heavy boat. See what you can do.

Her answer came seconds later.

I'm already on it. I'll have details for you in twenty minutes. I arranged for two Suburbans. They'll be waiting at the FBO.

Thank you!

I felt truly sorry for any team that didn't have an analyst as good as Skipper. Without her, our team would spend a lot of time lost and helpless. Well, perhaps not helpless, but certainly less capable.

Before the twenty minutes expired, my phone screen filled with the details she promised.

Reroute to St. Ignace if you can. The runway is thirty-eight hundred feet. We have a team there with a pair of heavy boats. Your contact is a guy named Hooty, and here's his number in case you get there before he does.

I climbed the metal steps leading to the cockpit and took a knee. "We need to reroute to St. Ignace. It's thirty-eight hundred feet. Can you do that?"

Gordo glanced over his shoulder, "I thought about that, but we'll stick out like a sore thumb at that little airport."

"I'm okay with sticking out," I said. "We're not trying to sneak up on anybody."

He nodded. "Whatever you say. You're the boss."

Tubbs reprogrammed the GPS, and the autopilot made the barely noticeable turn.

* * *

The flight took just less than two hours, and I couldn't wait to put eyes on our local contact. I couldn't get Hootie & the Blowfish to stop playing on a continuous loop inside my head, but when I met Hooty himself, the music vanished.

He looked nothing like Darius Rucker, but I've never seen anyone who looked more like an actual owl than Hooty.

He stuck his hand in mine. "It's nice to finally meet the great Chase Fulton."

I chuckled. "Ha! There's nothing great about me. I'm just a grown-up kid with better toys."

He said, "Speaking of better toys, I've got a couple that might be exactly what you're looking for."

Clark and I rode with Hooty while the rest of the team followed in an SUV that Skipper had arranged.

I said, "It's pretty rare for teams to intermingle, so it's nice to know we're not alone."

Hooty said, "We don't get the big jobs you guys are used to. We're just a small team of four and mostly cold-water operators up here."

I shivered. "I'll stick to warm water. Tell me about your boats."

He motioned through the windshield as we pulled up to a commercial dock on Lake Huron. "There they are. We plucked Irina and Tatiana off the island, and we have them in very comfortable and very safe surroundings. I've got three solid men on them, and nobody saw us exfil them."

"Thank you for that," I said. "May I assume they're unharmed?"

"You may," Hooty said. "And I intend to keep them that way."

We walked across the gravel lot and onto a finger pier.

He said, "Here they are."

Neither of Hooty's boats could hold a candle to the capability of our Mark V, but both were perfect for our local mission.

I pushed against the bow of the first boat with my boot. "We couldn't ask for anything more. Are you coming with us?"

"If you need me, I'm in."

"Give me just a minute to make a call." I stepped away from the group and dialed the op center. "What do we know about Hooty?"

Skipper said, "He's solid. He was a Coast Guard rescue swimmer before switching teams and going through the Air Force Pararescue course."

"Is he the team lead up here?"

She said, "He is, and his team is hardcore, so you've got nothing to worry about with Irina and Tatiana. They'll keep them safe."

I stared out over the water. "We're going to take Hooty with us for local knowledge. Are you still tracking Taylor?"

"I am, and you'll be happy to know you beat them there by a few minutes, but you need to get your butt in gear. They'll be on the ground in less than ten minutes."

"We're moving. We'll be on open-channel comms in three minutes." I ended the call and turned back to the boats and my team. "Our targets will be on deck in ten minutes, so let's hit the water."

We split into two boat crews. Hooty was at the helm of the lead vessel, and Clark managed boat number two. We powered southward across the Straits of Mackinac and toward Round Island. The ferry landing passed off our port side, and we turned east.

Hooty pointed at a massive resort. "That's Mission Point. We're going just around the corner, past Lover's Leap, to Arch Rock. That's where the house is."

We slowed as we approached the landing, and Hooty laid the boat alongside the small dock as if he could do it in his sleep. Clark made a nice approach as well, but not like Hooty.

"That's the house," Hooty said. "It's dense trees north and south. The only access road is in the front. The only other way out is the water."

We exited the boats and walked the property. I committed every exterior detail to memory and let a thousand approaches play out in my mind.

Mongo stepped beside me. "It's high ground with limited access. I could defend this place by myself."

"That's not exactly what we're here to do," I said. "We don't want to protect it. We want it to look vulnerable."

"How do you think they'll do it?"

I studied the small house carefully. "They seem to be big fans of fire and explosives, so I don't know why they'd change their M.O. for this one."

Mongo said, "This one's a little different. There's a pretty good fire department just minutes away. I'm not sure fire works in this case."

I pictured how I would assault the house, and I called a team huddle. "Here's the plan. I want Gator up high for overwatch. Hunter, I want you by the access road. Kodiak and Mongo will watch the water. The rest of us will be inside."

Hunter said, "I realize it's been a while since I played cops and robbers with you guys, but I'm capable of more than just babysitting the street."

"I don't think you understand," I said. "You're not babysitting. These guys have proven to be very good at retreating. If we scare them off before they get inside, they'll run straight back to you."

Hunter grinned. "I like the sound of that."

"Let's settle in. We're just minutes ahead of these guys, so time's running out."

"What about the boats?" Hooty asked.

I said, "Lash number two to yours, and tow it out of sight to the north. I think they'll either hit overland or by the same landing we used."

"Sounds good," Hooty said. "Do you want me to collapse back on the dock after they arrive?"

"I do. We want to limit their exfil routes as much as possible."

Skipper came through the bone conduction device on my jawbone. "Sierra One, Ops. I've got some bad news."

"Send it," I said.

"They broke into two teams. One is headed for you on the water, and the other is in a gray work van. You've got maybe five minutes before they're on-site."

"We're moving into position now. Do you have a head count?"

She said, "Three in the van, and two on the boat for a total of five."

"How are you watching them?"

"I've got a satellite, temporarily, but that won't last much longer. Can you put a drone in the air?"

Mongo answered for me. "Drone four will be airborne in thirty seconds."

We moved inside the house with Hunter out front, Mongo and Kodiak by the water, and the rest of us well hidden inside the two-bedroom house.

Skipper said, "I've got good comms with drone four, and I'm feeding video to each of your phones."

I checked the screen, and a bird's-eye view of the property showed up in brilliant clarity. "Everybody, report contact. Remember, we want these guys alive, if possible, but no matter what happens, Timothy Taylor does not leave this property a free man."

Everybody acknowledged the command, and the scene turned silent. The gray van pulled into sight on my screen, and Hunter said, "Contact front. One gray van with three occupants."

The driver backed the van into the trees, making it difficult to see from the road but giving them easy access to load a pair of hostages.

Kodiak reported, "Contact. Inbound to the dock in a deep-V hull outboard."

"Let them come," I said. "Report weaponry."

Hunter spoke softly. "I see rifles and grenades. They look like incendiary and not frags."

Gator said, "I've got both teams in sight, and I can confirm the grenades in sight are burners, not bangers."

As I waited for them to draw closer, I thought, *I guess they're running home to their old friend, the firebug.*

The boat landed alongside the small finger pier, and two men tied off and climbed the slope toward the house and tree line. The team from the van spread out and walked the perimeter until they met the waterborne team from the back.

As the sun sank lower in the western sky, I watched every movement of each of the five aggressors as they did everything my team and I would've done if we were planning to hit a house wrapped in trees.

"These guys are doing everything right," Clark said through the open-channel comms.

"They're pros," I said. "But they're expecting to hit two women, not us."

Mongo said, "Don't get too comfortable. If they're planning to hit Irina, they have to know she's former FSB. They'll expect her to fight back."

I glanced down at my screen and felt an instant of panic. "Where did they go?"

Skipper said, "Take it easy. They just moved behind their van."

"They're gearing up," Hunter said.

"Roger," I said. "Let them come by you. We'll have them in a crossfire once they're between you and the house."

He whispered, "Roger."

I glanced from my position of concealment and saw a strand of blonde hair—that could've been Anya's—hanging by a closet door. From my place of concealment, I moved until I could reach the hair. It took only a slight tug for the wig to fall from the plastic head on which it had been perched.

I lifted the head and slapped the wig back on top. A few seconds later, I had a somewhat believable dummy under a blanket, on the couch, with the television playing a show I didn't recognize. The scene was set, and we were ready to lock horns with Taylor and his team. The only remaining unknown was just how hard they planned to hit the house.

We didn't have to wait long for an answer to that question. Ten minutes after I put the wig on display, where Irina's head should've been, Taylor's gang closed in.

I said, "Here they come. Let's make 'em rethink their career choices."

Chapter 29
Up In Smoke

Back in my hidey-hole, I felt far more confident than I should have. Hunter took position in front of the home, and Mongo and Kodiak held the same position in the rear. We had our aggressors in a classic crossfire situation, and one command from me could drive them into the ground where they stood. Drilling holes through bad guys in my backyard at Bonaventure was one thing, but doing so a thousand miles from home, where I didn't know the dog catcher's name, let alone the chief of police, was quite another. Waiting for Taylor's crew to penetrate a physical barrier was the catalyst I needed to issue the command to execute.

To avoid backlighting my silhouette, I turned the brightness on my phone all the way down and watched the video feed from Skipper's drone in a high hover above the house. They were coming, and they obviously had no qualms about breaking a barricade. The living room window became their first victim of the night.

A pair of rifle rounds pierced the triple-pane glass, and the plastic mannequin's head exploded beneath the blonde wig. My pin was pulled, and the grenade I would toss would be the full might of my team.

"Gator, do you have the shooter?"

"Affirmative."

"Execute."

Although his rifle wore a suppressor, it was far from silent. The report of the weapon sounded more like a thump than the crack of a rifle.

In the same tone Singer would've used, Gator said, "Shooter down."

I watched closely to gauge the aggressor's response to losing their rifleman, but they showed no reaction, as if it never happened. They continued pressing toward the house, and I slipped from cover and into the closest bathroom.

After opening both the hot and cold valves, I plugged the tub and let the water collect. If Taylor's next move was what I expected, a hundred gallons of water would certainly come in handy.

I've always preferred bare-knuckle fighting, but what lay ahead for me demanded gloves. I pulled them from my kit and slipped them on, hating everything about the feeling of holding a weapon with a layer of leather between me and the grip.

I didn't have to wait long for Taylor's next move. It came exactly as I predicted. One of his men stepped beneath the same window the bullets came through, and he beat a hole the size of a shoebox with the butt of his weapon. Almost before the shards of glass hit the floor, a thermite grenade landed beside the sofa where the much-dead mannequin lay with a hole in her wig.

The thrower backed away, and I low-crawled to the burning grenade designed to reduce the house to ashes in minutes. I was designed to do the opposite, so I threw the bath mat over the flame spewing from one end of the device and rolled it quickly into a burrito of unimaginable spice. A ghost pepper didn't have anything on the tasty treat I had in my gloved hand.

I crawled backward, keeping the flaming, mat-wrapped incendiary grenade well away from my face, and tossed the whole burning mess into the waiting bathtub as water continued to pour from the faucet. I yanked the shower curtain down and flipped the switch to start the shower. Keeping everything flammable away from the grenade and covering everything in sight with a wall of water was the only way to slow the awful work of the fire starter. I had no way to know if it would work, but it had to be better than letting it burn on the living room floor.

While I was playing fire prevention specialist, my phone vibrated in my hand. I believed that anyone who would be calling me was part of the operation, but I glanced down at the screen just the same.

Before answering, I said, "Skipper, I'm receiving a call. Can you ID it?"

"Stand by."

In her next breath, she said, "It's Taylor. Answer it."

My sat-phone was configured so every member of the team on comms with me could hear both sides of the conversation.

"This is Chase."

"Ah, Dr. Fulton. It's your old adversary again. I have some exciting news for you."

My warped sense of humor wouldn't be denied, and I said, "I'm sorry, but I have a lot of adversaries. Could you be more specific?"

"This is no time for games, Fulton. Your giant's wife just absorbed two rounds of seven-point-six-two through the top of her head, and the little ballerina is about to get a taste of Hell on Earth."

"I don't believe you."

"Would you be convinced if I told you the address?"

I laughed. "*Knowing* an address isn't the same as occupying that address. I know the address to the White House, but I've never lived there."

"So, you want to play games, do you?"

I said, "None of this is a game, but if you'd like to settle it man-to-man, I'm more than willing to oblige."

He chuckled. "Only a fool would accept such an offer from you, and I am no fool. I am, however, smart enough to stay at least three steps ahead of you. For example, I know you are nice and cozy at McConnell Air Force Base while I, on the other hand, am burning down the house you thought Irina and Tatiana would be safe in. There is no place on Earth that is safe from me."

I said, "Oh, that must mean you're in the Pacific Northwest on Puget Sound." He hesitated, so I continued the chess match. "You're wasting your time. There's no one in that house. You walked right into my trap, just like I knew you would."

He said, "It would appear that you are the fool in this situation, so-called *Doctor* Fulton. I knew the house on Puget Sound was a decoy. I'm far smarter than you could imagine and on an entirely different body of water."

I was clearly being baited, but I couldn't resist. "Where's your designated marksman?"

"What?"

"Your rifleman," I said. "Where is he?"

The line was silent long enough to be my reward, but taking our little game one step closer to eternity made me happy.

I said, "He's the dead guy lying facedown, about fifteen yards behind you, with a bullet hole made by my sniper."

He still didn't speak, but hearing his breathing rate shoot through the roof was all the confirmation I needed.

"And, there is one more thing. Why isn't your thermite grenade burning the house down yet?"

The line went dead, and Taylor yelled in Russian, "Retreat! Abort! Abort!"

I stood from my concealment and headed for the door. "Let's invite them to stay, boys."

Hunter closed from the front of the property at the same instant Mongo and Kodiak collapsed from the rear. The retreat Taylor ordered was about to go up in the smoke he'd planned for the house.

I called, "I'm exiting to the rear."

Gator said, "Clear of friendly fire to the rear."

I stepped through the door with my rifle poised for the fight I wanted more than anything else in that moment, and the sound of footsteps hustling across leaf-covered ground was music to my ears. A retreating force is a confused, disorganized gaggle of mistakes, and my team and I were about to take full advantage of every one of those errors.

The sound of one body hitting the ground brought a smile to my face, and I said, "Let me guess. Mongo just got one."

Before anyone could answer, a second thud filled the air, and Hunter said, "Mongo ain't alone. I got one, too."

A single shot rang out, and it didn't sound like any weapon we brought to the fight.

I said, "Who's shooting?"

Hunter said, "Squirter front. He put one round in my guy's face as he ran by."

"Cut him down," I ordered.

Hunter's rifle fired twice in rapid succession. He asked, "Did you mean down or dead?"

"Down is my preference."

"Then I guessed correctly," he said. "He's on his face and losing a lot of blood from one leg."

I ran a mental inventory. Gator killed the gunman, Mongo put one man down, and Hunter got two. "That's four. Does anyone have Taylor?"

Hunter said, "Negative. Neither of mine is Taylor."

Mongo groaned. "Mine, neither."

Taylor obviously wasn't the rifleman because I talked with him after Gator did his work.

I rolled my phone faceup in my palm, but the drone footage didn't show any movement. "Find Taylor. Do not let him escape."

My team was on the move in an instant, and I said, "Skipper, do you have him?"

"I'm working on it," she said. "Give me a second."

I moved toward the water without cover or concealment and paid the price for my error on the third step. A bullet hit my ankle, throwing me from my feet and depositing me onto the ground. It hurt, but not as badly as a shot to my real ankle would have. "Find the gunfire, but I want him alive!"

"Got him!" Skipper called. "He's headed for the water."

"And you're sure it's him?"

"A hundred percent. Is anybody hit?"

"I am, but it's okay. He took out my prosthetic. I can't run, but don't worry about me. Stop Taylor." I rolled over to assess the damage, and I didn't like anything I saw at the end of my leg. "Sierra One is down but unhurt. Move on Taylor. I'm retreating to the house."

Mongo had other plans. He grabbed me with his enormous paw and yanked me from the ground. "He's heading for the boat, and I figured you didn't want to miss it."

Without my prosthetic, I weigh around two hundred pounds, and Mongo tossed me around like a rag doll while barely breaking stride. He tossed me into our borrowed boat and followed me over the gunwale.

I listened as an outboard engine roared away to the east. "Gator, do you have the boat?"

"Negative, but I'm scanning."

"You've got to kill that boat, Gator. Find him!"

Mongo fired up our engine, and a boot hit our bow.

Hunter stepped aboard. "It looked like you guys could use a push and another trigger-puller."

"Welcome aboard," Mongo said as he crushed the throttle full forward and we accelerated in pursuit of the one man I wanted more than any enemy.

"Don't let him get away," I ordered as I pulled myself onto a seat.

Mongo yelled over the wind and roar of the engine. "Are you sure you're not hit?"

"I'm sure. It was just my robot. No flesh."

I maneuvered to the bow of the boat and lay down beside Hunter. "Looks like it's you and me again, old pal. Sorry to throw you out of the kettle and into the fire."

He gave me a playful elbow strike. "Don't be sorry, brother. Be better."

Mongo yelled from behind the wheel. "He's running for Canada."

I set my jaw. "I don't care if he's running for Hell. We'll chase him into the darkest pit the Devil can dig."

Chapter 30
Isn't It Ironic

With every ripple on the water, Hunter and I bounced in the bow, making it all but impossible to get off an accurate shot. But that didn't stop us from trying.

I said, "You're aiming for the engine, right?"

Hunter laughed. "I'm aiming at that moving thing that's outrunning us. If I get lucky and hit the engine, I'll take it."

I flipped my selector switch back to safe and rolled onto my back. "This thing is falling apart."

Mongo yelled, "He's pulling away. We need some air support."

Skipper answered since we were still on comms. "I'm on it. How long can you keep Taylor in sight?"

Mongo said, "Maybe fifteen more minutes, but he's got more engine and less weight than us."

Skipper finally said, "Gordo will be on comms in minutes. And don't worry too much about losing Taylor. I've got a good track, and the drone is faster than both of you."

"Did you fly the drone out here?" I asked.

"Of course I did. I wasn't giving up the one big advantage we have."

The sat-com crackled inside my head. "Sierra One, Gordo."

"Gordo! It's great to hear your voice. We could use a little help out here. Do you guys have night vision?"

"What we have is far better than night vision. We've got synthetic vision built into the airplane. Tell me what you need."

"I need you nose to nose with a bad guy in a boat that's faster than mine."

"Skipper sent me the drone feed, so I'm tracking. We'll be airborne in five and on scene fifteen after that. Can you stay with them that long?"

I said, "We'll try, but it's not looking good."

Gordo asked, "How far are you from the Canadian border?"

"Way too close for my comfort."

"Don't worry. We'll get him stopped before he gets there. We're rolling now."

Hunter and I began tearing the boat apart and throwing everything that wasn't essential overboard. Making ourselves as light as possible was the only way we'd have any chance of keeping up with Taylor, and I'd given up on actually catching him.

Mongo wrestled the controls as we gained fractions of a knot every time we tossed something into the water.

He said, "Maybe you should throw me overboard."

I said, "We consider you mission-essential, so stay where you are."

My night vision showed Taylor's boat riding high in the water and not changing size. "We're matching his speed."

After giving chase for fifteen more minutes without losing ground, I saw the beautiful sight of the C-130J roar overhead, and Gordo said, "Ahoy, matey. Got anybody who needs a good rattling?"

I said, "I can't tell you how happy I am to see you. Can you slow that boat down?"

"We can give her the old college try. We'll make a head-on pass and see what happens."

Although Gordo and his crew had all the lights out, the shape of the airplane and the heat from her four engines glowed like fire in the sky. They flew well ahead of Taylor and performed a fighter-pilot maneuver I never would've expected from a cargo bird. When the talented hands aboard the Herk rolled out dead on, nose to nose with Taylor's boat, I loved everything I saw . . . except the gunfire.

The runner was pouring lead into the air, but the Herk never faltered, coming and growing in size with every passing second. When she was inside a mile of the target, they turned on every light they could find, and Taylor's boat lit up like a Christmas tree.

I yelled, "Nice work, Gordo. Keep it up. He's sending a few bullets your way."

"We figured that out, but I think we'll survive a little smalls-arms fire. Slider's working on a plan that should get your boy's attention. Is it the end of the world if we sink her?"

I said, "I want Taylor alive."

Gordo said, "We'll do what we can, but we're not in the business of letting bad guys live after they shoot at us."

"You'll get your licks in. I promise."

They reversed course and spent more time flying away than I expected.

"Are you coming back?" I asked.

"In the turn now. We need you to back off about a hundred yards. We've never tried this before, so I'm not sure it's going to work the way we planned."

Mongo heard Gordo's instructions and pulled the throttle back to give our airborne contingent room to work, even though we had no idea what they were about to do. Our ignorance was short-lived. When they passed overhead again, I tried to make sense of what I saw.

I punched Hunter and pointed toward the sky. "Is he doing what I think he's doing?"

Hunter grinned. "I hope so. Who are those guys?"

"They're a bunch of misfits, just like us. They just happen to have a better ride at the moment."

The reason for extra distance between us and Taylor became instantly clear when the fifty-cal rounds poured from the back of the Herk.

Apparently, Slider had moved the technical Hilux to the ramp and climbed on the M2 machine gun. Glowing tracer rounds laced across the water like needles in front of Taylor.

Hunter shook a fist in the air. "They're doing exactly what you think they're doing, and I'm loving every minute of it!"

The slowest speed the Herk could fly was still more than twice the top speed of our boats, so Gordo made a crop-duster turn and dived back into the fight. I could only imagine what was going through Taylor's mind as he was eating airborne fifty-cal fire in the middle of the night on Lake Huron. No matter what he thought, there was nothing he could do about the assault other than scream into the darkness.

I tried to put myself in Taylor's position. *What would I do? How would I get out of the situation he's in?*

When it hit me, I yelled, "Mongo, full throttle and bear away forty-five degrees to the north."

He didn't question the order, and in seconds, we were screaming across the water again on a diagonal course.

After another burst of full-auto fire, Taylor made his move, and I was rewarded for my good guess. He yanked the controls hard over, and Mongo said, "He's heading for the shoreline."

I yelled, "Cut him off!"

It was a race for the border, and I was determined to outrun him on our diagonal course. It was working, and I braced for the fight of my life. We cut the corner and had him in our sights. His only options were to continue for the shoreline and pray we weren't stupid enough to open fire on him in Canada, or he could turn back outbound and deal with Slider and his Ma Deuce on open water.

Mongo yelled from the helm. "This is as smooth as it's going to get. If you're going to shoot, do it now."

Hunter nestled behind his M4, just like I'd seen him do a thousand times before, and I waited for the report. It came in the form of a 5.56mm rifle crack, but Taylor didn't change course or speed.

Hunter said, "I'm going to cut the boat out from under him. Are you okay with that?"

"Just get him stopped and still alive."

Hunter's thumb found the selector and cycled it to full auto. The next report of his rifle was the chainsaw sound of lead leaving the barrel in mass. That did the trick, but the instant Taylor's boat slowed in the water, a wall of blue lights illuminated the space between us and the shoreline.

"Who is that?" I called out.

Skipper answered. "Is it blue lights?"

"Yes, and a bunch of them."

"That would be the trusty Coast Guard."

"Ours or theirs?"

"Ours."

I said, "Put me right on top of him."

As Mongo closed the distance to the crippled remains of Taylor's boat, I disconnected and removed what remained of my prosthetic.

We pulled alongside the demolished boat, and I scanned the surface. "Find him!"

Mongo shut down the engine, and the three of us listened for sounds only humans make.

Hunter shot a finger through the air. "Over there!"

Mongo turned the key and crushed the throttle. He put us just ahead of the swimming Taylor, and I pulled my pistol for a press-check. A round was loaded and waiting to do its terrible work should it become necessary. I laid my rifle beside Hunter's leg and rolled over the side.

Before Taylor realized how bad his day had just become, I was on him. My first strike was an elbow shot across his nose. Those blows tend to get—and keep—a person's attention, and it worked perfectly with Timothy Taylor.

While he wiped blood from his nose and face, I said, "Ironic, isn't it?"

"What are you talking about?"

I sent another shot toward his face, but he ducked it and shot inward, catching me just under the right arm. His grasp was like a grizzly bear's. I'd picked a fight with a man half my age and in the best shape of his life, thanks to the eighteen months he spent at The Ranch. Unable to outmuscle or outswim him, I had to match him blow for blow to control him.

As he focused on dragging me beneath the surface, I delivered a series of headshots, followed by a knee to his gut. If he had any air in his lungs before the strike, it was long gone afterwards. He now needed a breath far worse than I did, and my lungs and I were intent on keeping him underwater as long as possible.

Taylor's movement became that of a man in desperation. He threw punch after punch to my ribs and gut, but each of them was a little less powerful than the previous, so I set my mind on waiting him out. He finally stopped striking and began kicking for the surface, expending more energy and air than he had to burn.

We broke the surface, and I took a long, deep breath. "That's rude. You didn't let me finish my point about irony."

He gasped and pawed at the water. Taylor may have been a world-class scuba diver, but in the water without a tank and regulator, he was little more than an average swimmer.

I said, "Before you interrupted me, I was trying to tell you how ironic it is that we met underwater and that we'd finish this whole ordeal in the same environment."

He continued fighting for air, and the blue lights grew closer with every passing minute.

"Ready for some more?"

He said, "You're going to die right here, Fulton. If it's the last thing I ever do, I promise you that you'll never leave this water alive."

His right arm had been below the surface for too long, so I kicked with the one foot I had left, closing the short distance between us. My hunch was right, and he raised a pistol from the water, bringing it to bear on my head.

I was too far away to snatch the weapon, so I threw a Hail Mary. "You'd better empty that barrel of water before you pull that trigger or that thing will blow your hand off."

He took his eyes from me just long enough to watch the last bit of water drain from the muzzle and for me to close the remaining distance. I drew my Glock and sent two rounds through his right hand and his pistol. He bellowed as if I'd torn off his arm, and I moved in.

It took almost no time to subdue him in a headlock that left less and less blood finding its way to his brain. The fight was over, and I had won. Mongo's fist came across my shoulder, and he grabbed Taylor by the chin. I let him slide from my grip as Mongo hauled him aboard our borrowed boat.

Hunter sent a crushing knee to Taylor's sternum and slapped him several times, making certain he had the Russian's attention. "Hey, man. We've been trying to reach you about your car's extended warranty, but you haven't returned our calls."

Taylor spat a mouthful of water, blood, and saliva, but he lacked the strength to launch it far enough to hit my partner.

Hunter shook his head. "That was weak, dude. You've gotta do better than that."

I crawled aboard with Mongo's help and made my way to the bow, where Hunter was still having a field day with Taylor.

"He's all yours, Chase. He seems to have some stuff he wants to get off his chest."

I lifted my broken prosthetic and slammed it against Taylor's face. "You shot my mechanical foot. That's going to cost me ten grand. I guess I'll take it out of your flesh, you piece of garbage."

He growled in Russian, "Killing me doesn't end this. I'm just one man, and if killing one man wrecks the mission, the mission was poorly planned."

I said, "So, you're telling me that killing you only delays the inevitable?"

"Exactly. I am only one soldier. The line behind me is endless."

Hunter said, "Don't let him get in your head, Chase. There are no more. You know that."

Taylor smiled as if enjoying himself, and the blue lights reflected off his skin. "You have to turn me over to them. It's the American law."

I reached up with an open hand. "Give me a sat-com."

Mongo put the radio in my hand, and I made what I prayed would be my final transmission of the mission. "Op center, Sierra One. Call off the Coast Guard."

Almost before she answered, the blue lights turned black, and the night, once again, belonged to me.

"Maybe you haven't noticed," I said, "but I don't spend much time worrying about that American law thing. You might say in a world of black and white, I deal in shades of gray."

Rather than maintaining my offensive position, I made the potentially fatal mistake of giving Taylor both time and space to act. He took full advantage of my foolish error and drew a knife from his belt. His first thrust was to push me backward, but it didn't work. Instead of withdrawing, I turned and let the strike pass harmlessly.

He then swung wildly, slashing through the air at anything close enough to strike, leaving Hunter and me no choice but to back off and let him exhaust himself. That turned out to be the worst call I could've made.

As if possessed by some force beyond his own strength, Timothy Taylor drew the blade across his own wrist, opening the skin and spraying blood. Hunter made the first move, but I was only an instant behind him.

He caught Taylor's open wrist and clamped both hands around the wound. I blocked high to protect my partner from the crashing downward blow Taylor was undoubtedly going to throw next. The strike came, but it wasn't aimed at Hunter's head or my hands. The glistening blade of his fighting knife sank to its hilt in his own neck.

Hunter and I released our quickly dying prisoner and relaxed against the gunwale.

My partner said, "I never saw that one coming. How about you?"

"Nope, but I guess that means we won't be interrogating him. The good news is that we have at least two more prisoners who are still breathing. Maybe they'll have an interesting story to tell."

Chapter 31
Everybody Needs a Mongo

Hunter and I collapsed onto a pair of seats while Mongo brought us about and pointed our bow to the west.

"Is this how you expected any of this to play out?" Hunter asked as we raced across the choppy surface of Lake Huron.

"I knew there'd be a fight. They always want to fight."

He laughed. "You'd think they'd learn, wouldn't you?"

I let the memory of the previous few days wash over me, and I threw an arm across Hunter's shoulders. "Thank you for doing this. I've missed having you aboard."

"Don't get all mushy on me. This is just a part-time gig for me. I have to get back to my real job soon."

"You've got time to stay a few days, don't you? It'd be nice to catch up and hear about your exploits in far-flung corners of the world."

He said, "As much as I'd love that, I have to get back to Africa. My boss"—he pointed toward the sky—"doesn't like it when I skip out on work."

"I guess you're right, but stay at least long enough to see Singer when he wakes up."

"I think the boss would be okay with that."

The lights of Mackinac Island came into sight at the same instant a set of blue lights appeared on our starboard bow.

I asked Mongo, "Who do you think that is?"

"My bet would be the Coast Guard. Do you want me to stop? We can outrun 'em if you want. I'm not sure I want to explain why we've got a dead guy and a couple gallons of blood in this boat."

Hunter put a hand to his ear. "Is your sat-com working?"

I said, "No, it's full of water. What's going on?"

He motioned for Mongo to slow down. "Go for Hunter. Sierra One is with me. We're safe and still breathing, but I can't say the same for Taylor." Hunter listened intently for a moment, then said, "Roger. That's great news. We were starting to get a little worried out here." He made a slashing motion across his throat. "Shut it down, Mongo. According to Skipper, the blue lights are ours."

The big man stared into the distance at the oncoming lights. "That's definitely not ours. The American Coast Guard doesn't have any light configuration like that."

Hunter joined the big man in staring down the oncoming vessel. "Hey, Skipper. Are you sure that's an American boat?" Relief shone all over his face. "Thanks, Skipper." He said, "It's our boys, but not our boat."

Mongo relaxed. "So, am I supposed to heave to?"

Hunter nodded, and we drifted to a stop on the black water of the Great Lakes, under an obsidian sky dotted with a billion pinpoints of light. The ship lay alongside our much smaller vessel, and she was a beauty.

Hanging over the portside rail, Clark Johnson waved and yelled, "Check us out! We upgraded."

The Hero-class patrol vessel glistened in the beams of her floodlights and ours.

I said, "Nice ride, but what are you doing on a Canadian vessel in American waters?"

He yelled back, "Tie off and come aboard. I think you've got your geography a little screwed up."

I looked up at Mongo. "We're on the American side, aren't we?"

"Absolutely. It's more than thirty miles to the border."

I stood on the one foot I had left, and a crewman lowered a rope ladder from the ship. "This ought to be interesting."

Mongo turned his back to me. "Hop on. I've got you."

Hunter wore the look of a man lost in disbelief. "Are you going to carry Chase up that ladder?"

The giant furrowed his brow. "Sure. He's just a couple hundred pounds, and he's missing half of one leg. I could probably throw him up there."

Hunter shook his head and reached for the ladder. "Everybody needs a Mongo."

Just as promised, Mongo hauled me up the ladder as if I were a lightweight backpack, and a petty officer handed me a crutch. Although I didn't like surrendering my dignity for an aluminum crutch, hopping around on one foot just wouldn't do.

Two sailors descended the rope ladder and hauled Taylor's body aboard the ship while Hunter, Mongo, and I were reunited with the remainder of our team in a cramped compartment with two men in windbreakers and New York Yankees hats.

The first of the two men said, "You're probably wondering who we are and what's going on. I'm not going to answer the first question, but I'll take the second one. We're taking custody of and responsibility for Timothy Taylor's body, as well as the rest of his team."

I glanced at Clark, and he sent a reassuring nod, but I wasn't ready to surrender our booty to a couple of guys dressed like idiots. "So, you two are CIA, and as such, you can't operate inside the U.S. That's why you want me to believe we're in Canadian waters. How am I doing so far?"

The second man said, "We can neither—"

I cut him off before he could finish his ridiculous statement. "Maybe if you guys were wearing Braves hats, I wouldn't be so hesitant, but it's tough for a Georgia boy to trust Yankees fans."

That broke the tension and turned the conversation into a chat among friends instead of an official political action.

Man one said, "There is one little issue we need to clear up." He had my attention and said, "Did you fire a fifty-cal out the back of a cargo plane over the lake?"

I looked at the faces of my teammates. "None of us did anything like that. I'm afraid I don't know what you're talking about, but it sounds like a pretty cool idea."

"That's what I thought you'd say. For the record, we never met, and none of us was ever here in Canadian waters."

I said, "We're not in Canadian—"

He held up a hand. "Trust me. If any of us ever has to testify before Congress, we were one hundred percent in Canadian waters when we took custody of Taylor's body and his team."

* * *

The flight back to Bonaventure was as peaceful as a ride in the noisiest of echo chambers could be. We even managed to catch a little sleep.

When Gordo and company brought the Herk to a stop on the ramp, I stuck my head into the cockpit. "You guys aren't leaving right away, are you?"

Gordo said, "No, we need to get some rest before we go anywhere. We're running on empty."

We shuttled everyone to the house and assigned showers and beds. My first order of business was to replace my missing prosthetic, and it felt nice to have an even number of feet again.

Inside the op center, Skipper sprang from her chair and gave each of us an enormous hug, but the hug she gave Gator seemed to last a second longer than the rest of ours.

I couldn't find a reason to discourage either of them from chasing what they were feeling. Gator proved himself to be worthy of all of our respect, and that's exactly the kind of man I wanted in Skipper's life.

The analyst said, "Nice work, guys. I know I dropped the ball a few times along the way on this one. Thank you for not making me feel like an idiot."

I said, "None of us would ever feel that way about you. You're the glue. We're just the broken pieces."

"I've got some good news," she said. "Actually, it's three bits of good news."

"Let's hear it," Clark said.

"First, Singer is awake and doing great."

A roar of relief and celebration rose from the team, but Skipper wasn't finished.

"You can go see him at eight in the morning if you're awake. Thing number two is the world's best neurosurgeon. I found him, and he's very optimistic. He's doing Disco's surgery tomorrow." She hesitated for a moment before pointing to a small monitor tucked away in a corner. "That yellow dot over northern Europe is Anya and Penny on their way home."

"What's their ETA?" I asked.

"Some time in mid-afternoon. They'll have at least two fuel stops."

"Can we call them?"

She pointed toward a headset. "I've already got the number dialed. I'm just waiting for you to push send."

The satellite phone connection took several rings to establish contact with Penny's phone moving through the air at five hundred knots, but she finally said, "Chase? Is that you?"

"It is. We're home safe and sound. There are no new injuries, and the bad guys are in the bag."

"That's amazing news," she said. "It's so good to hear your voice. We'll be home in a few hours."

I drew in a full breath in anticipation of just how badly my next question could go. "How did things go with you and Anya?"

Part of me expected a stern scolding for leaving her with the Russian, even though she asked for it.

"It was so good. She's a remarkable woman and absolutely hilarious."

I dared not speak. Agreeing with her out loud couldn't result in anything good.

Penny softened her voice. "It makes sense now."

"What does?" I asked.

"Why you fell in love with her. There's so much more to her than how she looks. I never thought I'd say this, but I actually like her a lot. But that doesn't mean I don't hate her."

"Hate her?" I said. "Why would you hate her?"

Penny didn't hesitate. "For being older than me but still looking like she's twenty-five. All women hate her for that."

I finally relaxed. "I'm glad to hear you two hit it off. It's all over now, and I can't wait to get you home."

"It won't be long, now. Thank you for calling. I love you, Chase."

"I love you, too, Penny. I'll see you soon."

I pulled off the headset and turned to see a room full of wide-eyed faces awaiting my report. "They're good. Let's get some sleep. I want to see Singer at eight."

* * *

Sleep came, and I was grateful. When the clock buzzed at seven, I stretched myself awake and strapped on my foot. We poured into the hospital as a team, but the nurses would have nothing of it.

"Three at a time! And I mean it. No more. Do you understand?"

Her admonishment did little to deter us from sneaking the whole family into Singer's room when she wasn't looking.

Singer squirmed in his hospital bed and looked as if he were on the verge of shedding a tear. "I can't believe all of you came. It sounds like I missed quite a party."

We spent fifteen minutes laying out every detail of what happened in the previous few days, but Nurse Ratched caught us before we finished our tale.

"Out! All of you. I mean it."

I protested. "What about the three-at-a-time rule?"

"That was the rule before you broke it. Now, get out."

After a little negotiation, she allowed Hunter to stay, but she kicked the rest of us out.

When Hunter emerged from the room, he pulled me aside. "Hey, listen. I need to clear up something I said when all of this started."

I wasn't sure where we were going, but I was intrigued. "Sure, what is it?"

"Remember when you asked me about turning the other cheek?"

"Yeah, I remember."

He said, "I gave you two pretty bad examples of the point I was trying to make. I talked about King David and Goliath, and if I remember correctly, I think I tried to make a point about Lot and his wife taking the other citizens of Sodom and Gomorrah with them instead of leaving them behind for God to judge and punish."

I nodded, and he continued.

"Well, neither of those examples are good ones. The Bible is the owner's manual for our lives, but sometimes, I tend to look in the transmission chapter when I really need to know about the headlights."

That made me chuckle, and I said, "An owner's manual . . . I like that."

He said, "Exactly. What I should've told you when you asked about turning the other cheek was how that passage is not about facing a physical enemy. Goliath had to be killed, and the Sodomites had to be punished. Yes, we should love everybody, but at no point does God instruct us to just roll over when we're faced with a mortal battle. I'm sorry I didn't lay that out when we talked on the phone."

"I understand," I said. "As much as I don't want to admit it, I was scared, and I needed a pep talk. You did that, and it worked."

We left the hospital and hit the diner for a late breakfast. Our flight crew joined us, and I began laying the groundwork for recruiting all three of them.

Gordo said, "We've got a good thing going right now, but we'd love to lend a hand until you replace your Gulfstream."

I wiped my mouth. "We'd appreciate that. Our chief pilot is having surgery tomorrow, but by all indications, he's probably on the road to retirement. We tend to put a lot of miles on our teammates."

Gordo nodded. "We'll give it some thought, but in the meantime, we're just a phone call away."

*　*　*

I shook the hands of every member of the security team and compensated them generously for their dedication and diligence.

When the sun passed her zenith and afternoon officially arrived, in true family fashion, the whole team showed up at the airport to welcome Penny and our favorite Russian home.

Standing beside Hunter, I said, "Do you think Taylor was bluffing when he said that thing about a long line of soldiers waiting behind him to get to us?"

Hunter said, "Of course. He was just lashing out. We wrapped this one up and tied a nice little bow on top."

"I hope you're right. I'm not sure I could live the rest of my life knowing—"

Skipper squealed, "There they are!"

I looked up to see Anya's Citation with the landing gear extended and the plane perfectly aligned with the runway. My heart fluttered as the thought of holding Penny in my arms again flooded over me. Perhaps it was time to walk away and leave the battlefield to younger, stronger operators. Maybe I had shouldered my share of the burden long enough. Maybe it was time to climb aboard the sailboat with the woman I adored and disappear across the distant horizon. I watched the jet grow larger with every passing second and believed I was only minutes away from changing my life forever.

Mongo squinted against the sun and motioned to the east. "Is that a Stinger?"

A trail of white smoke streaked from somewhere over Cumberland Sound, directly toward the Citation, and I watched in horror as the missile clipped the tail of the descending jet.

The Earth stopped spinning, and I struggled to comprehend what I was seeing. Anya's jet was hit, and it was only seconds away from safely touching down on the longer of our two runways. My world went silent, and I felt life draining from my very soul.

The Citation clipped the perimeter fence and slid sideways onto the runway with flames escaping the fuselage like chaotic fireworks. I ran toward the burning airplane with every ounce of force my body could produce, but it felt like my boots were mired in tar. When I finally reached the wreckage, I yanked open the door and threw myself inside.

The cabin was empty, so I turned to the cockpit where Anya and Penny still sat, buckled into their seats, but neither of them showed any sign of life. I leaned across my wife and thumbed the belt release. She collapsed into my arms, and I dragged her backward from the burning machine.

Kodiak leapt into the fire and returned seconds later with Anya in his arms. I hefted Penny over my shoulder and sprinted away from the wreckage until Mongo showed up and lifted her from my grip. He deposited her on the grass beside the taxiway and stuck a pair of fingers to her neck.

Kodiak called from several feet away. "I've got a faint pulse and shallow respirations."

The universe collapsed around me when I looked back to see Mongo starting chest compressions on my wife, and what happened in the next several minutes is a void in time and space. I can't remember anything between the moment Mongo began CPR and the moment the ambulances pulled away.

The first of the two busses sped off from the scene with lights and sirens at full strength, but the second vehicle—the one containing Nicole Bethany "Penny" Thomas's body—neither sped away nor ran its lights and sirens.

Author's Note

First and foremost, I want you to know how much I truly appreciate the astonishing gift you've given me by including my work on your reading list. Being your personal storyteller has been a dream of mine for half a century, and thanks to you, that dream has come true. I'll never be able to adequately thank you, but I make this vow: I will do my best to make every story a little better than the one before, and I'll never take your support for granted.

I'd like to ask a favor of you before we go any further. The dramatic ending of this story will change the projection of the rest of the series. With Penny deceased, we will no doubt get to see Chase like we've never seen him before. I would ask that you not mention her death in your social media comments or in your online reviews of this story. Knowing the ending would greatly decrease the emotional effect of the scene, so please don't rob future readers of that experience with spoilers. If you'd like to talk about the ending with me, I would love to have those conversations. Please feel free to email any time. I always treasure interaction with readers like you.

With that bit of clerical work behind us, let's talk about my use of the term "illegal" in this story. We can't turn on a television or read a news article these days without seeing stories about illegal immigration, but that is not the meaning of the term in my writing. In the intelligence world, an illegal is a person who has been placed inside another country under an alias to live as a citizen of the country. When I write about the Taylor family being illegals, that is the definition I'm referring to.

I hope I sparked a bit of curiosity with the brief reference to the Rivet Amber project. That program was real, but I used it fictitiously. To my knowledge, there is no evidence to support the theory that the Russians had anything to do with her disappearance. It is likely that she crashed in the Bering Sea, but as you know, I love tossing tidbits of historical truth into my fiction.

We had quite a bit of fire in this story, and that wasn't intentional. It just played out that way while the story was coming together. I am by no means an expert in anything, especially not arson investigation. I relied on input from Rueben, a friend of mine, who just happens to be a well-qualified and experienced arson investigator and reader of my stories. The chlorine and diesel fuel combination was his idea, and I wouldn't dare take credit for it. I mentioned in the story that such techniques were standard tradecraft for Russian operatives, but the truth is that I have no idea if the Russians, or anyone else, ever used that technique. It made the story more believable, but like much of the tradecraft writing, it's not real.

I need to make a geographic apology. The terrain and population of Plainview, Texas, were wildly exaggerated in this story. Although it generally aligns with my description, it's not desolate, rugged desert. I needed such terrain to make the story work, so, once again, I made it up.

Ah, the honey bucket story. You knew I'd have to discuss that tidbit in this author's note, so here we go. Believe it or not, that story is based in truth. I did, however, take a great deal of literary license with the truth to make it more entertaining and hopefully humorous. My dear friend, Lieutenant Colonel Gary Bray, a retired Air Force C-130 pilot and Delta Airlines captain, shared the original story with me, and I couldn't wait to put it on paper. Gary is, of course, the inspiration for Gordo, the C-130 commander. The setup about the South American classified operation is true. The gastrointestinal distress following a meal is true. And as crazy as it sounds, the honey bucket is a real fixture in the C-130. The C-5, C-17, and C-141 crews enjoyed an airline-type lavatory, but not the Herk drivers. They got a bucket and a bag because the Air Force has a terrible sense of humor. Thankfully, Gary's story didn't include a loadmaster sliding out the back of an airplane, but this is a thriller novel, so having people dangling from cargo planes high above the equator is a requirement.

I'd like to make one more confession before we wrap this up. I hope you are endlessly curious about something that popped out of Singer's mouth when we woke him up in the hospital. He called a nurse Rose, but her name was Tiffany. I intentionally wrote that scene as an enticement to leave you aching to know who Rose is. I'm not willing to tell you anything about her in this note; instead, I'd like to direct you to the source. If you've not read *Singer — Memoir of a Christian Sniper*, Rose will be a mystery, but those of you who have read that book know precisely and painfully who Rose is. I hope you'll grab a copy of Singer's fictional memoir and pull back the veil over the mysterious Rose.

I'll step out of the confessional now and close with one final thought. Although the agonizing final scene of this story would make a pretty good place to stop the series, that's not going to happen. If you'll indulge me a moment longer, I'll tell you a little history about this series. When I wrote the original manuscript for *The Opening Chase*, it was meant to be a stand-alone novel with no book number two. In fact, everyone died in the original ending. Killing everyone in book number one doesn't make for a very interesting series, so, as you know, we didn't print my original ending. When I hired Sarah, my editor, for that first project, she insisted that I change the ending and write a second book with the same characters. Now, thirty-two books later, I'm so glad she did. The original manuscript was 136,000 words. It went to print at 92,000 words, and we kept most of the characters alive. You may remember a line from that first book that mentioned God hearing the prayers of an assassin. Because of that line, the original title was *The Assassin's Prayer*. I liked the title, and who knows? I might write another story someday with that title just because I think it sounds cool. I almost forgot what I was trying to explain in this paragraph, but I'm back on track now. Although the series could end with this book, I have absolutely no plans to ever stop writing this series. I'm in love with the story, and I can't wait to see what happens next. I hope you'll stick around, and we'll figure it out together.

Cheers,
Cap

About the Author

Cap Daniels

Cap Daniels is a former sailing charter captain, scuba and sailing instructor, pilot, Air Force combat veteran, and civil servant of the U.S. Department of Defense. Raised far from the ocean in rural East Tennessee, his early infatuation with salt water was sparked by the fascinating, and sometimes true, sea stories told by his father, a retired Navy Chief Petty Officer. Those stories of adventure on the high seas sent Cap in search of adventure of his own, which eventually landed him on Florida's Gulf Coast where he spends as much time as possible on, in, and under the waters of the Emerald Coast.

With a headful of larger-than-life characters and their thrilling exploits, Cap pours his love of adventure and passion for the ocean onto the pages of the Chase Fulton Novels and the Avenging Angel - Seven Deadly Sins series.

Visit www.CapDaniels.com to join the mailing list to receive newsletter and release updates.

Connect with Cap Daniels:

Facebook: www.Facebook.com/WriterCapDaniels
Instagram: https://www.instagram.com/authorcapdaniels/
BookBub: https://www.bookbub.com/profile/cap-daniels

Also by Cap Daniels

The Chase Fulton Novels Series
Book One: *The Opening Chase*
Book Two: *The Broken Chase*
Book Three: *The Stronger Chase*
Book Four: *The Unending Chase*
Book Five: *The Distant Chase*
Book Six: *The Entangled Chase*
Book Seven: *The Devil's Chase*
Book Eight: *The Angel's Chase*
Book Nine: *The Forgotten Chase*
Book Ten: *The Emerald Chase*
Book Eleven: *The Polar Chase*
Book Twelve: *The Burning Chase*
Book Thirteen: *The Poison Chase*
Book Fourteen: *The Bitter Chase*
Book Fifteen: *The Blind Chase*
Book Sixteen: *The Smuggler's Chase*
Book Seventeen: *The Hollow Chase*
Book Eighteen: *The Sunken Chase*
Book Nineteen: *The Darker Chase*
Book Twenty: *The Abandoned Chase*
Book Twenty-One: *The Gambler's Chase*
Book Twenty-Two: *The Arctic Chase*
Book Twenty-Three: *The Diamond Chase*
Book Twenty-Four: *The Phantom Chase*
Book Twenty-Five: *The Crimson Chase*
Book Twenty-Six: *The Silent Chase*
Book Twenty-Seven: *The Shepherd's Chase*
Book Twenty-Eight: *The Scorpion's Chase*
Book Twenty-Nine: *The Creole Chase*
Book Thirty: *The Calling Chase*
Book Thirty-One: *The Capitol Chase*
Book Thirty-Two: *The Stolen Chase*
Book Thirty-Three: *The Widow's Chase*

The Avenging Angel – Seven Deadly Sins Series
Book One: *The Russian's Pride*
Book Two: *The Russian's Greed*
Book Three: *The Russian's Gluttony*
Book Four: *The Russian's Lust*
Book Five: *The Russian's Sloth*
Book Six: *The Russian's Envy*
Book Seven: *The Russian's Wrath*

Stand-Alone Novels
We Were Brave
Singer – Memoir of a Christian Sniper

Novellas
The Chase is On
I Am Gypsy

Made in United States
North Haven, CT
15 November 2025